Asymmetrical Woman

Aliza Ross

Black Rose Writing | Texas

ISBN: 978-1-68433-644-9
PUBLISHED BY BLACK ROSE WRITING
www.blackrosewriting.com

Printed in the United States of America
Suggested Retail Price (SRP) $19.95

Asymmetrical Woman is printed in Georgia Pro

*As a planet-friendly publisher, Black Rose Writing does its best to eliminate unnecessary waste to reduce paper usage and energy costs, while never compromising the reading experience. As a result, the final word count vs. page count may not meet common expectations.

Cover Art by Tereza Dimitracopoulos

Asymmetrical Woman

"Reality doesn't impress me. I only believe in intoxication, in ecstasy, and when ordinary life shackles me, I escape one way or another. No more walls."
– Anais Nin

Prologue

I rummaged through my daughter's toy chest and pulled out the brightly painted masquerade mask that she made at school. I adjusted the string around my head, above my ears, as I walked down the hallway back to my bedroom. Positioning myself face down on the bed, supporting myself on my knees and elbows, my silk tank top bunching at the small of my back, I waited for Jonathan to come out of the shower. I turned to look at myself in the full-length mirror leaning against the wall. *Oh god*. The mask was ridiculous, hardly Kubrick. I scanned the room, mentally noting the other grenades. There was a mirror behind our slatted headboard and on our spinning armoire as well. *But I have to do this. I have to know he can do this.* I licked my fingers, slid them between my legs, and prepared a pillow to smother my face in.

When I heard the water turn off, I pulled at my nipples until they were darting out of my tank top, waiting nervously. Jonathan stepped into the bedroom, a towel wrapped around his waist, his hair already gelled. He made a beeline to his dresser without looking at me.

"The nanny already took the kids to school. It's an empty house. You can have me now, if you like," I offered.

"Nah, I have to get work," Jonathan said, searching for matching socks in his drawer.

"Nah?" I asked, a pang of nausea sweeping through me.

"No, it's okay," he said, his face buried in the drawer.

"But it's not," I muttered.

Silence.

"I need this, Jonathan," I whispered, my throat raw.

I felt him frowning even though his back was to me.

He turned to me and saw the mask. His eyes softened, and he faked a smile. "The mask is kind of hot, but I really don't have time."

I felt sick from his rejection, but I couldn't blame him. He was probably more scared than I was that his body would betray him; that the mask would get knocked off at some point and he'd suddenly go limp.

I turned onto my back. As I watched him collect his briefcase, I swallowed, trying to keep the desperation out of my voice. "I understand... I would never make you stay with me if I look like this forever."

Chapter 1

One Month Earlier...
He was by far the most handsome man at the dinner party in the West Village loft. His eyes were sparkling with confidence, his charisma unmatched. He wore a brightly colored shirt and only I knew that there was a small hole on the bottom tucked neatly away in his slacks. He flashed his perfect smile at his five partners' jokes as he attracted the amorous eyes of their wives. Any woman with a pulse would have been hard-pressed not to appreciate Jonathan. Any woman, that was, except for me—his ungrateful wife.

Jonathan rose from the dining room table and raised his glass, preparing to toast his partners and their newly formed venture. William, the host, swallowed the last of the white wine that had been paired with the first course—goat cheese, beets, and edible purple flowers—cleared his throat, and lifted his hand to signal Jonathan to wait. As all eyes were fixed on William, I took the opportunity to subtly move some of the cheese off of my plate and onto Jonathan's. William pressed a button on the underside of the table so that its center spun counterclockwise until a carafe of red wine was directly in front of Jonathan. "That one is for the toast," William said.

Jonathan filled a crystal goblet and raised it. "Here's to changing this industry. I'm inspired by what we're doing here, guys. I'm passionate about Envirex and certain that our investment company is destined for success. Over the last few months, we've really started to grow." Jonathan bent his knees to sit but then rose again. "And... to my beautiful wife for supporting me when I had the vision for this company a year ago."

Normally, I'd have belabored the point that *I* wanted to be the object of Jonathan's inspiration and passion, and all else to be an afterthought. I'd have wanted him to acknowledge me, not just as the "beautiful wife" supporting his success, but as the woman whose brilliance inspired him. Who in her own right, just four years ago, had been named as a "rising star" and one of the "Forty Under Forty" attorneys in New York City. Instead, I was imagining being bare in the center of the dining room table under the track lighting, hands outstretched behind me, legs spread displaying slick soft skin, nipples erect, head tilted back, lips slightly parted, my long chestnut hair cascading into a waterfall of curls beneath me. With a touch of a button, William was controlling in front of which guest I would end up. The selected guest would rise and begin touching me, groping my breasts and squeezing the flesh between my legs, as if to determine the ripeness of a cantaloupe, until William would raise his hand to signal that the table was about to turn again. Once all the guests had the opportunity to inspect me, he'd announce the one that would get to probe me first while the other men watched, gripping their stiff cocks, waiting their turn.

"I'm certain that she's grateful to finally have me out of her hair," Jonathan added. Everyone laughed, knowing that Jonathan hadn't worked since selling his technology company and making a fortune four years ago. "I look forward to many more dinners with my new partners and our wives as we embark on this journey." Jonathan clanked my glass and the others within reach.

I smiled awkwardly, wondering, as I always did when these fantasies flooded my consciousness, whether they were in response to, or the cause of the sexual neglect I felt from Jonathan. Or was I just overly aroused tonight because of last night's events? *Oh my God. Last night. Don't think about it.* If Jonathan were the sort of man—and he wasn't—who became aroused just knowing that I wanted him to take me over the marble sink of his partner's bathroom, it might have diminished my disgust for him. It would have been an antidote against the fact that he was always tired or irritable—and worst of all, focused on my flaws.

"The pomp of that dinner filled the air, but not my stomach," I told Jonathan as we walked outside to hail a taxi. The mild May air was refreshing. "A six course tasting menu. It wouldn't fill up a three-year old."

Jonathan nodded.

"I already have a headache. I think it's from mixing the wines, but then again, I think I've had the same headache since last night." *Last night. Don't think about him!* I figured it'd take twenty-five minutes to get to our apartment on Central Park South, and about forty-five minutes for a food delivery. I dialed our usual diner and ordered eggs over easy with fries for me and a hamburger for him. "Don't get me a Deluxe. I don't want fries," he interjected. I lowered my voice and added, "Make it a Deluxe." I knew the grease would go a long way to averting hangovers for us both.

The children were asleep when we got in. By the time Luisa, our nanny, summarized their evening, the food had arrived. As I undressed, Jonathan cued up the DVR to where we'd left off on Bill Maher. I took an Ambien and we sat in bed with our pore-clogging cuisine on our laps. "Before your sleeping pill hits, don't forget that we're supposed to see that couples' therapist tomorrow at noon," Jonathan reminded me. His bitter tone always accompanied any mention of my sleeping pill, its side effect of amnesia, or our problematic sleeping patterns.

"Okay, I'll remember," I assured him. How could I have forgotten? For years, I'd harassed Jonathan to make an appointment with a couples' therapist because I felt that we weren't having enough sex and that the sex we did have was obligatory. I'd found the therapist's business card thumb-tacked to a bulletin board at the Jewish Community Center on the Upper West Side where I took our four-year-old, Ella, for swim lessons. "I hope you're ready for this guy to take my side that you don't bang me enough," I said, smiling.

"I hope you're ready to confess that you're a nut job," he retorted. "You do realize that for all your complaining, we've never gone a week without fooling around? We're doing better than just about every couple we know."

"That's because all of our friends cheat on each other, and we don't." I tried changing the subject. "What do you think we're going to talk about tomorrow?"

"I think we'll tackle our underlying issue," he said.

"That you're the only man on the planet who won't give his begging wife anal?" I asked with a naughty smile, trying to keep the mood light.

"No, Alix. Your addiction issues," he said, growing irritated that I was once again trying to simplify our issues as only lack of sex.

I shifted uncomfortably. "Are you talking about sleeping pills, wine, sex, or exercise this time?" I asked, my face falling a little.

"All of the above, baby," he said with a sad smile. "But first, the sleeping issues."

"You know I only take my sleeping pill as prescribed because if I don't, I'll be up all night. Don't you want me to get the sleep I need?" I tried to gain his sympathy back a little.

"I'm not getting into this with you right now," he said. I'd struck a nerve. "You can't lawyer your way out of this one. You don't take the pill to go to sleep. You stay up and do who knows what, and you don't let me sleep either. You mix it with alcohol. Then you blame me if you miss your window, that precious time when the pill is hitting you, and claim that the reason you aren't asleep is because we didn't have sex. And then you don't remember anything in the morning. You say that you need sex, exercise, and sleeping pills like I need oxygen, so everything has to revolve around those things. I'm not sure anyone is going to view that as healthy," he said. "Do you really not see how this has impacted me, Alix?"

"I can see why me *not* taking Ambien affected you, back when I was pregnant," I answered. Jonathan and I had been mostly sleeping in separate beds (except his was actually a couch) since midway through my pregnancy with our now eleven-month-old, Charlie. During the pregnancy, I'd abstained from taking sleeping pills. That meant facing sleepless nights without the crutch I'd been leaning on ever since law school for over fifteen years.

The pregnancy hormones and insomnia formed an absinthe-like cocktail that drove me to watch porn on my phone and masturbate until I could finally fall asleep. Mostly, massage porn—the kind where an innocent girl got so unexpectedly turned on by a professional masseur rubbing her inner thighs and buttocks, inching ever closer to her private parts, that she ended up getting screwed on the table. The part that brought me over the edge was witnessing that moment, that critical turning point, where the masseur, unable to resist being so close to forbidden areas, crossed the line. Jonathan was sick of the bed shaking, my moaning, and the light from the screen of my phone as I surfed from video to video to find the one worthy of orgasm. That was when he started sleeping on the couch.

"And then what happened?" he asked, becoming irate.

"And then when Charlie was born, you chose to keep sleeping on the couch rather than have sex with me." I knew I was slightly distorting the issue. Jonathan had volunteered to do the middle-of-the-night feeds with the breast milk I pumped, so that I could take my Ambien and get undisturbed rest to recover from the C-section. He knew that if I woke to feed the baby, I wouldn't fall back asleep. Plus, he didn't trust me to care for the baby on Ambien. Though he'd done the same when Ella was born, it didn't wreck him because he wasn't working. He did dishes, house chores, and took care of the bills. And he grew more and more tired. What he did not do—and what I would have traded all that for—was make me feel like he still wanted me.

"Right, because unless we have sex every night, you can't sleep, regardless of how I feel about it."

"Every other night, actually," I corrected him, growing annoyed. For me, negative feelings were all the more reason to have sex—to regain equilibrium and control. I spent most of our marriage guarding our sex life like an overprotective mother, demanding an explanation whenever there was a lag. That pressure basically killed off his spontaneity and lust, which I concluded from a heap of self-help books. So over the last year, I'd made a conscious effort to change. I no longer initiated sex. I no longer discussed it. I let him approach me and pretended to be okay with the decreased frequency. But I quickly decayed. My resentments grew. I nagged about unhung jackets, milk cartons left out. I involuntarily became increasingly mean and bitter towards Jonathan, which in turn removed any impetus for him to want to sleep with me. It was a vicious cycle.

"Anyway, I'm sorry. We'll talk about it in therapy. I just hope you're ready to talk about your mother," I added trying to lighten the mood again.

"What does my mother have to do with anything?" he asked. Jonathan was practically the only person I knew who'd never been to a psychologist.

"Therapists like to talk about moms. I guarantee he'll ask about her. And, I'll be happy to explain that you're transferring anger towards her onto me. Don't you think it's bizarre that she's also an insomniac? And that I'm no longer litigating at a big firm? I'm practically a stay-at-home mother like she was." I sighed. "Maybe that's why you aren't attracted to me anymore, because you aren't supposed to want to fuck your mother."

"Your sleeping pill must have already hit. You're talking nonsense," he said. "Just because you were a psych major doesn't make you a shrink."

"You'll see. You'll have to contend with Freud." I laughed, suddenly feeling the rush as I absorbed the Ambien. "Anyway, are you planning to stay in bed tonight and wear your teeth?" I asked. As if my sleeping pills weren't enough of an issue, Jonathan had sleep apnea, and I needed him to wear a snore guard so I wouldn't be woken up.

"Tomorrow is Monday. I need a good night's rest so I can be fresh for the week. I'm not wearing my snore guard tonight," he said.

"I have a busy week too, and I'm willing to deal with your breakthrough snores," I said, referring to the noises he made, even with the guard.

"What's so busy about your week?" he asked doubtfully. I willed myself not to get annoyed realizing that my busiest week didn't compare to the long, stressful hours he worked.

"I have a big mediation Friday. Four parties, and they each attached a hundred pages worth of exhibits." I'd used connections at my old firm to get me onto a prestigious roster of volunteer mediators for court-ordered mediations. I only got paid if the mediations went beyond two hours—they rarely did. Although it was only occasional, the intention had been to keep my head in the professional game while the children were younger, and eventually return to litigation. But I liked it and was good at it. Over the last three and a half years, although the courts had only sent me a couple dozen cases a year, I felt more than competent, and was now ablaze with the prospect of building my own mediation practice.

"What kind of case?" he asked.

"Employment discrimination. And I have a call with Dan Shapiro tomorrow—one of the personal injury partners at my old firm. I want to gauge his interest in joining my company."

Jonathan shook his head. Either the name didn't ring a bell or he was reaffirming his disapproval of my business. I didn't clarify.

"Are you at least staying for frozen yogurt?" I asked, referring to my ritual of bingeing on a gigantic bowl of frozen yogurt every night. The frozen yogurt had to be a particular brand, eaten out of a particular bowl. Before taking my first bite, I always pressed the cold bowl into my cleavage and then against each nipple.

Jonathan looked wide-eyed at the half-eaten hamburger in front of him and pushed out his stomach as if that answered the question. In the past, he'd always join me with his own frozen yogurt. We'd pause the television relentlessly to exchange commentary, jokes, or whimsical business ideas, and of course, have sex while my frozen yogurt melted on the nightstand. I'd curl up into his armpit and he'd tickle my back until I fell asleep. But the demands of parenthood had slowly eroded the pleasure of being up late. He began leaving to sleep on the couch within fifteen minutes of finishing his frozen yogurt. Then he began leaving before he even finished the last bite. And finally, he'd started skipping the frozen yogurt, and the conversation, and the sex.

Jonathan's absence from the bed gave me anxiety. I drank just a bit more wine with my Ambien and masturbated repeatedly, which helped chase away the thoughts about how discontented I was with our marriage. I shouldn't have to be doing this myself, I'd lament, moments after coming. My heart rate would rise, then fear would set in that I wouldn't be able to fall asleep if my emotions were running amuck, so I'd find another video to watch. I knew that my sleep rituals were debilitating for both of us, and though I wanted to change, I also knew that I intensely needed them.

"Okay, will you pretty please just bring me my bowl from the freezer?" I asked, finishing the last of my fries.

Jonathan nodded, left, and returned with my bowl.

"Thank you. I love you," I said, and tilted my head up to meet his for a goodnight kiss.

"See you in the morning," he said.

Almost as soon as Jonathan left the room, my phone blinked with an email. *Evan!*

"I'm going to be at Lee's Art Shop by your apartment tomorrow. I'd give anything to just see your face for a moment."

Do not respond! I told myself. *You drank, you took your pill, and more importantly, you're married with two beautiful children!*

I reread his message, my finger poised over the screen.

Chapter 2

Five months earlier, in early December, I had received a friend request on Facebook from Evan Roth, my childhood sweetheart. We were thirteen the summer his family moved from the farms of upstate New York to our urban Queens neighborhood. Instead of attending camp, I was puffing on a cigarette in the park with the usual bunch of rowdy kids when I first noticed Evan. He was throwing a softball, underhand, to a girl—probably his sister— who appeared to be about seven. He had a sunburnt nose and forehead, dirty blonde curls framed his high cheekbones, and a sweaty white t-shirt stuck to his athletic body. I lost interest in the crowd around me. My eyes followed him as he picked up a tattered backpack and took the girl's hand to leave the schoolyard. I put on lip-gloss, pulled my hair out of its ponytail, and pushed up my padded bra to create an illusion that I had breasts.

"Hey, wait up!" I called, running to catch up with him. "You're new, aren't you? I'm Alix. I live just down the block." I pointed in the direction of my family's red brick house.

He stared at my face rather than where I was pointing. He seemed unable to find his voice. When he finally spoke, his voice cracked. "I'm Evan." He cleared his throat. "That's my sister, Joy. We just moved here," he said, looking down at his feet.

"Well, see that big tree next to my house," I told him, "I put down a cardboard box and an old doormat in there. And I've got a few cigarettes. Come by there tonight at 9:00 and I'll teach you everything you need to know to get by here. Okay?" I had plenty to teach him. In the schoolyard, you fit in better if you acted dumb, poor, and disenfranchised. You never mentioned friends from nearby neighborhoods or things you did with your family that required money. You never admitted to being Jewish, except to other Jews. I didn't know if he was. I would introduce him around the neighborhood and show him the one minimart that would sell beer to underage kids.

"Okay," he agreed.

That night, while my older sister, Sabrina, was fighting with our parents, I headed out to the tree instead of intervening on her behalf the way I normally did. I was always protecting her; pleading with our parents to lessen her punishments, doing her homework for her, cleaning the dishes she was asked to wash, pretending I hadn't seen her steal ten dollars from their dresser. Once I took the spray can she was using to do graffiti when we had heard the school guards coming and let her run away because one more violation and she'd be suspended. It was like I felt guilty for the lousy relationship she had with my parents. As if each of my glowing report cards and gymnastics trophies drew attention, by comparison, to the lack of hers.

Evan showed up and we lay under the big tree smoking and talking for hours. I told him that my sister got all of my parents' attention because she was struggling at school and always getting herself into trouble. His parents favored his little sister. I told him both of my parents were high school English teachers. His father taught art history at Queens College—they'd rented a house here to ease his daily commute from upstate. They'd kept their house upstate and planned to go back on weekends. I told him that I counted everything that could be counted and had to read cereal boxes from back to front without interruption. He told me that he washed his hands a lot and got out of bed several times at night to check that the stove was off. I told him that I had recurring nightmares of waking up in a concentration camp because my grandparents had horrified me with their stories about World War Two and that I starved myself earlier that year out of guilt for what they'd been through. He told me that he kept a BB gun under his bed because he'd always been scared a rabid animal would find its way to his room. We both loved the group Air Supply, camping, and sugar—not syrup—on our French toast.

We both hated the feel of construction paper on our bare hands. I told him I'd already gotten to third base, and he said he was taking it slower than most kids. I told him I was going to live in Paris and be a teacher when I grew up. He said he'd like to own a chocolate factory.

"Can we kiss?" I asked him that first night under the tree.

"I never have," he said, looking at his sneakers.

"It's cool if you don't, but if you wanted... I can, you know, be your first," I said.

"Sure." He turned his head toward me and I kissed him gently.

We met every night under the tree for the next five weeks. French kissing became the norm, and dry humping followed. I marveled at my saturated panties after every encounter and explored the parts of my body that he did not until I collapsed in spasms.

"I'm going to have a growth spurt next year. My mother was a really late bloomer, too," I said apologetically the first night Evan's hands wandered into my bra, which my father had secretly taken me to buy after my mother insisted I didn't need one. She reminded me frequently that I wouldn't need one until I was much older. After all, I was just like her.

"That's why I keep pushing your hand away, when you try to, you know, touch me down there," he said. There'd been numerous occasions when I had tried to grip him, anxious to feel the swelling I could see through his pants. Feeling how hard he was beneath my hungry fingers created a wanting, a longing, to feel his flesh. But he always pushed me away, and now I knew why. I wasn't enough for him. I had been lying on my back on the cardboard box. I sat upright immediately, tears welling in my eyes, feeling shamed, inadequate.

"No, not because of you! You're perfect. It's just that... me too. The doctor said I'm a little delayed, you know, with puberty," he said in a hushed voice, face beet-red.

"Oh," I said, wiping my tears. "Don't be embarrassed. I promise that doesn't matter to me." I felt like a character from one of my romance novels, comforting him, about what I wasn't even sure. "Tomorrow night, after the party, do you want to give more a try?" I suggested.

"What party?" he asked.

"There's a party in that big parking lot in Bayside. I hear there will be pot. If you can get out, it's going to be awesome," I told him excitedly.

"No, I'm gonna skip it. You have to be home by 11:30, right? Let's sneak out and meet under the tree at midnight, okay?" he asked.

"Sure," I told him, but I was disappointed.

I went to the party as planned, but I couldn't stop thinking about Evan. The usual pissing contests between the boys as to who was tougher, did more drugs, or had more sex seemed irrelevant to me that night. Getting buzzed and being hit on by the older boys was suddenly unappealing. As I pulled on a joint, I realized that I would have much preferred to be under the tree reading him a sentence from *To Kill a Mockingbird*. He was right to avoid these parties. Sirens interrupted my thoughts as the police arrived at the party.

"We're not here to bust you for drinking," an officer called out. "We're investigating a hit and run. A little girl, hit by a blue vehicle."

We scattered like roaches.

I hitched a ride home, wondering who'd been hit, ashamed that we'd all been more concerned about getting in trouble than helping the police. By midnight, I wasn't merely eager, but almost desperate to meet Evan. I waited an hour for him to show up, but he never did.

By the next afternoon, I learned why. The little girl who'd been hit was Evan's sister. An article in Newsday reported that she was in critical, but stable, condition. The police were investigating. Anyone with information should call.

Evan must need me, I thought. But he hadn't called, and his phone rang unanswered. I wanted to help him, but not force myself on him. I started toward his house, then turned back, repeatedly. By the time I brought myself to walk by his house, a week later, a moving truck was being loaded in front of the house, a "for rent" sign staked on the lawn, and no sign of the family. I walked home tasting my tears. I mailed him a letter, hoping it'd be forwarded to him, but he never wrote back.

The next and last I heard of him was a month later. Newsday reported that the eight-year-old victim of the hit and run had died from related injuries at the Golistano Children's Hospital. The investigation was ongoing. Nobody I'd ever known had died. I couldn't imagine my own sister dying. I struggled to comprehend that Evan's had—that a girl I'd known, his baby sister, no longer existed.

***

Nearly twenty-five years had passed when I received Evan's first Facebook message, six-month-old Charlie sleeping on my shoulder. Immediately the warmth of that summer love enveloped me once more, as if I'd stumbled upon a favorite childhood toy. According to his photo, he had sideburns, my pet peeve, but a handsome face. He was living in Tribeca.

After a few polite email exchanges, he explained what had happened that summer. He'd been in the street throwing a ball to his little sister. As Joy lunged to catch it, a blue car came speeding down the street, hit her, and sped away. His parents, devastated, dumped their rental house and moved back to the country for Joy's treatment. She would later die unexpectedly of a brain contusion. The driver was never found. He'd thought about me often through the years, wondered what had happened to me, but couldn't bring himself to contact me because I was too much of a reminder of life in Queens. Now he was writing a memoir, seeking closure, and thought I could help. Could we meet to discuss it in more detail he wanted to know.

Instinctually, I wanted to comfort him. I told him I'd help however I could. We planned to meet in a few weeks.

In the meantime, we continued corresponding until we'd caught up on the twenty-five years that had passed. We'd both gotten heavily involved in drugs and drinking the year that followed our summer together. As teenagers, we'd both been through rehab and therapy and had thrown ourselves into expressing our struggles creatively. He emailed me short stories and scanned copies of paintings he'd done twenty years prior. Children whose faces were half-infant and half-prematurely aged. I sent him the poems I'd written during my brief stint in a psychiatric ward, exploring my sexual identity, which I'd never shared with anyone. The themes in our writing eerily paralleled each other's. We had both excelled in college. He had majored in biology. Now, he was working as a physical therapist—a path inspired by a physical therapist that had helped his sister before she died. We were both married to spouses we loved, but self-admittedly hypersexual. He had an eight-year-old daughter. We analyzed each other's words in excruciating detail, deconstructing the psychological nuances in all. Less than a week after reconnecting, it was as if we never had left the shadows of the old tree.

"I feel like you already know me better than anyone," he wrote. "We've been through the same stuff. I can't wait to see where we go in real life."

"The same stuff? I went through nothing but whippings from my parents, and an occasional paper cut. Your sister died! Where do you want to meet?"

"I'm vegetarian, but I'll go anywhere. A café in Paris with espresso and chocolate-covered pretzels?"

The night before we were supposed to meet, I had misgivings. Jonathan had recently started his new investment company, I was breastfeeding Charlie, and three-year-old Ella was regressively attempting to breastfeed, envious of the new baby. Each time I crafted an email to Evan, I could feel something building deep in my stomach, an intangible pull. It felt as if I were cheating on Jonathan. *It's not like you're going on a date,* I thought. *You're just meeting an old friend to talk about his sister's death. Still, this can't be a good idea.*

I sat at my desk and drafted an email to Evan: "Evan, I'm so sorry but I won't be able to meet you tomorrow after all. – Alix." Before I hit the send button, Jonathan walked over to me. I minimized the screen and turned in my swivel chair to face him.

"What's up?" I asked.

"Where are my black pants?" he said impatiently.

"I have no idea."

"Why is all of my stuff missing? Nothing is ever where it's supposed to be," he mumbled, and stomped into the laundry room to pick through the dirty clothes.

I deleted the last half of my email. Instead, I wrote: "Evan, I'm so sorry but I can't meet you unless you understand that I'm not quite back to my pre-pregnancy condition yet. These are my kids, and me, just before this last pregnancy." I attached a picture of me with both kids, and one of me in a tiny bikini.

Within minutes, he wrote back: "Why do you care what I think of how you look? At this point, I was hoping you'd show up in sweatpants because your mind has blown my mind and I'll probably have my stomach in knots anyway. Now, you send me this picture. You're killing me, here. I'm at your mercy. You like to drive people crazy. I'll have my revenge."

"Jonathan?" I called out. He was looking out the living room window with his telescope. How I loved when he used to stand behind me as I peered through it, instructing me, passionately explaining what I was looking at. Now it seemed ridiculous: ten grand on a telescope to see the smog of New York.

"What?" he asked with annoyance.

"Jen just emailed me..." Jen was my closest girlfriend since we met in law school. Jonathan had never cultivated much of a relationship with her because she was single and preferred to go out with just me. "She has an extra ticket to La Boheme at Lincoln Center tomorrow." *Does a show buy me enough time?* I wondered. "And she wants to have dinner. I'll ask Luisa to stay late."

***

It was an uncharacteristically warm December evening. There was a line to get into the midtown bar. I scanned the people waiting. My eyes fixed on the tallest man. He was at least six foot, two inches, broadly built, young-looking, high cheekbones. He was running a strong, knuckled hand through his thick hair. His eyes caught mine. I was as in awe as I'd been twenty-five years ago. Automatically, I sucked in my stomach.

"I didn't expect you to be this handsome, Evan Roth," I told him, smiling from ear to ear. I stood tippy-toed, on my four-inch heels, to give him a kiss on his cheek. It was one thing to correspond virtually with an old fling from childhood. It was quite another to have been overcome with the urge to press my body against his, to suck his cheek. He smiled, blushed, and shifted awkwardly in his polished shoes. He tried hard to fix on my eyes, but his eyes betrayed him as he took in my shapely legs and the cleavage under my open short jacket. He was disarmed. I wondered if I'd have had this effect on him—or he on me—had we not been love-struck as teens?

"Should we go inside?" he asked.

"It's too crowded. We won't be able to talk." I cocked my head to signal him to follow me. He wiped his palms on his thighs and I realized his must be as sweaty as mine. I walked a few paces in front of him, trying to shift the weight of my rear to accentuate its roundness, but my nerves were stiffening my hips and thighs. We were now a few doors away from the bar.

"I don't mind if we just walk," he said.

I turned to look back at him over my shoulder.

"Neither do I," I said, holding his gaze until he caught up. It felt awkward walking beside him, as if we were slow dancing at a sixth-grade prom, not knowing how close to get and struggling with our steps. But had there not been an overwhelming attraction, walking aimlessly wouldn't have been an option. After all, we both had spouses and children waiting for us at home.

"Where are you tonight?" I asked, imagining his wife at home with his daughter waiting for him. I knew from the scarce photos on Evan's Facebook wall, that he and his wife, Amy, looked happy and clearly in love on their wedding day. I knew from Amy's public Facebook page that she was a few years older than me and Evan, a part-time social worker, and though she posted daily photos of food she prepared—grape leaves, pasta, baklava, chickpea salad—and of their daughter, there were almost none of Evan.

"I'm honestly too overwhelmed to dissect what you're asking me. Do you mean emotionally or intellectually?" he asked.

"Where does your wife think you went tonight?" I clarified.

"I'm at work," he said, looking intently at me for a reaction. *That look.* I imagined his beautiful full lips, gently tugging and pulling between my legs, his tongue circling me, holding me still with his large hands on each thigh, looking up at me. "And then I'm at massage class," he continued.

"That's random. Why didn't you just tell her you were meeting me—an old friend?" I asked, raising an eyebrow and smirking. My heart was fluttering somewhat, and though my nerves made me feel a bit like I was observing myself, I could feel my usual confidence returning.

"I'm really taking a massage class. I just joined a new practice. We offer full-service treatment, from physical therapy, homeopathy, and massage to meditation. The current owner, my partner, is transitioning out. I need to have working knowledge, at a minimum, of every facet of the business," he said. "As for my wife, well, she'd be peeved if she knew what you looked like," he said more to the pavement than to me. My confidence was officially restored.

We'd continued walking up 6th Avenue. It didn't seem safe to stop. If we did, I'd want to feel him pressed against me. Please don't let his feet get tired, I thought.

"How's the father-husband thing working for you?" I asked.

"My daughter is my world. And because of that, my wife is too," he said.

"Children change everything, don't they? I swear I forgave my parents by the time Ella was one for everything I thought they'd done wrong. But my sister never had kids. She still blames them for everything—doesn't get it. I bet becoming a father made you comprehend your parents' loss on a whole new level," I said. He pursed his lips. "Why did you say that because of your daughter, your wife is your world too?"

"She's a wonderful mother. Takes good care of me. I'm a lucky man," he said, unconvincingly.

"I'm relieved to hear you're happy," I said, eyeing him suspiciously. "How many times have you cheated on your wife?"

He looked at me bewildered and said nothing for a few moments. *Was he counting affairs or offended by my candor?*

"Twice. What about you?" he asked.

"Never have. I couldn't do that to Jonathan," I said. "In fact, I can assure you that I'll never meet with you again."

"Why's that?" he asked, smiling.

I just smiled back. There was moisture pooling between my legs.

We'd already walked fifteen blocks. We sat down at the next restaurant we passed. Evan sat back in the chair, with his feet extended so far that I wondered how the waitress wouldn't trip over him. I took him in, his broad shoulders, long torso, chiseled face.

"Writing a memoir, a new business... impressive. Must be satisfying."

"So what would be satisfying for you?" he asked.

"A paycheck," I said, ashamed, and only half-kidding. "I've been toying with the idea of starting my own business, a mediation practice. I enjoy the volunteering—it's the perfect mix of law and psychology—but I need more."

"A woman like you most definitely needs an intellectual outlet," he said. "I imagine you're pretty good at persuading people to sacrifice things they thought they wanted, simply to please you," he said.

"Would you?" I asked, but didn't wait for an answer. "I vow to work out a business plan by my next mediation, which is next month," I committed, more to myself than to him.

He swirled his beer. "I had a rough few years after that summer. But why do you think you ended up in trouble right afterwards?" he asked.

"I'm not sure," I said. "I was an overly analytical kid and got consumed by my own anxieties. I had sexual energy, but objectively I was just a skinny little girl. And there was all this meaninglessness surrounding sex and objectification of girls around me... it was my first existential conflict." I forced a laugh. "I think I believed that by basically exploiting myself under the guise that I was living in the moment, that I could control how men saw me and compensate for being just a little girl."

"Did I play in?" he asked.

"When you left, I felt like nobody got me the way you did. Whether that feeling played a role in my precipitously losing my virginity, sleeping around, getting a dumb butterfly tattoo on my butt, and getting high... I don't know. I think you provided a brief respite from an inevitable path I was on," I said.

"But why were you so sexual at that age to begin with?" he asked.

"Everyone is... I just didn't repress it. What's with your self-proclaimed hypersexuality? Is enough never enough, like me, or do you literally not get enough?" I asked.

"The latter," he said, frowning.

"Maybe you create problems in your marriage so you have an excuse for going on excursions?" I suggested.

"I never thought that to be the case," he said. "My wife doesn't seem to want any affection—nothing physical—or even conversation beyond what she gets from our daughter. All she has left for me is to do lists—literally, yellow post-it notes with tasks for me." He shook his head. "But I admit that I do like keeping a little piece of me, sexual or otherwise, to myself," he said.

"That's not my nature," I said thinking about how I'd demanded that Jonathan and I synch our lives as if individuality threatened the very core of our relationship. We'd morphed from two autonomous, highly functional individuals into one unified dysfunctional self. We'd chosen to depend solely on one another for our happiness and our definitions of self, with our highest ambition to go into business or do something artistic, like creating a documentary or a play together. We hadn't considered what we'd do if we stopped making each other happy.

Four hours, four sangrias, and three untouched appetizers had passed before I considered how late it was.

"I sent you a letter," I said. "Right after you left."

Evan fumbled for his wallet. I opened my pocketbook prepared to argue about the check. He pulled out a piece of paper, folded many times over and handed it to me. I opened it:

"Dear Evan,

I can't believe what happened. Please write back or call me. I'll be under the tree every night thinking about you. 'I'm all out of love, I'm so lost without you.'

Love, Alix"

"I cannot believe you have this!" I said, overcome with nostalgia. I folded the letter, handed it back, and he put his hand over mine. I wanted to put my whole body into it.

"In my book, I want to detail Joy's death and how I coped. I want to finally make peace it with it." He looked at me intently and took a deep breath before continuing. "Did you ever learn who the driver was?"

I shook my head.

"I want to find out. I'm going to go back there, talk to people. If you still know people in the neighborhood, if you remember anything, even rumors, I'd have a starting point. Does your family still live there?"

"My parents live in the same house, and Sabrina nearby," I said.

Sabrina had gone from living with my parents to living with Paul, her childhood boyfriend, six blocks from my parents' house, and marrying him, not out of love, it seemed, but out of fear. She'd always craved security. When my parents had thrown out her favorite tattered blanket, she'd said, "I don't care," but bit her lower lip. When I later heard her crying, I retrieved it from the garbage. They never knew she slept with it and hid it for years after. She was phobic of everything: strangers, airplanes, driving to the city, closed spaces, open spaces, the list goes on and on. She was petrified of tests—or maybe failure—so she'd cut school on test days. She became the first woman in our extended family not to get a graduate degree. As a hairdresser, if she had too many clients on a given day, she had panic attacks. I caught up with and surpassed her delinquency by the time I was fifteen and reversed it by college; Sabrina never hit bottom, just continually fed on it, and therefore never had a reason to come up. Though she seemed to have stopped getting into serious trouble at about the same time I'd started, she remained stunted.

"They'd know if your old neighbors still live there. Do you remember old Mr. Timble, the neighborhood drunk?" I asked. "He waited at the door for Bear Tavern to open every day. People thought it was him. He drove a blue Toyota. His house was a shambles. My parents said he was 'bringing down the property value.'" He shook his head. "But, it's been decades. Why now?" I asked, hoping I didn't sound judgmental.

He sighed. "Cassidy, my daughter, is the spitting image of Joy. She talks like Joy, sticks her pinky out when she throws a ball, takes the crusts off her bread like she did—everything about her."

He showed me a photo of Cassidy eating an ice cream cone, her dirty blonde curls and smart blue eyes, the same as Evan's, the same as Joy's. I made a pained face.

"She's beautiful. If this weren't a digital photo, I'd swear it was Joy."

"Wild, isn't it? She just turned eight. That's how old Joy was, when it happened. I keep flashing back. I get night sweats. I mean, the uncanny resemblance has always evoked memories of Joy for me. But it's gotten worse—Cass is now older than Joy ever was. There'd been many times, over the years, that I felt this burning urge to find the driver. But then I'd talk myself out of it, for my mother's sake—she couldn't have handled me reopening the wound—sometimes she'd just start crying when she was with Cass, and I knew why. But she passed away six months ago."

"I'm sorry, Evan," I said. I shuddered now, first imagining a car hitting Ella or Charlie, and then his mother's suffering.

"It was expected—she was sick for a while. But with my mother passing, Cassidy turning eight, finding you on Facebook... it's like the Perfect Storm. I need to do this now and I'm thinking..."

He paused. I nodded to encourage him to continue.

"People might be more willing to talk to me if you came along," he said. Inadvertently, the violent images subsided and were replaced with a flash image of us having car sex. I shook my head clear and immediately berated myself for having the capacity to weave sex into such a grim conversation.

"Yeah? You think Mr. Timble is going to confess to the brother of the kid he ran down? I'm sure I'd have more success talking to him on my own," I said, immediately realizing that casually saying "the kid he ran down" likely jolted him. I had a tendency, as Jonathan frequently reminded me, to speak bluntly without considering the emotional impact on others, even when my intentions were good.

"Would you do that for me?" he asked like I'd offered him a kidney, apparently unscathed.

"Yes," I said. "And then I'll talk to the neighbors. Now, when I will myself up from this table, please do not kiss me goodnight, really," I said, nervous that I was being presumptive, and possibly the only one of us compartmentalizing the seriousness of his agenda with the lightness of our flirtation.

Evan tilted his head down, and then looked up. "But I'd like to."

"You mustn't," I said, feeling very Victorian with my choice of words, and left.

When I got home, Jonathan was up waiting for me. I could almost feel my glow dimming as I asked him about his day. But then, in a completely uncharacteristic display of desire, he slipped his hand into my underwear, and pushed two fingers into me. Did he unconsciously perceive that he was being threatened? What on earth had gotten into him, I wondered, as he pulled off my clothes and bent me over the couch? Why was I looking for a reason rather than enjoying the moment? I quieted my mind and lost myself.

Chapter 3

"Look, Joanne, I know you're pissed that you weren't promoted. And, as a woman, I completely get how it feels to *know* you're being treated differently. And then to feel like you were fired for reporting it on top of that?" I said, shaking my head, as if I were talking to an old pal rather than the Plaintiff in the mediation whom I'd just met.

Joanne exhaled deeply, her heavy breasts settling on her stomach. "Finally, someone who gets it."

"But the truth is, you're going to have a really hard time proving that it wasn't because of your lateness."

Joanne's attorney nodded. "I've explained that to her," he said. I put my hand up to stop him from speaking.

"I know you've asked for a hundred thousand dollars. And naturally, you want to punish the company. But if you go to trial, you may end up getting nothing. And trial will be grueling. They'll do everything possible to embarrass you. It's January, the beginning of a new year. Let's think about what you really need to move past this so you can take control of your future."

Joanne looked at her attorney, then back at me. "I'm in debt. I have two kids. I can't get another job in sales without a recommendation letter from them," she said. "I've been trying for months. What I need is money and a recommendation letter."

"If their position, even if it's incorrect, is that you weren't doing satisfactory work, the letter is a tough ask. Look, you mentioned that you were once denied a request to transfer from sales to HR, right?"

"Yup. Again, a man got the position. They said I wasn't qualified," she said.

"Now I'm not sure I can do it. But if I got them to agree to pay for an HR course and pay you the equivalent of your salary for three months would you be willing to walk away and make a fresh start?"

Joanne perked up. "I'd do that!"

I went back to the conference room where I'd left her former employer, Scott, and his attorney. "She's really stuck on the recommendation letter."

"Absolutely not," Scott said. "She's the worst salesperson in history—when she even shows up! That's why we fired her."

"I hear you. But unfortunately, she tells a good sob story. She's going to make a convincing witness. Look, you're a businessman. Even if you win, you know the time and cost of taking this to trial. Between us, my sense is she's more concerned with having a job than punishing you. Maybe she'd be interested in switching career paths. I don't know if I could get her to go for it, but would you be willing to pay for her to take a six month course to get certified in something else and give her a small amount, maybe six months pay while she trains?"

"Six months?" he said. "No."

"Tell me what you would be comfortable with."

"Three months. Tops. Her base salary, not including commissions."

A half hour later, a term sheet was drafted.

I got home late. The kids were asleep. Jonathan was in the dining room. "Hi," I said. "I settled the case." He shushed me, with aggravation, because he was on the phone. But, I didn't mind. I'd just settled a case. I had another notch in my belt for my future business.

In the four weeks that had passed since meeting Evan, the prospect of having my own business had made me more tolerant of Jonathan. I felt alive, inspired, and energized. "Sorry," I mouthed, then changed into workout clothes and got onto my elliptical machine in the den.

Jonathan came in and sat, hunched, on the couch next to the elliptical machine, his thumbs working his phone.

"I'm ready to start working again," I told Jonathan from the elliptical, eager to share my excitement and get feedback on my ideas.

"Good. Think about where you want to be two years from now, once Charlie is in school," he said, still pecking away.

"I'm thinking about where I want to be *four months* from now," I said, a little disheartened. "I spent the last few weeks working on some ideas to build a mediation practice."

He finished whatever thought he was typing. "I thought your plan was to wait until the kids were older and then go back to your old firm if you wanted to work again."

"Because it's more acceptable for older children not to see their mother?" I asked, hoping I'd made my point without sounding too antagonistic.

"No, you should do it part time," he said. "Your firm had a decent policy in place."

"The mommy-track?" I asked.

Being "mommy-tracked" — silent consent to less-demanding, lower-profile, less time-consuming work—was one solution, because bearing a child and having little to do with its day-to-day rearing was instinctively distasteful. But for women like me, who had—prior to having children—prided themselves on their careers, being mommy-tracked was not only unfulfilling, but as nauseating as morning sickness.

"So I can do unimportant work, knowing I'm resented for being only half-in, and then use my spare time to organize play dates, plan meals, and deal with all the household stuff?" I continued, increasing the intensity of the elliptical as if it could decrease the building tension.

"That's the point of good part-time policies, so that you aren't pigeon-holed into busy work and can still balance family life," he said.

"I was a litigator, not a bank teller! If you need a preliminary injunction by morning, you work tirelessly to get it done. You don't get to tell a client, 'Hey, I'm part time and I want to be home in time to put my kids to sleep tonight so you have to wait.'"

"Please. Not everyone is an extremist like you. Don't tell me every lawyer out there is working around the clock, like you used to..."

"Not the mediocre ones! All we have carved out for ourselves, with these mommy policies, is that it's acceptable to be mediocre at everything."

"Making a couple of hundred thousand a year working part time is demoralizing?" he said sarcastically.

"I'd rather be *just* an exceptional mother, or *just* an exceptional woman in the professional world," I said. "But now I am neither and I am failing even at mediocrity."

"And you starting a mediation business is the solution?" he asked.

"It'll be more fulfilling to help people avoid the trial process instead of helping rich companies get richer, or helping banks avoid taking responsibility, or making my entire existence revolve around hitting billables. Why are you trying to talk me out of my own business?"

"I'm not. But, I just started Envirex. We can't both have our own companies right now. The kids still need a lot of your time." *No, they need a mother who doesn't lie to them that she's going to work when she's really just escaping the tedium of home life.*

I thought about the countless times I'd been told, "You're so lucky to have the money to stay home, to do what you want." But my freedom felt like a responsibility. The pressure to take advantage of it was overwhelming. I thought it was what had driven Jonathan back to Wall Street. I'd become lethargic about the greater picture, the point, the meaning of life. The children consumed me. The countdown to a glass of wine and an Ambien consumed me. Jonathan's lack of desire consumed me.

"Um, no, I think I'll just go ahead with my own company," I said, as if I were merely disregarding his opinion on what takeout we should order. Now I increased the incline on the machine and switched into a reverse motion. "For most of the last four years we were both semi-retired, stay-at-home parents. Six months ago, you decide to start a new company, and what? You expect me to fall into the role of primary homemaker now while you're out sowing your oats?"

"I expect you not to intentionally make my life more difficult," he said, over the buzzing of the elliptical as it continued shifting gears. "You don't just wake up and decide to start a business. It's a long process to even formulate a business plan, to think about the structure, and it can't just be on a whim... it's a huge commitment."

"I want to create something big, on my own terms," I said.

"Well, then, I guess we'll talk about it when the time comes," he said, and turned away from me. "I'm going outside to smoke."

I imagined the encouragement he'd have given to anyone else with a business idea. He didn't even ask me to elaborate.

"I've already filed the articles of incorporation," I said, casually. "I'm working out the Operating Agreement."

He stopped in his tracks and turned back. "You're so fast! With everything," he said, shaking his head in disbelief, but impressed. I relaxed.

"I'm taking the kids to my parents tomorrow," I said. Jonathan rolled his eyes, as I knew he would. Though he was nothing but pleasant with everyone in my family, once the boundary between Manhattan and Queens was crossed, he seemed like a basketball player crouching to board an airplane.

"I already have..."

Before he could say, 'calls to make,' 'a haircut,' a 'breakfast meeting,' I added, "You don't have to come."

Jonathan went outside to smoke. I called Sabrina.

"Hi, Mom is babysitting the kids tomorrow at her house if you want to see them," I said.

"Tomorrow is laundry day. Can't do it. Where are you going?"

"Remember that kid Evan Roth, my boyfriend when I was thirteen and you were fifteen—the one whose sister died after the hit and run?"

"Yes."

"He reached out to me on Facebook. He's trying to track down the driver. He asked if I'd talk to Mr. Timble and see what I could find out."

"Oh," she started seriously, and then switched into a teasing tone, "Super-I-can-do-everything-Alix. So, now you're a detective too? Going to uncover something the police missed twenty-five years ago?"

"You're always so negative," I said.

"Involving yourself with an old boyfriend... Does Jonathan know what you're up to?"

"No."

"Why are you *really* helping him?" she asked.

I thought back to when we were kids. Once, I'd pretended to be sick so I could stay home from school with the Rottweiler—Momo, I called him—that I'd found, snuck in through the garage, and hidden in our basement the day before. Momo had never barked, and I felt I could have walked him, fed him, and cared for him undetected for life. Then Sabrina barged into my room, barely glanced at me, and threatened to tell my mother I was faking, unless I told her why. I showed her Momo and invoked, "Nellie," our code word, inspired by Little House on the Prairie, for keeping a secret. Now too, I thought, hanging up, she always knew when I was up to something.

***

The screen door was ripped. A broom with dead-ends leaned against the house on the front porch. I knocked. A woman in her early thirties opened the door.

"Hi, I'm Alix Beck. My parents, the Goldens, live a few blocks over. Does Edward Timble still live here?"

"No, I'm his daughter, Lisa."

"Lisa! I remember you. You and your brother used to run to our corner barefoot for Mr. Softee." She nodded, as if she recognized me and stepped out, pulling her acrylic cardigan together.

"My father passed away a few years back. Cirrhosis."

"I'm sorry to hear that," I said.

"Can I help you?" Lisa asked.

"It was a long time ago. But I wanted to ask him if he knew anything about the car accident that happened on 188th Street. You were young. I don't know if you remember."

"You kidding? I spent third grade dodging the Camuto twins' spitballs for it. 'Child Killer' was written on our sidewalk for months. It's been awhile since anyone asked about that. Why are you?"

"I'm in touch with the family. They're still hoping to find the driver. Sometimes people are more willing to talk years later when they know nobody can go to jail. So I'm retracing the police investigation."

"Oh," she said. Her face hardened. "He didn't do it, you know. He was a drunk, but he never killed anyone."

"If you don't mind, how do you know?"

"I remember the cops came here looking for him right after the accident. He'd been home drinking all night. He was so drunk they couldn't wake him. They asked my mom where his car was parked. She told them it'd been in the body shop by Seven-Eleven since he banged into a tree two days before. 'Yeah, we'll see if he banged a *tree*,' the cop said. You could tell they didn't believe her. They were looking for a blue car, and dad had a dented fender, and everyone knew he drank. But then they confirmed that the car had been at the shop just like she said. Didn't matter. People believe what they want to believe."

"Must have been hard for you, with the rumors. Anyway, I'm sorry to trouble you. Thanks for your help." I took a step down the stairs, visualizing the auto shop and the guys in overalls always working outside. And then I paused.

"Hey Lisa," I said, turning to face her, "Wasn't your older brother, Jason, a mechanic at that auto shop?"

Lisa closed the door with an eye roll.

I sent myself an email before starting the car: "Follow-up w/J. Timble. Lied to protect Dad? Or was Jason driving? Check if auto shop still exists. Ask Sabrina if she knows where Jason lives."

Jonathan called as I drove towards Evan's old house.

"Did you take all the money from the top drawer?" he asked. "I left two thousand last Friday and there's nothing left," he said.

Like I always did when Jonathan questioned me about money, I suddenly felt the stinging prick of the conversation we'd had about a prenuptial agreement when we were engaged. While I was having dress fittings and engraving his wedding band, he'd been speaking to a financial adviser. He waited until the wedding was just a few weeks away to broach the topic.

"What do you think about a prenup?" he'd asked casually, as if we were discussing whether to paint the office. Immediately, his rehearsal was evident. The hours of preparation, the false starts I hadn't noticed, the already worked-out clauses of the agreement, becoming as transparent as the diamond on my finger.

"It's a fine idea," I said. Relief rolled over his nervous face. "We'll need a graph," I said, straight-faced, racing to the kitchen for a paper and a pen. I half-expected to find a notary in there. "Let's outline the terms." I made a chart of ages—under 20, 20s, 30s, 40s, and education levels—College educated, Graduate Degree, Ivy League.

"What is this?" he asked, as I assigned dollar amounts in the second column.

"This," I said, as I wrote, without looking up at him, "is 'The Monetary Penalty' column on cheating." This, I said to myself, is your death certificate, your extradition papers. "Since I haven't a clue how much money you have, I'll just use five million dollars as a total, and make a legend right here..." I made an asterisk at the bottom of the page, unwittingly pressing down hard enough that the pen pushed through the paper, "... to clarify that the numbers should be adjusted upwards as a percentage of actual numbers." I assigned the gravest penalty, four million dollars to the twenty-something categories and Ivy Leaguers—because I considered them the biggest threats.

I figured my overreaction would be both sobering and funny to Jonathan. He started laughing, genuinely amused, as if he didn't understand that he had just flung my heart against a wall with a slingshot and was now watching it dribble down. "Listen, if you don't want..." he began.

If? Because it was possible that I did? Wait, was that, could it be, I thought it was, my lunch about to shoot from my mouth onto the framed photo of us at the Eiffel Tower?

"Let's agree that if you cheat on me, there will be penalties based on the woman's age, education, and my age. We'll need to assign monetary values to each of my aging features, maybe a hundred thousand dollars per millimeter of breast sagging? A thousand per wrinkle? Because I'd certainly need to be compensated for giving you my best years."

"Alix... I..."

"No, it's fine. You want to make sure your financial capital is protected, and I'll do the same for the emotional and physical capital I'm investing."

"I don't think these agreements are supposed to be emotional agreements. I don't think it's about emotion at all." *Exactly.*

"Is marriage?" I asked.

He was silent for a few seconds, looking apologetic.

"It is," he said. He kissed my forehead.

"Not a business agreement, then?"

"No."

"Then why are you treating it like one?"

Did he realize he was? Was he just being reasonable, thinking about the statistics? *This must be what the rich do*, I thought. *I'm just beneath him... them, so I don't get it. Do you want to marry an unreasonable man? No.* Then why did the mere question make me feel dirty, make me want to tear up my law degree, make me feel like a child? Make the half a million that I'd managed to save—a half a million that'd given me the right to unapologetically fuck whoever I wanted—seem like pennies in a piggy bank? Because he was announcing his fear that I was only a scheming whore out for his money. Weren't we in the throes of idealized love, inhabiting that interminable place where logic and reason were beautifully overshadowed by passion and faith?

There was something both shameful and shaming about his request. I knew it symbolized something about both of us, something I wouldn't dare tell another soul. I couldn't tell my girlfriends, coworkers, or parents—definitely not my happily married parents who had earned the same teacher's paycheck every week, took sabbaticals every seven years together, and had no lives outside each other. He was making me choose between appearing greedy or giving up the romanticized ideal. I was ready to hurl his ring across the room, but I didn't.

"I'm not treating our marriage like a business agreement," he said.

"Just cold feet?" I asked.

"Definitely not. I want nothing more than to marry you. This could be beneficial for both of us," he said, hitting the first of ten bullet points his adviser gave him to persuade me.

"Alright, so let's be logical," I said. "What sort of agreement are you suggesting for *our* benefit?"

"I haven't thought about the details."

"Chocolate filling or vanilla?" I asked.

"What?"

"The wedding cake. Those are the details *I* was focused on an hour ago," I said, feeling my chest tightening with something rancid. "You want to spend the next few weeks before our wedding negotiating a prenup? Should I get a lawyer, or do you think I can negotiate this minor issue on my own behalf? Who's your lawyer? I'll reach out."

"I don't have a lawyer. I just..."

"Right, just a financial advisor. Fine. Business it is. My projected income is over a million dollars a year, assuming I make partner in the next two years. Part of marrying and starting a family means I'll be risking that income—*millions!*—either because I'll be taken less seriously as a result of getting married, everyone counting down until I'm pregnant, or because we decide it's better for me to work part-time after kids. You've already said that's what you expect. How can that be addressed in the prenup? And how can you ask me to lessen your risk? Marriage isn't about hedging. Imagine if I get pregnant, stop working, and then you leave me, and I can't get back on the career path? How could I ever be comfortable having a kid? Or what, if after thirty years together, you decide to trade up for less fleshy arms and live eggs, leaving me without a pot to piss in?"

Surely he'd realize how insulting this was, the drops of lemon juice he was leaking into the milk.

"I've thought of that. There could be a sunset provision, if it would make us feel more comfortable, so that the agreement would be void after a set amount of time." *A sunset provision!* With a thump, the entire wedge of lemon was lodged in the milk.

"I see. How many years of my life would my internship last?" I asked.

"I don't know, five years?"

Geez, I'd just called myself an intern and he was letting it stand, uncorrected. I couldn't swallow the lump in my throat. My eyes swelled with tears, realizing I'd have to call off the wedding.

"Okay, so you're sure that five years is enough for you to feel confident that I'm not scheming to take all your money? Or is that how long it'll take you to decide if you really want to spend your life with me, while ensuring that I don't get away in case you decide you do? Jesus, how rich *are* you? Would you really want a 'sunset provision' anyway? Let's say I do fall in love with someone else, in year one, and want to leave you. You want to incentivize me to keep it secret and stay for another four years so I can outlast the sunset provision?" I asked.

"Most marriages that fail, do so in the first few years. So I was just suggesting a way to..."

"Buy fate? You can't control everything. You think I really think I can prevent you from having an affair if you want to? Should money be the reason not to cheat?" I felt like I was in another reality. What happened to our talks of traveling the world, living in Europe for a year, having two adorable kids, doing something creative together, harassing our great-grandchildren to take us to lunch? "The bottom line is you're saying you don't know me well enough to marry me, and that's okay. It's only been two years. I'll love you as much in five years as I do now. We can marry then, if we still want to." I gave a tissue an unladylike blow, wondering if I'd be able to recover from this insult. "Believe me, I'm in no rush to deal with the paperwork involved in changing my name, or to stretch my perfect peach and have kids. This is *bogonia*," I said, invoking our made-up word for bullshit.

"It's just something we felt I should raise as a possibility," he said. "I'm not waiting to marry you and I'm not waiting to have children."

"Did 'we' feel it was a good idea to meet in secret and wait until the twelfth hour to raise it too?" I wondered at what point a prenuptial agreement came up. Was it when he made his first, second, third million? Was it when he met a girl from Queens without a pedigree or trust fund? Or was he always this way, made so by his greedy father, his unhappy mother?

"It wasn't in secret..."

"It wasn't with me."

"I don't want you to feel like it was behind your back. It's not unusual for..."

"... for a man who's been divorced and has children from another marriage to have a prenup? No, it's not."

"Can I finish?" he asked.

"I don't think we should get married," I said, cutting him off, unable to separate emotion from logic.

"What?"

"This isn't how it's supposed to be," I said.

"Come here, Alix," he said, realizing I was about to come undone.

"You're asking me to walk into the woods blindfolded, while you're leaving a trail of breadcrumbs for yourself. If we're doing away with convention, let's do away with convention. Why even bother to get married? It's an unnatural state. The idea is that you can't imagine *not* being with this person for the rest of your life. But you're doing the exact opposite." I looked at him with teary eyes and his got a bit teary too.

"We *are* getting married. In five weeks, as planned." He sighed. "No prenup." He touched my arm. "Can we pretend I never raised this?" he asked.

"No. Fuck it. Draft it up however you like. I'll sign whatever you want."

"I don't want a prenup anymore. I'm sorry. It was only a thought, a passing thought. Just forget the whole thing."

But I never would. He'd effectively gotten what he wanted anyway because the request, alone, ensured that I would never view his money as my money.

The air in the room became the air between us. That's the air that would recirculate. I called my father that night, crying, telling him only that I had a feeling that I was marrying more money than I'd realized.

"Mazel Tov. So why are you crying?" he asked.

"Because it's a complication," I said. Because by not walking away from him then—and from his treating our marriage as an arms-length agreement rather than an eternal squeeze of the hand—I had taken the first step away from myself and towards a man who'd risk upsetting me rather than his portfolio.

"Daughter, you are the complication," he said.

"Well? Did you spend two thousand?" Jonathan asked.

"I paid Luisa, bought groceries, and I got the kids more winter clothes. Would you like me to start leaving receipts on your pillow?" I asked. "I have to go. I'm parking."

Chapter 4

Evan's old house was on the corner at the end of a block that led to the service road of the Long Island Expressway. The most likely eyewitnesses would have been his next-door neighbor and the one across the street.

I rang the bell at the house next to his. A plaque on the door read, "The Martins." A dark-skinned woman with an accent I couldn't place opened the door, introduced herself as Anita, Jack Martin's caregiver, and invited me in. The house smelled of curry. I told her about the hit and run and asked if she could help me.

"Jack's been living here forty years. Wife is long dead. I've been with him two years now. His memory isn't right. No point talking to him," she said, but took my coat and led me to the living room. Jack was sitting in a floral-upholstered armchair, staring at a ballgame, remote in hand.

"Molly," he said, smiling at me.

"No, it's not Molly," Anita said.

"She looks like Molly," he said.

"I hope Molly is pretty," I said.

"This is Alix, an old neighbor of yours."

"Sit down," Jack said, motioning to the tufted once-white couch. "I don't get many guests nowadays. My children live in Texas. My friends are old. I used to have card games here every Thursday. Roberta would make her famous pecan pie." He went on to tell me how she'd defrost her pies and they'd still be delicious, the right way to play poker, the night he made seven hundred dollars with only a pair of eights.

Twenty minutes passed before I asked him if he remembered the accident.

"You bet I remember."

"Did you see it?" I asked.

"You bet we did. Roberta said it was because we lived so close to O'Hare. All the Chicago dust. People couldn't see where they were going." Anita got up, taking an empty plate to the kitchen, shaking her head. She glanced at me, silently saying, "told you so."

I thanked Jack for the information and left. I was bothered by the smell of curry in my hair. Then I realized how trivial the thought was and thought about what Evan might be feeling on his old street had he come. I emailed myself: "Find Jack's children?" Then, I called my mother to check on the kids.

"We're about to leave to the park," she told me, "Should I wait for you?"

I felt bad that I'd already left her with the kids so long. But I saw a light on in the house across the street, and it was more inviting than another day at the park. "No."

I crossed over to the house and knocked on the door. A woman I immediately recognized—Mrs. Springfield—opened it. Her poodle used to relieve itself on my parents' lawn during the five-block walks she'd take him on. I introduced myself.

"The Goldens' kid? I remember you," she said, a look of disapproval on her face. "You were always smoking on the porch." *And you were always a nosey-body.*

I remembered when I was sixteen and came home to a suitcase and some of my clothes on the front lawn. My mother demanded my key and said I wasn't welcome until I signed a contract to obey curfews and stop 'using pot.' Mrs. Springfield stared from across the street while I banged on the door, holding her dog's leash taut so he couldn't lead her away. My father watched me from the living room window. He didn't share my mother's certainty that "Tough Love" was appropriate. But he shared her commitment not to let the constant battling with me interfere with their otherwise idyllic marriage.

"You still smoke?" she asked.

"Yes. The only time I didn't was when I was pregnant."

"What can I do for you?" she asked, eyeing my wedding ring a little too long.

"I was hoping you could tell me if you saw anything the night Joy Roth was hit."

Her beady eyes widened. "Come in," she said. We sat at her kitchen table. There was a hanging plant over her kitchen sink and four glass jars filled with pickles on the windowsill.

"Why on earth are you asking about that all these years later?" she asked.

I explained that the family was still hoping to find the driver.

She got up, filled the teapot, pulled at her earring.

"I was watching TV on the couch that evening. I heard a car coming. Then boom, I heard a thud. I thought the car hit my dogwood tree. When I looked out the window..." she shook her head, "the little girl was lying all twisted on the street. The car backed up and zipped away. I hollered for my husband to come up from the basement. Took his fat ass forever."

"What kind of car was it?" I asked as she dipped a tea bag in and out of her cup.

She cocked her head to one side and put her hands on her hips. "The kind you drive. Am I a car expert?" She suddenly got very still, didn't blink. "All I saw was that it was blue," she said slowly.

In all the depositions I'd taken, I was always on guard when the witness made sudden head movements as I asked a question and then made no movement while answering. I took it to mean that the witness was lying or scared.

"Did you get a look at the driver?" I asked.

"No, just the car," she said.

"Then what happened?"

"Mrs. Roth came right out, hollering, 'Help!' It was awful. The ambulance came, then the cops. The poor girl was loaded into the back on a stretcher with her parents. Her brother, a fine boy— used to help me move my garbage cans from the curb—he stayed outside talking with an officer."

"Did you go outside?" I asked.

"No, my husband said I'd only be in the way. Then another police car pulled up and they came here."

"What did you tell them?"

"Same I told you," she said, picking at her chipped nail polish.

"What shade of blue was the car?"

She stopped picking at her polish and looked like she was thinking hard. "Dark blue."

"Is there anything else you can think of from that night that might help me?" I asked.

"No," she said, again very still. I felt like she was holding something back, but decided not to push her, yet.

"Thanks for your time," I said, standing. "Hey, are those pickles homemade?" I asked, hoping to get a sense of her mannerisms when she was relaxed.

Her shoulders dropped. She clasped her hands together, grinned, licked her lips. "Oh yes, dear. You need salt, water, kirbys, garlic, and fresh dill. You have to watch them carefully and make sure the lid is tight. You can add shallots or peppers." She was speaking quickly. "For the half-sour, don't let them stand more than a week," she said, wagging her finger.

"I'll try it," I said. "Have you had horseradish pickles?" I asked, as we got to the front door.

"Never heard of it," she said.

"You know what? The next time I visit my parents, I'll bring you some from a flea market near me."

As I walked towards the car, I added to my notes: "Pickles/follow-up re: Mrs. S—hiding something."

Then I called Evan and downloaded what I learned on his voicemail. "Also, I'm having my body perfected in a few weeks—don't ask—so it'll be awhile before I'm on my feet and can revisit this. In the meantime, try to locate Jack's children online and ask them if they saw anything, and do a free criminal record search on Jason Timble."

Motherhood had taken its toll, not just on my marriage, but on my body too. I ran and lifted weights daily. Within eight weeks of having Charlie, I'd gotten back to my pre-pregnancy weight. But my stomach was distended and my intestines seemed to wander like a live wire just under the surface of my abdomen. Even small quantities of food created the discomfort and appearance of being pregnant. I'd made an appointment with a plastic surgeon.

"Well, Mrs. Beck, you have an umbilical hernia and severe diastasis, a separation of the abdominal muscles. The hernia is easy, but the only way to repair the diastasis is an abdominoplasty—a tummy tuck," the surgeon had told me.

I was ecstatic that there was a solution. That I'd need a massive surgery to fix it didn't deter me.

"How bad will the scar be?" I asked.

"It's going to extend from hip to hip," he told me.

"I have no choice, right?" I asked. I remembered how distraught I'd been in the hospital after having Ella, seeing the bandages covering my C-section incision as I hunched past the bathroom mirror with Jonathan holding me up. Despite the joy of a new baby, I collapsed into his arms crying that I'd never be the same woman to him. He had cupped my chin in his hands and looked into my teary eyes, "I'll love you no matter what. You're still beautiful to me. Scars are nothing." But I'd remained self-conscious about it, always hoping that Jonathan would acknowledge that the scar bothered me and trail small kisses along it before moving downward with his mouth. He never did.

"Your stomach won't ever look any different if you don't do the surgery. Are we doing your breasts too?" he asked.

What! How had the plastic surgeon's office turned into a car dealership, trying to convince me to purchase add-ons? I hadn't even considered doing my breasts. Sure, they weren't as perky as the full double D's they'd been before breastfeeding, but I'd thought I had another good five years left before I qualified as "needing work."

"No, I'm only doing this to alleviate the discomfort—so I can eat a meal without feeling it and seeing it travel through my innards," I told him, inexplicably insulted.

We set a February date for my abdominal surgery, and I paid the hefty three hundred dollar consultation fee. As the receptionist handed me the receipt, though, I turned and said, "You know what, since I'm paying for the consultation anyway, maybe he should take a look at my boobs." Ten minutes later, I'd been scheduled for a breast augmentation as well.

Despite Jonathan's insistence that our dry spell had nothing to do with physical attraction, I was certain that if I could have my pre-pregnancy body back, I could have my pre-pregnancy identity and marriage back.

"You really ought to start making me feel like you want to ravage me, now, before the surgery," I told Jonathan after my appointment.

"Why's that?" he asked.

"Because if you don't, and suddenly start wanting to have sex all the time after I get new tits, it's just going to confirm that I was right all along. That all this time you just weren't attracted to me."

Jonathan didn't initiate more sex before the surgery. To the contrary, it gave him another distant point after which things would, in his mind, change. It was easier, for both of us, to wait for external change.

***

Evan texted back, rather than calling: "Got your voicemail. Can't talk right now. Thank you so much. I won't ask, but I can say with absolute certainty that you don't need perfecting."

I felt like a freshly fluffed pillow from his text. I couldn't help but stare at it, until my phone showed an incoming call from Sabrina.

"Hi," I answered.

"So, did you learn anything, Sherlock?"

"Not really. The neighbors didn't see anything. I have to confirm it, but I still suspect it was one of the Timbles. Do you know where Jason Timble lives?"

"No idea," she said.

"I'll follow-up," I said.

"I guess this is what happens when you don't have a full-time job," she said and I thought she might be right.

Chapter 5

"Alix, I can't believe it's been nearly four months since we met. I'm not sure why your presence affects me so, but my writing has taken off since we've reconnected. I attached my draft so far. Also, I emailed Jack's kids. They said nobody in their family saw anything. I did the background check on the Timble kid, too. If you're willing (no pressure) we can discuss all of this in person – Evan."

Twelve weeks had gone by without any communication with Evan. I had the tummy tuck and breast surgery. I spent the recovery time working on the business, and delighting in my refurbished body, and wondering why Evan hadn't inquired about either, and wondering why I had the silent expectation that he would. His lack of communication made me minimize what I thought I'd been feeling for him, and left me indulging in the possibility that I had glamorized our encounter. But now that he'd emailed my doubts were stymied.

I replied: "Glad my 'presence' affects you so. Not much to discuss until I revisit Mrs. Springfield. I did the search on Jason Timble, too. Two DUI's and currently in Rikers for dealing marijuana! Maybe he did take the car for a joyride that night." I stopped myself from adding that I'd be happy to question Jason at Rikers as inmates topped my list of sexual fantasies, realizing it would likely sound insensitive.

Days later I was chapters into his draft:

"Alix was intense and had a sexual magnetism that I, and all the other boys, were drawn to. But she picked me. When she asked me to join her at the party that night, I wanted to please her. But I was brewing with insecurity. I suggested meeting her later that night instead. I was going to surprise her with a charm bracelet and tell her she was my charm."

With a lingering smile, and feeling stupidly inflated and helplessly drawn to him, I emailed: "Let's discuss your draft next Saturday night. I can't stay out late this time because I have a big dinner with Jonathan and his partners the next night (who throws dinner parties on a Sunday?!), and I need to be fresh."

There was no way that the seeming intensity of our first meeting could be replicated. I had invented it. He was happily married, only doing book research. This was safe and in no way ethically questionable. That's what I told myself as I walked to meet him at a restaurant on the Upper West Side, his draft rolled up in my pocketbook. So why had I lied to Jonathan that I was meeting an old colleague for dinner to discuss the new business? And why had I manhandled my own breasts to determine if the implants were noticeable? I walked past a candy store and saw chocolate covered pretzels in the window. I stopped to take a photo to show Evan, and then decided it'd be a nice gesture to bring him some.

The smell of fresh tar from street repairs filled my nostrils as I crossed the street towards the restaurant, in obscenely high heels, trying to concoct a clear picture in my mind about what Evan looked like. Our emails, reading his draft, the passage of time, and my idealization of him converged to confuse my memory. I stumbled over the unpaved portion of the street and clumsily stretched my arms out to avert the fall, when to my embarrassment, I saw Evan trotting towards me, and within seconds, his two hands were now firmly gripping me around my rib cage. Blood rushed to my cheeks.

"You're a strong woman. But also fragile." He removed his hold on me slowly enough that I had time to recuperate and imagine pressing my breasts against him. *Oh lord.* It hadn't been my imagination; the charge between us was already igniting the air, and he was still breathtakingly handsome.

"Good to see you," I said.

"Surprised to see you," he said, as we walked into the restaurant.

"Why is that?" I asked, as we followed the hostess to a table in the back corner.

"Because I figured our meeting was an outlier in your life, that I happened to catch you at the right time in the right place, and that you meant it when you said you wouldn't meet me again. I'm actually a little disappointed that you no longer think this is dangerous."

"It is definitely dangerous," I said, relieved but panicked that he felt something too. He nodded in agreement. "You might just fall in love with me," I added.

Without flinching, Evan leaned across the table so that his face was closer to mine, and asked, "What makes you think I'm not already?"

Instead of fainting or kissing him, I said, "Because if you were, you'd have been more aggressive about seeing me again."

"Had I done that, you wouldn't be here right now," he said, his eyes so vulnerable and intense that the walls below my cervix constricted.

"Do you understand what you are doing to me looking at me like that?"

"Do you realize that I can't maintain eye contact with you for the same reason?"

"What are we supposed to do with this?"

"That's completely up to you," he said. "I'm not going to push you, and I'll respect your boundaries. But since you may not let me see you again, can I just look at your face?"

His words left me speechless, as I obliged, looking away from him towards the irrelevant humming of the restaurant, wanting desperately to go somewhere, anywhere, where we could be alone.

"I could never get tired of looking at your face," he said.

"Don't you think marriage, by definition, kills this?" I asked, turning back to him.

"Why is that?" he asked seemingly in complete agreement.

"I think it's probably chemical. I wish I could always carry this feeling, even if we never actually *did* anything," I said.

"Maybe we're fortunate for already being happily married, and the trick is to only see each other once a year?" he suggested.

"Is that what you do with your other, um, diversions?" I asked.

"I've been thinking about that. Those two times... I wish I hadn't," he said, looking at me again with those vulnerable and expectant eyes.

"Because you realize how poetic it would be if we lost our marital virginity to one another?" I laughed. "Once a year, huh? That's brilliant. But probably not realistic once this begins, not that it *will* begin. But if it did, every ninety days is probably more appropriate."

We both looked at the waiter approaching to take our order. "I no longer have an appetite," I said, smiling.

"Me neither," he said.

"I need air," I said, fanning myself playfully.

"If you creep out of here before we order, I'll follow."

"Let's go to the park," I said, and got up.

When we got outside I fumbled through my oversized pocketbook and retrieved the paper bag with chocolate-covered pretzels. His draft lay at the bottom of my bag, still unmentioned. Evan opened the bag and breathed hard through his nose. "That's sweet," he said.

We walked one block in complete silence before entering the park. My mind was racing. Where was this going? What would constitute cheating? This was already an indiscretion, so I might as well allow it to play out. No, I hadn't done anything wrong yet. I could spend an eternity fantasizing about what this would be like. But I wanted him badly. The thought unleashed another wave of wetness between my legs. My head started hurting behind my ear, probably from the stress of indecision. An available taxi stopped at the red light on Central Park West. Get in it, I told myself. There is no going back if you don't.

"Don't," he said reading my mind, "not yet." That he read my mind made me think of Jonathan, how he'd cringe knowing someone else had.

We walked into the park until we got to the jogging path. Evan sat down on a bench, placing the pretzels beside him. I stood in front of him, my feet positioned between his as if I were about to give him a lap dance. I wished he would let himself go, slide his hands up my thighs, and end the spinning and indecision in my mind. I wanted to kneel before him, expose him, and feel him in my hands, until his legs tightened and he came in my mouth. Jonathan was disappearing to the back of my thoughts as my body took over. I looked away from Evan, down to the shadow we were casting on the concrete path.

"Between the idea and the reality, between the motion and the act, falls the shadow," I said, knowing he would recognize Eliot's quote. "I want to sit on you, just for a moment... because I need to feel you, and then I have to go," I asked more than said, knowing it required that he consent to frustration.

"That's fine," he said.

Evan placed one hand on each of my thighs. I closed my eyes and looked upward to the open sky as he slowly began moving his palms up my thighs, his thumbs getting closer to the front edge of my panties. His fingers gently slid under the thin straps on my hips to find my waist and then back down to my hips, thighs, with his hands now caressing, then gently parting my behind. I moaned. I took a step back so that he had to withdraw his hands from under my dress and could no longer reach me. He was visibly excited, bulging in his pants.

I stepped forward again, and this time straddled him, placing my knees on either side of him on the bench, holding myself up so that my body wasn't touching him. I eased myself softly onto the base of his bulge, moving my hips forward so that I could feel the stiff length of him beneath me. Evan groaned. His girth shocked me. I knew that if I traveled his length again, I would come. *Jonathan.* Goddamit. In this sensual moment, my tortured mind could not let go. I had to stop.

"I'm so sorry. I have to go," I said, leaning down to press my forehead to his.

"It's okay, Alix," he said. "I'm a patient man."

"There's no point seeing you again, not until I'm ready for this," I said. "I'm never going to be able to be near you without all roads leading here."

"See you in ninety days, baby," he said. "Maybe."

Maybe. Maybe. No! I barely slept that night, pushed him out of my mind to the best of my ability, and reinstated my role as Jonathan's faithful wife before we arrived at William's apartment the next night for dinner.

Chapter 6

The morning after William's dinner party, Jonathan woke me at 6:30 a.m. for the morning routine. There was still a dull pain in the back of my head under my left ear. The French fries had failed me. I checked my phone to make sure that I hadn't responded to Evan's email that he would be at Lee's Art Shop post-sleeping pill, and forgotten. *Oh no.* I had. At 12:09 a.m. I had written, "It's been less than 2 days. You're breaking protocol. There are 88 to go... and that's assuming I get my arms around what we're talking about. In which case, I'd need to get my arms around you. Is that even possible? You're enormous (everywhere). I bet nobody has held you since you were a boy. I would hold you, if it were physically possible. It's probably not. Poor you!" *Oh geez. Humiliating!* There'd been so many times that I'd awakened to messages, usually sexual, that I'd sent and forgotten as a result of the sleeping pill, insisting that I couldn't be held accountable for my words or actions. I reread the words, "I would hold you" and shook my head with embarrassment. What was I thinking!

I was dreading the drilling from the construction site outside our building that would begin promptly at 7:00 a.m. and end at 7:01 a.m., like a rogue rooster abusing its power to wake the ranch, before really picking up again at 7:20 a.m. I brushed my teeth, put on my gym clothes, got the kids dressed, scrambled four eggs, printed the mediation documents I planned to review in the afternoon, and went downstairs to smoke a quick cigarette before letting Jonathan leave for work. By the time I got upstairs, the construction outside of our apartment had already begun.

With my headache, the banging seemed amplified. I headed outside with my double stroller, dropped Ella off at school, returned home to leave Charlie with Luisa, and went back out into Central Park for a four-point-two mile run, certain I could sweat out the alcohol and beat the headache that was nagging the left side of my skull. Or was it in my ear? I couldn't tell, but it was getting annoying.

My morning runs were as critical as my morning coffee. That's where the to-do list was mentally written and the day's meals were planned. Tonight would be pea soup. It was also my therapy, and today Evan was dominating my session. I jogged past the bench we'd been on not forty-eight hours ago. I glanced over to see if the chocolate pretzels were still on the bench. They were not. Eighty-eight days to go. *Wrong countdown,* I scolded myself. One hour until real therapy.

My phone rang exactly half a mile before my run should have ended and five minutes before scheduled. I slowed to a walk, retrieved the phone from my armband, and took the call anyway. This was important.

"Hi Dan. So, what do you think?" I asked.

"I read everything you sent. The idea is basically to create a spinoff firm that capitalizes on the reputation of our firm."

"Well, that's a simplification. The novel part of this, the selling point, if you will, is that each mediator is specialized in his field. So the client saves money on mediator prep time and knows he has expertise and training from a good firm. There'd be a steady flow of business just from referrals. Obviously, I'd want you for med-mal and professional negligence cases if you came on board. I want to ferret out anything that isn't complex litigation by emphasizing a business judgment philosophy towards settling, rather than the touchy-feely mentality. We aren't looking for emotional epiphanies, but financial ones. So think about who I could bring on for real estate and entertainment matters."

"The startup costs will be sizeable," Dan said.

"Don't worry about that. I'll shoulder it."

"In exchange for greater partnership?" he said, more than asked.

"I just want the right talent so I'm not going to get hung up on the initial investment," I said.

"Let's meet and flesh it out more next Thursday," he said. "I'm heading to Greece for three weeks the following week. I'm definitely interested. Oh, by the way, I gave your contact info to Madeline Schwartz, the President of that rescue organization you did that dreadful internal investigation for. Something about fundraising she thought you'd be interested in."

I hung up with Dan. There was no time to shower before the appointment, so I jogged straight out of the park to the therapist's office on West 57th Street, thinking about the impression I'd make on him: An Upper West Side woman in sweaty gym clothes who hadn't bothered to shower to meet her husband at therapy, and then wondered why her sex life was in the dumps.

Jonathan was already sitting in one of three chairs in the small waiting room that was carved out of what was otherwise a studio apartment. I sat next to him. A short middle-aged man came out from behind a closed door, and introduced himself as Dr. Stearns. He shook our hands, and asked us each to fill out a new client intake form, and then left.

"Can we agree that I don't need to admit to recreational drug use? It's not something I want on a form," Jonathan whispered, referring to the pot he occasionally smoked.

"Yeah, and I'm obviously going to answer no to this question about whether I have a history of drug or psychiatric treatment, right?" I asked. Jonathan knew that my parents had strong-armed me into agreeing to rehab at sixteen by threatening to kick me out if I didn't. I'd spent two angry weeks in rehab before the facility transferred me, for another two weeks, to an adolescent psychiatric ward. He also knew that I'd never believed those measures were warranted. Ultimately, I'd been diagnosed with a "drug-induced depression" and spent a "sober" year on anti-depressants.

"Of course, and this bit about smoking... do you think it will affect insurance or anything if we admit to being smokers?" he asked.

"Probably. Just say no. Hey, what'd you write for thirteen?" I asked, "about what brings us here."

Jonathan flipped the pages to show me: *My wife is nuts.*

I laughed. "Look at mine!" *My husband is a dick.*

"What about number eighteen, have you ever had homicidal or suicidal thoughts?" I asked in a serious tone.

He flipped the page again to show me his answer. *I might kill Alix (just kidding) if she doesn't match my socks.*

I laughed again, showing him mine. *I feel like killing Jonathan when he leaves the iced tea pitcher empty (but I won't).*

Doctor Stearns returned to collect our intake forms and said he'd review them and come back.

"Do you think this time counts towards our fifty minutes?" I asked Jonathan when he left.

"Probably," Jonathan said as we united in our defense mechanisms.

"Remember when you thought about transitioning into family law and wanted us to start going to marriage counselors just so you could win them over and have them send you clients?" Jonathan asked with a grin.

"Yeah, that was genius," I said.

"Well, I wouldn't have married you if you weren't," he said, reminding me that despite the office we were in, he still loved me. I had the urge to jump onto his lap, wrap my arms around his neck, and tell him how much I loved him, like I used to. But I was no longer comfortable showing affection, only anger. I flashed back to his toast at our wedding. "Alix told me not to forget to tell all of you how beautiful I find her. That's obvious to everyone but her. What she doesn't realize is how much beauty there is in her beyond the physical. She has no idea how her inner beauty trumps all else." I pushed the thought out of my mind. He no longer believed that.

Dr. Stearns returned and ushered us into his office where I was faced with the choice of one of two armchairs or a couch to sit on. Despite his unimpressive looks, I'd immediately envisioned him bending me over the armrest of the couch and forcefully taking me while antagonizing Jonathan, "see what your wife wants." I chose the armchair as if rejecting the couch would help me focus on positive marriage thoughts.

"So, what brings you here today?" Dr. Stearns asked.

Reflexively, Jonathan and I looked at each other.

"Shall I?" I asked Jonathan. "Why don't you, so that I don't mischaracterize," I said.

Jonathan shrugged. "We've had some underlying issues for quite some time now, and we both have different opinions and perspectives about those things, and while there are merits to both sides, we don't see eye to eye, and things have definitely reached a really bad point for us lately, and I..." he paused and in a higher pitch continued, "I think she needs to talk to someone." I watched Dr. Stearns as Jonathan used so many words to say almost nothing. I was happy that Jonathan had already begun to dig his own hole by implying I was the only one who needed to talk to someone. I waited for Dr. Stearns to turn to me. Jonathan always complained about me cutting him off so I was careful not to.

"We're in a sexless marriage and Jonathan has poor communication skills," I said.

Jonathan laughed. "Alix has a tendency to exaggerate," he said in a condescending tone.

"About the sex or communication?" I asked.

"We do not have a sexless marriage. Granted, it's been a little light lately because we're fighting incessantly. But for the entire eight years we've been together, we've never had a sexless marriage," he said.

"There are different definitions of sexless," I said. "But this last year has probably met them all."

"You mean this last year that you had a baby, major surgery, and I started a new company?" Jonathan asked, shifting in his seat and turning his legs toward the wall.

"And it's not so much about frequency as the fact that I don't feel desired anymore," I said.

"Anymore?" Jonathan stressed. "If nothing else, I've been consistent all these years. It's not like when we first met, I wanted sex every day and then lost interest and waned."

"Do you agree that Jonathan has been consistent through the years in his sexual desire?" Dr. Stearns asked.

"I suppose." I thought back. "When we were dating, spending our weekends together, he was voracious on Friday and Saturday. Made me feel like he had never touched me before.

Then Sunday, nothing. I always left his apartment wondering if he was still into me. When he gave me the ultimatum about moving in together..."

"Ultimatum?" Jonathan interrupted, looking bewildered.

"Call it what you want. You said I had until the end of the year to move in with you," I said. "I asked him if moving in would mean more sex, and he assured me that it would. The day we moved in, I naturally expected to christen the apartment. But Jonathan was all tired from the move—and he's not the sort of man who goes through the motions just because it's a birthday, or a holiday, or to commemorate *the day we moved in together*," I said. "Don't get me wrong. I appreciated—still appreciate—that he is genuine. But, when I sat on our coffee table, legs wide open, and he rejected me..." I shook my head.

"Is it satisfying when you do make love?" Dr. Stearns asked.

"Absolutely," I said. Jonathan was technically good at everything.

"Alright, that's a good start. Why don't you both tell me what your goal is, what you hope to accomplish by coming here," Dr. Stearns said. "Jonathan?"

"What do you mean?" Jonathan asked.

"Some couples want to work on staying together, some need help separating, some aren't sure what outcome they hope for and we figure it out. Do you want to stay married to Alix?" he asked Jonathan.

"Yes," Jonathan said without hesitation. "Let's keep it in perspective. We are planning to stay together, buy an apartment—we recently saw a place we loved—go on family vacations. Our life is on track. I just want us to work out our issues," he said.

"What about you, Alix? Is your goal to stay married?" he asked.

"I don't know," I said, and though I knew Jonathan had turned his head to look at me in disbelief, I continued looking straight at Dr. Stearns. "I don't want to stay together at the expense of completely losing who I am or at the expense of my children's well-being. I mean, children shouldn't grow up without seeing their parents express love for one another." Dr. Stearns nodded approvingly. "I feel like a horse that's been broken. I'm so full of resentment that I do things that are so out of character, or at least out of character with respect to how I see myself, although that's the problem. Jonathan sees me, or rather, I feel that Jonathan sees me in such a negative light now." I shook my head reflecting on my own words. I'd been complaining about sex for years, but that alone could not be fueling my anger.

"He no longer knows me—not as I want to be known. It's like he's stripped me of my identity by no longer treating me as a sexual being. We fall in love with ourselves, right? Because being in love is really just loving who you are in someone's else's eyes, and now when we fight, everything out of his mouth just cuts to the core of who I am. He knows my hot buttons. But he can't control himself. I never go below the belt…"

"So, those are character attacks, and I'm going to give you some rules about fighting that I want you to look over at home. Jonathan, how do you feel about what Alix just said?" Dr. Stearns asked.

"Well, I'm surprised. I'm not sure what we're even doing here if she doesn't want to be married to me anymore. That's what she's saying," he said. "That's what she's saying," he repeated, his face flushing, palms now face up in the air.

"That's not what I'm hearing from Alix. What are the hot buttons you were referring to, Alix?" Dr. Stearns asked.

"I've told him that ignoring me when I ask him a question is the equivalent of smacking me in the face. I mean most people, when you ask them how they feel about something or what they meant, either answer the question, or, if you stay silent long enough, feel compelled to fill the gap. Not Jonathan. He will literally just stare at me silently, endlessly, rather than answering me." I paused, and took a deep breath. "I've told him that questioning me as a mother, particularly in front of the kids is off limits, and that any negative references to me working out is unacceptable. Mind you he never works out and doesn't seem to understand what I'm sure you, the rest of the medical profession and the world do, that exercise is a healthy outlet," I said, pressing my hand under my lower left ear where my headache was not only persisting, but getting worse.

Jonathan scoffed. "Not everyone exercises at the expense of everything else. We can't go anywhere until Alix runs in the morning. If she doesn't get her run in the morning, forget it... I'd rather give her that run than deal with the consequences," he said.

"Did you hear that, Dr. Stearns, he's *giving* me my run. I'm supposed to be grateful for it."

"Well who is with the kids when you're running?" Jonathan asked me directly.

"When are you ever with the kids when I'm working out? I go after you've left to work, and on weekends I take them with me to the gym!" I said with disdain.

"And it's not a problem that you sometimes do a second workout at night, on the elliptical in our den?" he asked.

"It's because I can't bear the tension between us, watching television or whatever, and not having sex. It's a replacement for intimacy... to pass the time rather than dealing with your rejection, silence, and utter disinterest in me," I said. "By the way," I turned to face Dr. Stearns, "the fact that I work out is what makes me a, quote, bad mother."

"I never said you're a bad mother. You're a wonderful mother, as long as all of your own needs are met first. Otherwise, you're angry and everyone in the house feels it," Jonathan said.

"Let's not have this fight right now," Dr. Stearns said. Why don't you tell me..."

"Haven't you ever been on an airplane?" I asked, helplessly aware that I'd cut off Dr. Stearns. "Mothers are supposed to put their oxygen masks on first... there's wisdom behind that. And I'm not the one with anger issues."

"Then why are you the one who has a conflict with everyone in her life?" Jonathan asked.

"Who do I have conflict with?" I asked.

"Other than me, you mean? Your sister, my mother, everyone..."

"You mean my sister who hasn't come to visit our kids, ever, and only calls me when she needs something? Your mother who criticizes everything from what I feed the children to the fact that I wear high heels?"

"So, let's not interrupt each other. Why don't you tell me what attracted you to each other in the beginning?" Dr. Stearns asked.

Jonathan's shoulders dropped from their tense position and

he looked at me with tenderness. "We met online. We had a connection right from the beginning. She just got me. She was sharp and untamed and full of adventure—she had just taken a trip to Cambodia on her own. I'd never dated a woman who even understood my business, let alone gave me sophisticated advice about it—she did. She was so real, and uninhibited, and funny... Not just witty, which she was, but deeply funny." He laughed, remembering something.

"Look at that, therapy works," I said. "That's the first compliment I've heard in ages. Jonathan doesn't give compliments freely. But when he does, you know he means it."

"I'd like to stick to the topic. Tell me about what you were attracted to in the beginning, Alix," Dr. Stearns said redirecting me.

"He's right. We connected immediately. We laughed, philosophized, we had our own dictionary of words we'd made up. We just made each other happy. And he thought the world of me. He was simple, confident, refined. I remember feeling like, who knew relationships could be this easy? My exes loved me because I was like their shrink slash prostitute. But the first time we had sex, it was like the first time I actually 'made love.' On our wedding night, I cried because we got married for all the right reasons and I was imagining the day he dies. We were inseparable," I said. I turned to Jonathan.

"When did things change?" Dr. Stearns asked.

My headache was distracting me so Jonathan was first to speak.

"Hurricane Sandy. Alix was pregnant and sick and bedridden for three days during the hurricane. We had no help. I was stuck in the house with our two-year-old, non-stop. Not easy. The first day that Alix was feeling better, the minute she woke up, she decided that, rather than giving me a break, she needed to go running in the wreckage outside. It was the final straw. So selfish." He shook his head. "That's when I realized that me, the family, everything, revolves around her."

"Good. What about for you, Alix?" Dr. Stearns asked.

"I'm not sure that there was one event that changed everything. I know that it used to warm my heart to see what a good Dad Jonathan was and now, sick as it is, I'm disgusted with how freely affectionate he is with the kids in contrast to me."

I shrugged, trying to pinpoint when things changed.

"As newlyweds, when Jonathan had made an obscene amount of money and stopped working, we set up charities, I took a leave of absence, we traveled, wrote comedy. We made a list of things we wanted to do together before we were sixty. I didn't want to do anything, even watch a movie, without Jonathan. Now, I'm happier without him, without being subjected to his constant criticism. I used to feel like we were a team, and that no matter what, at the end of the day, we had each other and all of life's annoyances were just background. But at some point, we just became platonic roommates executing chores, and all of life's annoyances became the focal point and our marriage mere background. I think if we were having enough sex, the nonsense we argue about would disappear. But now that's all screwed up too."

"What do you mean?" Dr, Stearns asked.

"I mean, the one thing I never had to overthink in life was sex. But now... I haven't let him go down on me in months. Why? Because I want to encourage him to fuck me with no pressure to make me come. Everything has become so routine. He goes down on me and I climax once or twice and then we quickly screw and call it a day. I never come from just straight sex anymore. I know a lot of women would love such a giving man but I'd be more satisfied if I knew he was just selfishly taking me because he wants me at that moment. Now, I feel like he just wants to get my orgasm out of the way. And I constantly fantasize about him fantasizing about another woman when we're together because otherwise I can't get around thinking about how he doesn't really want me," I added.

"How do you feel about what Alix just said, Jonathan?" Dr. Stearns asked.

"While I recognize we can be having more sex, she acts like nothing else matters. I'm not allowed to be too exhausted to screw. And I'm perpetually exhausted because she has sleeping problems. And not for nothing, I'm in my forties now," he said.

"Alright, I'm getting a good picture of where you are. Let's meet again next week at this time," Dr. Stearns said, standing up.

"Wait, we haven't even talked about addiction," I said, ignoring the prompt that the session was over.

"Yeah, this is really important," Jonathan said looking very serious, ready for me to disclose all of my addictive behaviors.

"Next week we can..." Doctor Stearns began.

"Jonathan is an addict," I blurted out. "He's addicted to making money and enough is never enough. And he's done some crazy gambling these last few years," I said, not knowing why.

Jonathan's jaw dropped as he stared at me in disbelief. "I don't gamble. She's talking about my trading."

"He doesn't trade like an ordinary person. His hobby is to risk millions and millions in options trading, for the thrill, for the money, without any regard to the impact it could have on me and the kids," I said. "I just wanted to make sure we all understood the difference between healthy outlets and unhealthy ones."

"Alix, one, I don't trade anymore. Two, I know what you're doing..." Jonathan said.

"We really need to end here. I have another client coming in," Dr. Stearns interrupted.

"She's trying to slant things," Jonathan continued, "to take the focus off her issues."

"Okay, we have to end here," Dr. Stearns said, growing impatient.

"Thanks, Dr. Stearns," I said, pleased at where the session was ending. I stepped forward to shake his hand. Then, turning to Jonathan, "I'll see you at home tonight. I'm going to take the stairs down." Jonathan was still seated as I raced out of the office. I didn't want to take the elevator with Jonathan. I couldn't face him. I was embarrassed. It was true that Jonathan took unsettling risks when it came to money, but he was hardly an addict and I trusted his judgment. As I walked home, I wondered if I'd diverted attention from myself because I couldn't face my own addiction issues or if I simply wanted Jonathan to feel what it was like to have a mountain made of a molehill.

Chapter 7

When I got home, I prepared the soup, showered, blew my hair, moisturized my scars, and proceeded to apply make-up, a routine I was so accustomed to that I could do it with my eyes closed in the dark. Pump the moisturizer. Apply generously. Smooth the primer around the eyes, followed by foundation. Suck cheeks in. Apply blush. Prepare the eyeliner making sure the tip isn't too wet. Close one eye. Apply... Wait. *What the fuck! CLOSE ONE EYE. CLOSE IT. CLOSE ONE EYE! Why won't my left eye fucking close?! Oh Shit, I'm having a stroke!* I stared in the mirror. My left eye was staring wide-eyed back at me clearly not responding to my brain asking it, begging it, to close. Each time I tried to close it, the right eye closed instead. I tried to get my eyeliner on without closing the lid. I ended up with a black thick smudge in the middle of my eyelid. I put eye make-up remover on a Q-Tip and tried desperately to create a clean line out of the smudge, as if fixing the make-up on my face would make the stroke go away.

I called Jonathan. "Don't panic, but you know how I've had that pain in my head the last couple of days?"

"Yes," Jonathan said clearly worried because I told him not to panic.

"Well, I still have it and now my left eye won't close," I told him calmly. "So, in case anything happens, I want you to tell whomever needs to know that the pain was behind my left ear and that I couldn't close my eye."

"What do you mean your left eye won't close?"

"It won't close. I can't put on my make-up. I can't blink. I'm home. I'm going to take Charlie to the gym kids class—it's forty-five minutes—and then go to the doctor," I told him.

"NO! You are going to leave the kids with Luisa and go the hospital right now," he told me.

"I'll call you after class when I'm heading to the doctor," I said.

I realized that something serious was happening. I knew I needed medical attention immediately. But I also knew that whatever was happening was going to be a "before" and "after" event. I would never have forty-five "before" minutes with Charlie again if I didn't go to class. Whatever was going on had been happening since the start of my headache days ago. What difference could another forty-five minutes make? The damage was done. I walked eight blocks with Luisa and both kids to Charlie's gym class and explained to her that I'd go back home to shut off the pea soup simmering on the stove after class, then to the doctor, and that she might need to stay late.

Luisa was from Ecuador. She was in her late fifties, and lived in the basement of her mother's house with her husband and two of her four children. She'd been our cleaning lady before I'd asked her to be our nanny. We paid her about thirty five thousand dollars a year to watch our children. Luisa didn't know, until I told her, not to put plastic containers in the microwave, what I meant when I said Charlie needed "a protein" for lunch, that cold sores were contagious, or why it was important to me to be on time, even to preschool. What she did know, though, was how to love my children. At this moment, I felt a heightened indebtedness to her.

As Charlie pulled himself up to a standing position on the colorful gym mats to reach for a toy snail, he flashed a proud smile at me. "I love you so much, little man... my little Manzi," I cooed at him and leaned in to give him a kiss, but my lips started tingling. "I might be gone for a bit. I need you to know how much I love you." I was suddenly very thirsty. My face started tightening as if the skin from my nose to my left ear was a twin-sized sheet being stretched to fit a king sized mattress. "Go, Charlie, get up there," I cheered as Charlie attempted to maneuver his way through an obstacle course. My own voice was bothering my ears. I sounded peculiar, and now the other mothers in the room were staring at me.

The class finally ended and Luisa and Ella were waiting for us outside.

"Your lip. Your lips are sagging," Luisa said in a hushed voice, tugging at the side of her own mouth to show me what she meant.

I walked back towards the apartment to turn off the pea soup. The blocks seemed much longer now. I picked up my pace. I felt my mouth pulling downward as if some magnetic force under the sidewalk were pulling it. The muscles on the left side of my face felt taut as if someone were stretching saran wrap over it. The faster I walked, the more the wind hit my face. It felt like a blow dryer in my eye. My eye was blurry, dry, and I couldn't blink. I began to jog, then run, all the while cursing myself that I hadn't sent Luisa home to turn off the pea soup instead. The faster I went, the dryer my eye got. My neck was wet. Why was my neck wet? Was I sweating? No, I was drooling. Suddenly, I felt like I was on an airplane, struggling to get my headset to work, like it was plugged in, but only half way, so the sound was going in and out. I was deteriorating. Would I make it another six blocks, or were my arms and legs next?

My heart beat erratically as I ran the rest of the way home. In my lobby, the elevator doors opened to expose a mirror. Those nine floors felt like an eternity as I looked at someone that wasn't, couldn't, be me in the mirror. It was as if someone had opened the pin of an inflatable toy and let the air out of half of it. My eyes, nose, and mouth looked like remnants of a melted snowman. My left eye was staring at me, soul-less, and wide-eyed, with no emotion. That eye made my face so unfamiliar that I almost felt as if it were rude for the stranger in the mirror to be staring at me. I reminded myself of a Dali painting.

Can I just look at your face? Evan's words haunted me.

As I walked down the hallway toward my apartment, the familiar smell of dill and parsley from the pea soup filled the air. The smell was usually comforting on some unconscious level—it was my mother's recipe. But as I inhaled it, only my right nostril flared, inflaming my sense of panic. Maybe I'm just dehydrated, I thought. Maybe my electrolytes are off. It was nothing Gatorade couldn't fix. I went into my apartment, turned off the stove, opened the refrigerator. No Gatorade. Vitamin Water should work. I stood before the full-length mirror in my dining room. I extended my arm and my leg to determine if they were numb. They weren't. I raised the Vitamin Water to my lips and allowed myself to feel hopeful that I simply needed to replenish, that nothing serious was happening. But the beverage fell right out of the corner of the left side of my mouth. I reached into my panties and checked to see if I could feel my own touch. I could. *At least my vagina is intact. And there is pea soup for the family to eat.* Both thoughts made me smile, except they didn't, because I couldn't. When I tried, the right half of my mouth bared teeth and the left half didn't move, a most inhuman expression.

I headed to the walk-in clinic, around the block, rather than the hospital emergency room, thinking I'd get medical attention faster. "Something's happening," I told the receptionist in a spooky voice, "I think I should see a doctor right away."

"Okay, I just need you to sign here and here and print your name and birthday there." I took the pen but realized I had no idea what I'd been asked to do. I stared at the papers in front of me blankly until the receptionist repeated himself.

"I'm sorry. I have no idea what's going on," I told him and my left cheek inadvertently puffed out while I spoke. He was looking at me as though I'd just begun to rip off a mask and reveal my true identity. And that's exactly how I felt—that I was being stripped.

He must have thought I was having a stroke because I was placed in a room right away despite the packed waiting room. The physician's assistant took my vitals and calmly asked me a series of questions. No, I haven't had chest pain. Yes, I could move the rest of my body. No, my limbs weren't tingling. *Why the hell are we looking for additional symptoms?* I wondered. *Isn't sudden paralysis enough to get a doctor in here right away?* After about a dozen more questions, the physician's assistant left and returned with the doctor. She was Indian, wearing a dress that looked to be made of hemp and open toe flat sandals. She washed her hands, introduced herself as Dr. Sayeed, and peered at my face.

"So, Mrs. Beck, I hear you're suddenly unable to blink your eye. And I see your mouth is drooping, too. Uh-huh. Raise your eyebrows."

I tried.

"Okay, you have Bell's Palsy," she told me, just like that. "It may get worse over the next day and then give it three weeks at the least to start improving. Most people recover."

Most? "Wait a minute... that can't be... is it because I can't raise my eyebrow? I've had Botox. You might be mistaken. I can never move my eyebrows."

"You should be happy it isn't a stroke," she said as she checked the reflexes in my knees.

I was speechless. She'd spent maybe three minutes speaking to me.

"You haven't even told me what Bell's Palsy is. How do you know it's not a stroke?"

"This is what Bell's Palsy is. It's one-sided facial nerve paralysis. Sudden onset and accompanied by a headache. Classic case. With a stroke, there's usually numbness or weakness in the arms and legs, and patients can still control the upper part of their faces and will have wrinkling in the forehead. You don't. You have Bell's," she said.

"Is this going to go away?" I asked.

"Probably. Like I said, most people start recovering in about three weeks," she said. "It's good that you got here quickly. Steroids help with the nerve compression."

"So, I'll be fine in three weeks?" I tried to confirm.

"Don't know. It could be four weeks or nine months until you fully recover. Everyone is different. Some people don't recover," she said without a hint of sympathy.

"What caused this?" I asked, realizing she wasn't planning to address the topic.

"Bell's Palsy is idiopathic. Nobody really knows what causes it," she said shamelessly.

I stared at her in defiant silence waiting for her to fill in the blanks.

"There are many viruses that are speculated to cause inflammation or compression of the cranial nerve, the facial nerve, which causes the paralysis," she told me. "We can take some blood to see if there's something like Lyme in your system that we need to treat," she said, as if it were neither here nor there to do the test. "Maybe Epstein Barr, shingles, herpes. Are you sexually active?" Dr. Sayeed asked waiting to check a box on her clipboard.

"Sure," I said, "but not nearly enough as I'd like to be," I added, flashing a sexy grin at the physician's assistant, forgetting that I was neither grinning nor sexy.

"Men, women, both?" she asked, and I could tell that she was straining to sound nonchalant.

"*These* days," I stressed, and then paused to make eye contact with the physician assistant, "only my husband." My one eye managed to make the desired eye contact but my lip drooped and the 'b' sound in "husband" caused my left cheek to blow up. Why was I trying to be provocative? It was so ingrained in me. My sexual innuendo was no longer cute. It was more like a tic.

"Have you been under any stress lately?" she asked.

"Nothing unusual," I said.

Dr. Sayeed marked her chart. It was decided. I had Bell's Palsy. Steroid. Antiviral. Eye drops. I was done. She had finished telling me everything she felt she ought to. Dr. Sayeed stood in front of me, like a black jack dealer who had just taken all of my chips, as if to say, "All done... Others need your seat."

"You mentioned Lyme disease. I was in Florida recently and definitely in tall grass. Do you want to check me for a tick?" I suggested.

"No," she shrugged.

"No?" I repeated in disbelief.

"No, we'll know from the blood work if there's something else going on." She excused herself. A technician came in to take my blood. When he left, Dr. Sayeed returned. "Things might get worse over the next day. You may experience hypersensitivity to noise. There's a real risk that your cornea can get damaged because you can't shut your eye. So tape your eye shut at night. Call us if anything changes."

Tape your eye shut. Goodbye. How is that okay? What kind of tape? Masking? Duct? Scotch?

"You know, I take Ambien and drink wine every night. Could I have messed up my central nervous system from long term use?"

"This has nothing to do with Ambien or wine. You can keep taking the Ambien," the doctor told me.

I kept asking questions. I didn't need answers. I just couldn't accept leaving the office with my diagnosis. I just wanted to sit there.

Realizing that I wasn't mobilizing and was having trouble accepting everything that'd been communicated to me, Dr. Sayeed asked the physician's assistant to bring up a website describing the symptoms and prognosis for Bell's Palsy. "Sometimes people get it better when they read it," she told me.

The three of us huddled over the physician assistant's laptop. Dr. Sayeed read aloud, nodding her head in agreement as she read, as though she were learning about the condition and diagnosing it at the same time.

"Okay?" she asked.

"Yes."

When I finally left the office, the outside world seemed as if someone had changed the aspect ratio on my television. The city seemed denser, foggier, and more overpopulated. The same bright lights and energy of New York City that prompted me to swear off ever moving out of the city were now disorienting instead of stimulating. I had a block and a half to walk to the pharmacy to pick up my prescriptions. As I crossed the street, an ambulance approached. The blare of the siren that had practically become white noise to me after living in the city for fifteen years, penetrated my skull and seemed to reverberate around what felt like an endless tunnel. I raised my left hand to my ear and stopped walking, sure that my head was about to shatter. The ambulance came closer. The siren filled every synapse in my brain like a tsunami hitting the shore. Everything else around me disappeared. The only thing that existed was my being and a high-pitched noise. I no longer had the walk light. The cars and taxis were now approaching and frustrated that some pedestrian was holding them up. The ambulance passed. *I'm so fucked.*

I had a half block more to go to the pharmacy. I dialed my general practitioner and set up an appointment for the next morning. Then I called Jonathan. Before the call went through, I saw him approaching from down the block. I felt guilty that he had to leave work early. A woman next to him was admiring him, his dark hair, dark eyes and healthy skin accentuated by his crisp white shirt. He could obviously see my disfigured features from far away because he averted his glance from my face down to my feet as he approached. He embraced me stiffly. After the lack of affection we'd been sharing, it felt as foreign as my new face. I looked up at him, knowing my expressions had now become unreadable, and said, "I'm smiling."

When we got home, it was already witching hour, the time to make sure everyone was fed, bathed, and put to sleep. I didn't want to scare the kids with my face so I kept busy picking up toys and doing laundry until Jonathan put them to bed. I undressed, not even bothering to check the progress of my now meaningless abdominal and breast scars, got into the shower, lathered my hair with shampoo and let the soapy water run down my face. I forgot that my eye wouldn't blink, though, and my eye felt like a prisoner being hosed down for a confession. It was exposed and vulnerable, and suddenly I was too.

"Listen," Jonathan told me as I scooped my frozen yogurt into the bowl. "You may not believe me, but there's something really endearing about you like this. If this doesn't heal, and it will, I'll still be into it." Well, perhaps I'd finally found his fetish. I took an Ambien and taped my eye shut with steri-tape.

Chapter 8

When I woke up the next day, I pulled the tape off my eye, and with it a few eyelashes. I changed Charlie's diaper as he quizzically looked at my mouth. He was searching for my usual smile. He started shaking his head "no," a behavior that always made me laugh wildly. I laughed, but half of my face didn't move. He reached up to touch the corner of my mouth. *Little man, how will you know I love you if I can't smile? And oh god, if this lasts, how will you learn to speak? It's not going to last. Eighty percent of cases resolve.*

At eleven months, Charlie had almost mastered what I had studied back in my college days majoring in neuroscience. There were two kinds of smiles: Smiles that activate the muscles in the corner of your mouth, and smiles that activate both the muscles in the corner of your mouth and your eye socket. The latter were real smiles. The former were fake. The way humans determine whether another person's smile is real or fake is to automatically mimic the smile they see. If it is real, the brain in the person being smiled at activates the same areas in the cranial nerve of the person smiling, and the brain interprets it as real. As a result, the reward circuits of the person being smiled at light up and it causes them to be happy. I couldn't give that to my son. All I could give him were the voice and gestures that usually accompanied my smiles, and hope that it'd be enough to communicate my love, to let him know that his very existence was my smile.

It was pouring as I walked Ella to school for early drop-off so that I wouldn't have to face anyone and deal with questions. I feigned anger as she jumped in puddles, wetting the princess dress she insisted on wearing.

"I don't like that face you're making, Mommy!" she shouted at me as I smiled at her to let her know I wasn't really mad.

"I'm smiling, Ella," I assured her.

"No, you're not. You're mad at me," she said as her outward anger softened and she let herself just be the four-year-old who craved Mommy's approval.

I crouched down in the rain and explained that I had something like a cold that made it impossible to smile. "Oh, well, you know," she told me, "you might not be able to chew either, right? So, maybe you can eat soft food like Charlie. Sometimes, if something is too hard for me to chew on one side of my mouth, I just chew it on the other."

"Don't worry," I said, "It's my job to worry about you, not the other way around."

I had three hours to kill before seeing my general practitioner. I set out to the park for my usual run, rushing past my doormen to avoid conversation. I brushed past the hot dog stand, the hagglers trying to rent bikes to tourists, and the vendor selling hats at the entrance to Central Park at Columbus Circle who were, as always, expecting an eye socket smile from me. I pretended not to see them. I stared at the pavement as I jogged toward the east side, ignoring the familiar faces of the members of my unnamed club—the joggers and dog walkers of the Central Park subculture that I crossed paths with most days. We shared an intimate space in the park. The only key required was a nod and a smile. Today, I had no key. And four point two miles didn't seem long enough to handle my anxiety. Instead of making the turn into the reservoir, I kept running north to do the big loop of the park, the full six miles. There was a walker in front of me who had some sort of physical disability. I'd seen her around the park many times. She was clearly fit, but she shifted her weight from one stiff unbendable leg to another as if she wore invisible braces. I felt an odd need to say hello to her today, as if it would fill some need for social connectivity that I sensed I was losing. I slowed up my pace as I gained on her, only long enough to overhear her exchanging information about a reverend with a couple of women next to her. It hadn't been twenty-four hours since I'd entered the world of the aesthetically challenged and already I was shedding my unyielding anti-religious stance, understanding why she'd cling to a place of acceptance, even if that place were a fiction. I ran past her and home.

"First and fifteenth, please" I told the taxi driver, as I hoisted myself into the taxi van to go to the doctor.

"Where?" he asked. My speech seemed to have worsened.

"First and fifteenth," I repeated, frustrated.

"Fourth and fiftieth, you say?" He waited to clarify before starting the meter.

"No, first, like first, second... first... and *fifteenth*, like one, five," I said. He began driving.

I was researching Bell's Palsy on my phone when the taxi stopped only five minutes later. I looked up at the street signs. I was on first and fiftieth.

"Jesus Fuck," I shouted, straining to pronounce the "F" in "fuck" and seeming more like somebody with Tourette's syndrome than Bell's Palsy. I took out my phone and typed the correct coordinates for the cab driver to see.

I continued researching Bell's Palsy in the waiting room of the doctor's office and then called my parents to let them know what was happening.

"Hello?" my father picked up his cell phone, and the sound of clanking in the background killed my ear.

"Hi, Dad, I have bad news. I have Bell's Palsy," I said.

"What did you say? How do I adjust the volume? Just a minute. Sharon!" he called to my mother, "Alix is on the phone. I have the heating technician here. Can you take this?" he asked. My father's love of literature and photography could only be matched by his obsession with fixing things in the house. I heard my mother yelling back to him in the background that she needed a minute, the dog let out a "mailman is here" kind of frantic bark, and my ear couldn't take it. She finally came to the phone.

"Half of my face is paralyzed. I have Bell's Palsy," I said.

"You're kidding. The Kleins' son had that, I think," she said. "It resolves itself, right?"

I was reminded of the time I had mononucleosis in my teens and needed exploratory abdominal surgery. "Don't you dare leave any permanent scars outside the bikini line," she told the doctors as I was wheeled into surgery.

"Yes," I said.

"Well, there are worse things. How are my grandkids? Wait. Hold on. I have a call waiting. Oh, it's the knee doctor for your father. Let me see if I can pick this up without hanging up on you. How do I do this? Hold on." I knew I was about to get hung up on accidentally.

My parents seemed to have given up learning new technologies at about the same time they retired from teaching fifteen years prior. My father worked two years more than necessary so they could retire at the same time, which was also how they ate, socialized, woke, and went to bed. All at the same time, all on my mother's time. They mocked marriages where household responsibilities or money weren't shared, were explicit about their sexuality and attraction—"your mother had triple diamond legs, an eighteen inch waist, and the most perfect giant breasts I'd ever seen when I met her"—united in forcing Jewish principles down mine and Sabrina's throats until it proved ineffective in keeping us in line, and then united in forcing Tough Love and Twelve Steps down our throats instead. My parents insisted that they were equal in every respect. There were, in fact, only a few times I'd ever seen my father put his foot down to my mother, once when she was dragging me by my hair to the kitchen to wash my cereal bowl and once when my sister, at nine, told my mother that she "h-h-hates" her and my mother, in a weak moment, retorted "you are being f-f-fresh," mocking her stutter. They'd set the bar high for an equal marriage and the bar low for individual growth outside the marriage.

"Mom? Mom? I'll just send you an email later. I have to go."

My doctor confirmed that I likely had Bell's Palsy. He thought the clinic should have given me a steroid injection at the office because every hour of nerve compression mattered, but I should be fine. I should get an MRI right away because there was of course—*of course?!*—the possibility that I had a brain tumor. His office would make sure I got an appointment for an MRI that night, at 6:30 p.m., and for the neurologist the next day.

I prepared plates for Jonathan to feed the kids before heading out to the MRI. Pea soup for Charlie *again.* How many days had passed that the pea soup could still be good? Oh, it was only last night. It also felt like a lifetime ago that I had met Evan, but it had been only three days. I grabbed the files for the employment discrimination mediation to review in the waiting room.

"What are you doing with those?" Jonathan asked.

"I figure there will be a long wait. I might as well prepare for Friday's mediation. Kill two birds," I told him.

He raised his eyebrows. "Don't you think you should reschedule?"

"No, I can't just cancel because I'm ugly. I'm about to launch my business. This isn't the time to slack. The more mediations under my belt the better. Right?" I asked.

He didn't answer.

"Is it that bad... like to the point where it will distract the parties?" I asked.

"I just think you have a lot going on and it might be smart to reschedule," he said. "You know, you're having trouble speaking. It's not like you're going to be working behind a computer. You're basically making a speech, moderating the room, caucusing face to face. It's your call," he said, seemingly concerned about my reasoning skills. Normally, I'd be reluctant to have the spotlight on me if I so much as had a pimple on my face.

"I'm sure this will start improving every day. I can't just hide," I said. "Could be useful. The first thing the parties can agree on is that I'm hideous," I joked.

"Where is the mediation?" he asked.

"New Jersey," I said.

"And how is it that you think you are getting to New Jersey?" he asked.

"I'm going to drive," I said matter of factly.

"Alix, you can't drive. Your ear, your eye. You can't get behind a wheel," he said softly.

I put the files down, recognizing that denial had set in. I would need to cancel the mediation, and probably every other event scheduled in the next few weeks, including my meeting with Dan next Thursday, and our appointment with Dr. Stearns.

***

It'd been a week. There was no brain tumor, just a bad case of Bell's Palsy that might or might not go away. The fucking construction was starting to wear me down. Earplugs didn't work. I didn't want to run into people I knew in my building. I kept my head down and my hair in my face. I pretended to be on the phone as an excuse for not acknowledging people in the elevator or the doormen. It was such work to not be friendly. I'd put on the same hooded sweatshirt, tied tightly around my face, every time I'd left the apartment to avoid the stares. But the dusty city, crowded sidewalks, horns, sirens, and loud conversations disoriented me and forced me back to the solitude of my apartment.

I couldn't handle the sound of Charlie or Ella crying. Their cries shattered my eardrum. I should instinctually have wanted to comfort them. Instead, I sent them out with Luisa, reminding myself not to smile as I said goodbye. It was an effort to talk, but my only mode of communicating. The human face shows over twenty emotions and thousands of expressions. Mine showed none with any accuracy. My eyebrows betrayed me when I wanted to raise them to show interest or curiosity. I couldn't form the surprised look Charlie deserved when he did something he was proud of. The sight of my face at rest, even, was disfigured. Charlie was better off not seeing it; not seeing me. My disobliging smile was confusing, scary. Playing peekaboo was more like a goblin dropping down from the ceiling of a haunted house than a game.

I found dead fruit flies in the corner of my wretched eye after I jogged. When the other joggers smiled at me, I waved at them in reply. I was infinitely thirsty. My salivary glands were malfunctioning. A crust formed around my mouth. My scalp tingled. I thought a cockroach might be crawling around in my hair. *Why does it only stay on the paralyzed side?* I wondered. It must have known. It sensed half of me was a carcass, vulnerable to hungry predators.

My reaction to the Bell's was as bipolar as my face. I wanted to be less vain and not allow myself to feel victimized. But I was insecure, obsessed with my appearance, and felt assaulted. I wavered between feeling like I was good for my children and doing them harm by being around them, craving love and acceptance from my family but also craving isolation and the freedom of nobody caring about me, so that nobody could be disappointed. But hadn't those concerns always lingered under my now deformed surface? Hadn't that hawk of inadequacy always circled my confidence?

I called my sister, who I had not yet told about my face.

"Hey, what's up bro?" she answered, clearly chewing, sounding, as usual, like a sixteen-year-old boy, talking to a buddy. "Crack any cases for ex-boyfriends lately?" she joked.

"I think I'm canceling Charlie's party," I told her.

"Was that supposed to be next weekend or the one after? That's good because I have a bride job anyway so I wouldn't have come, plus I've been eating like a pig. The last thing I need is one of your parties, all that food. I'm bloated. Beyond. I look like I was out drinking all night. Well, I was. Paul and I went out, so of course he was late to work, which means he'll probably get fired soon. He just can't keep a job. I really might just leave him."

Paul was Irish, a freckled redhead, with skin that seemed translucent when the veins in his thick neck bulged blue, when he was angry or drinking, events that occurred daily. He was raised by his paternal grandmother because his mother had died when he was three and his father left him soon after, and, as the neighborhood knew, mentioning that fact to Paul guaranteed a black eye. I'd always hoped Sabrina would outgrow him, but it was a lofty hope premised on her own hampered growth.

"And this morning my car broke down. I don't have the money to fix it. I asked Dad if I could borrow his and he acted all imposed upon. Can you *believe* him? Meanwhile you know he's going to expect me to drop everything when his shiny bald spot needs a trim, like I don't have a hundred other things going on in my life." In the past, I'd offered to pay for her to go back to school, paid for her to see therapists, and sent her expensive gifts. Though I'd normally have offered to pay to fix her car, I was too preoccupied with myself at the moment.

"So the reason I'm canceling the party..."

"Yeah the parents told me," she said. "That sucks, bro. Did I tell you who I went to dinner with? You know the girl from Housewives..."

I considered telling her that if she wanted to befriend the stars, she could just come to our building to visit the kids, but I realized she would just take it as me harassing her, again, about having no relationship with them. I said nothing.

"Hello? You still there, Alix?" she asked.

"That sucks? My life may be over..."

"Don't be dramatic. Remember Tom Moretti... no, no... Tom Franelli? Whatever. He had that. Back to normal in three weeks. Everyone gets that. People won't even notice. It's like an annoying cold. What's the big deal? You have no problems. You're the luckiest person I know," she said.

"I look like I had a stroke. How am I lucky?" I asked.

She was silent, limited by her envy. I didn't have to worry about the bills. Therefore, I was lucky.

"I have a hundred things to do. Later."

Get your shit together, I told myself when I hung up. *She's right. This is likely temporary. You'll be back to Evan, back to mediating, back to life, in no time. There are far worse things. You pathetic, annoying, wretch.*

Over the next few days, I sent nude pictures to my sister and my friend Jen in sexy poses wearing a mask to convince myself that I was in good spirits. I lip synced "Michelle, my Bell," and "For whom the Bell tolls" to Jonathan replacing "Bell" with "Bell's." I joked to my mother that the paralyzed side was prettier than the normal side of my face because at least there were no wrinkles. She told me I still had more wrinkles than she ever did at my age. I searched online for Bell's Palsy pornography just to see if it existed. It actually did not. I told Jonathan I had found a niche and needed to commercialize Bell's Palsy porn. His entrepreneurial eyes didn't light up. He was too concerned to humor me.

But the unbearable construction wouldn't stop. I cleaned out the linen closet, reorganized my drawers, tried to push away thoughts of Evan. I expected that under the circumstances, I'd naturally forget him.

The neurologist I'd seen last week checked in on me to see if I was suffering any side effects from the high dose of steroids. Since I hadn't improved and had pain, he thought we might need to increase the dose. "Have you been sleeping?" he asked me.

"No, but I'm an insomniac anyway," I told him.

"Have you been gaining weight?" he asked.

My tongue is numb. I have no appetite. I've eaten nothing but frozen yogurt for days. I eat it out of habit, not hunger. I've lost four pounds.

"No weight gain," I told him. "I've been exercising a lot."

"I imagine you need it for stress. I'm sure stress is what caused this to begin with," he said. This is the second time a doctor alluded to stress being the root of the Bell's Palsy. I thought about where my head was the day this affliction began. Couples therapy and contemplating an affair with Evan—undoubtedly, stressful.

"Any psychiatric issues from the steroid?" he asked.

When I stared into the mirror, I felt as disconnected to the image as I did during acid trips in my teens. My rot was apparent, like the bruised tip of a banana carelessly ripped from the bunch. I was an angry woman grappling with cheating on her loyal, loving husband because she wanted to be devoured by a man who was genuinely starved for her. I needed a restraint. Beauty was an all-consuming curse, giving way to feelings of entitlement and creating opportunities with other men. Ugliness stops entitlement in its tracks.

"I don't think so. It's probably fine to increase the steroids," I told him.

Three more days passed. Dan proposed dates to reschedule the meeting I'd canceled to flesh out the new business, reminding me that he'd be in Greece the next few weeks. Madeline Schwartz, head of the animal rescue organization, left a voicemail to see if we could meet to discuss her new non-profit. Jen called to see if I'd join her at Soho House for cocktails. Evan asked if he could join me when I return to Mrs. Springfield and when I was planning to. I only responded to Evan: "Things are hectic. I won't be able to go for at least three weeks. I'll touch base then."

It was a beautiful May morning. The sun was shining and the weather was warm. I took my steroids and checked my ugly face for progress, as I did each morning. Frown, nothing. Smile, nothing. Raise eyebrows, nothing. I was frustrated and despondent. *Stop feeling sorry for yourself. Be happy this is happening to you rather than your children. That'd be a tragedy. You're going to have a normal day and make them happy. They love you no matter what.* But Charlie seemed less interested in me. Ella didn't seem to mind—I was a perfect mother so long as I gave her high-fructose corn syrup.

"Try to smile," Ella asked me at breakfast. She laughed when I couldn't.

"I'm working late tonight," Jonathan said before leaving.

"Again?" I asked.

"Why—can't Luisa stay late?" he asked, distracted.

"Yes," I said, "but she can't console me," I added too low for anyone to hear.

"Okay, I'm going to close your eye. And you try to keep it closed, okay, Mommy?" Ella instructed. I obliged. We laughed at my failure.

"I want to be a mediator, a lawyer, and a mommy when I grow up, just like you," she told me and gave me a hug.

"You make me so happy," I said, and meant it with every ounce of my being.

"I think I'm catching your cold," she said and pulled her face so it was twisted. "See, I'm just like you."

I blew my hair out and put make-up on. I put on a camisole with no bra and white linen pants. I felt like a person. I'd walked about seven of the eight blocks to the playground with the kids. The sun was a blowtorch in my eye. My eye teared and took my mascara down with it. The blurriness was dizzying.

"Tell me a story, mommy," Ella asked. I ignored her because the sidewalk was a wavy mirage under my feet and I was concentrating on walking. "Please, from when you were little," she begged.

"I can't right now," I said. I felt a surge of self-loathing for my growing impatience.

There was a line for the swings. I waited for a turn, Charlie on my hip. He's so smart, I thought. He was learning to focus on my right eye to see what I felt. The ugliest face was the half-smile, but I had to smile and look at him and say, "wheeeee," while I pushed him on the swing. He needed that. So did the mothers next to me so that they could stare at my face with me seeming not to notice.

By the time we left the park, my face was tired. My heart was pumping too fast. I tried to conceal my misery. I'd absorbed the commotion and noise. I had no bearings. My head yearned for normal senses and function. Charlie started crying in the stroller as we walked home. I crouched down. Normally, a smile would have been enough to comfort him. I tried. "Don't cry, my love. We'll be home in a few minutes." He kept crying.

A teenager nudged her boyfriend, signaling him to look at me. My heart ached for Ella. She was bound to notice people were horrified by me, or worse, pitied me, her idol. How would she believe me when I told her beauty was on the inside amongst the whispers? How long until she'd realize that the last thing she'd want to be, was just like me? When the young couple caught me catching them staring, they averted their glance to my children. The girl remarked how cute Charlie was. Children are so easy to use to fill the uncomfortable gaps.

I used them to fill the gaps with Jonathan. I'd initiated no conversations with him since the paralysis began, except about the children. I knew he was as fearful as I was. There was nothing to say. At bedtime, Jonathan raised his eyebrows and smiled playfully at me while I brushed my teeth, his usual invitation to sex. But the interest was understandably feigned.

I looked at him and said, "You have to be kidding me. Do you have any idea what *this* will look like moaning!"

"It'll be hot, Alix. It'll be like I literally screwed you silly," he tried to joke, but his tone and the look in his eyes told me he was relieved that I'd declined.

A year ago, before I'd recoiled in response to our fading intimacy, I'd have been pleased. I'd have thanked him for doing me the favor of filling me.

But in that moment, and in his unconvincing eyes, I realized that the face in the mirror that I was growing accustomed to was no more ugly than the reflection of myself I'd seen in his disappointed eyes for quite some time.

"You should be mourning my face, not embracing it!" I blurted out, toothpaste dripping to my chin.

"What?"

"Always doing the proper thing, what's expected of you, huh?" I said, spitting toothpaste into the sink. "I don't want you to act polite. I want you to act like you've been robbed."

He didn't speak. We both knew I hadn't finished.

"*You* did this to me," I said.

"How did *I* do this to you?" he asked in the defensive tone he seemed to have suppressed since the Palsy started.

I nodded, knowingly.

"All this time, I've forced myself, I've pretended, that I could handle your rejections. That I could accept that you're just the conventional tired, stressed man, that my fears that you were diminishing me as a woman were an overreaction. That I could just ignore the stress I literally felt bubbling in me. That there's no price to pay for ignoring my instinct." I paused. "Well, *this* is what it looks like when you defy yourself too many times! Are you happy now?"

Jonathan walked away. I thought about Evan.

I decided, though I realized it was an irrational punishment for both of us, that I wouldn't have sex with Jonathan tonight. I'd play with my vile self instead. I crouched underneath the faucet so that the water stream functioned as a vibrator, imagining Jonathan's secretary seducing him. I wanted to release the tension. But I couldn't climax. And then there was a sudden massive pressure in my head.

"Jonathan!," I yelled.

He opened the bathroom door to find me sitting in the tub, both hands on my head.

"What's happening?" he asked.

"I don't know. My head," I said.

"I'm calling an ambulance," he said fidgeting with his phone.

"No, I think it's getting better," I told him as I tried to stand up.

"It happened out of nowhere?" he asked, handing me a towel.

"Just as I was about to come," I said looking up at him. His brows loosened as he processed that I'd chosen masturbating over sex with him and then furrowed again in worry.

"It could be the medication," he suggested.

My mouth gaped. Paranoia, rapid heartbeat, depression, disorientation, anorexia, insomnia, and blaming Jonathan for my brain malfunction were okay. Not being able to come properly, unacceptable. I put a towel on my wet head and left a message on the neurologist's service. "Hi, Dr, Bolchek. It's Alix. I think those psychiatric side effects from the steroids you mentioned are happening. I need to get off these steroids. It's an emergency."

Chapter 9

It was early June. With the steroids out of my system, my anger towards Jonathan settled. His attitude toward me hadn't fluctuated since the Palsy began—he'd been accommodating and concerned, but as emotionally distant as he'd been before the Palsy. Now, rather than focusing on what Jonathan hadn't been giving me, I thought about what I could no longer give him.

He'd been catapulted into being a single father. He was a widow, but without freedom. There was no one to accompany him to events or the children's birthday parties. He'd lost my attention, my ear, his image of home. He couldn't complain about the commute to work, long toenails, a headache, or our mounting marital issues. His daily concerns were rendered minute by the magnitude of my uncertain future. The present was only relevant to me to the extent it had to be experienced to get to the future.

I neatly boxed Evan away into the basement of my thoughts. I recognized that I could no longer attract him, or any other man. So did Jonathan. Despite his complaints about the effort I'd put into exercise and my body, he was secretly proud when other men looked at me. The underlying fear of losing his woman to another man no longer existed. Neutralizing that threat, I was simply a humming intrusion on daily life.

I no longer had the luxury to complain about not feeling desired or our unanimated marriage. Jonathan had wanted to work on our marriage before this. But what impetus could he have to work on it now? I surely had one. I needed stability. I needed him. And I needed to let him know that I could still be his wife.

I rummaged through my daughter's toy chest and pulled out the brightly painted masquerade mask that she made at school. I adjusted the string around my head, above my ears, as I walked down the hallway back to my bedroom. I positioned myself face down on the bed, supporting myself on my knees and elbows, my silk tank top bunching at the small of my back, and waited for Jonathan to come out of the shower. I turned to look at myself in the full-length mirror leaning against the wall. *Oh god.* The mask was ridiculous; hardly Kubrick. I scanned the room, mentally noting the other grenades. There was a mirror behind our slatted headboard and on our spinning armoire as well. *But I have to do this. I have to know he can do this.* I licked my fingers, slid them between my legs, and prepared a pillow to smother my face into.

When I heard the water turn off, I pulled at my nipples until they were darting out of my tank top, waiting nervously. Jonathan stepped into the bedroom, a towel wrapped around his waist, his hair already gelled. He made a beeline to his dresser without looking at me.

"The nanny already took the kids to school. It's an empty house. You can have me now, if you like," I offered.

"Nah, I have to get work," Jonathan said, searching for matching socks in his drawer.

"Nah?" I asked, a pang of nausea sweeping through me.

"No, it's okay," he said, his face buried in the drawer.

"But it's not," I muttered.

Silence.

"I need this, Jonathan," I whispered, my throat raw.

I felt him frowning, even though his back was to me.

He turned to me and saw the mask. His eyes softened, and he faked a smile. "The mask is kind of hot, but I really don't have time," he said.

I felt sick from his rejection, but I couldn't blame him. He was probably more scared than I was that his body would betray him; that the mask would get knocked off at some point and he'd suddenly go limp.

I turned onto my back. As I watched him collect his briefcase, I swallowed, trying to keep the desperation out of my voice. "I understand... I would never make you stay with me if I look like this forever."

"You won't look like this forever," Jonathan said and began pacing. He paced during most of our conversations, like a Polar bear in the zoo. I'd learned to time my questions so that I could see his expressions as he paced towards me, rather than away.

"Most people who recover have started by the three-week mark," I said. "That was last week, and there's been no change. I've been hiding and put everything on hold, assuming this was temporary. But at some point, we may have to accept that this is permanent and I'll have to adapt. I didn't want you to stay with me out of obligation before, and I won't make you now," I said.

"You're being ridiculous. This is going to pass," he said. I couldn't help but realize he failed, twice, to address, or protest, my remark about staying with me.

"It may not," I said.

"Let's see what the ENT doctor says today. If your hypersensitivity to sound is going to persist, we should think about moving to another rental to get you out of this construction noise. Why don't you stay at the beach house this week? Take Luisa and the kids there, if you feel up to driving. I'll come out on the weekend. Just go get some peace," he said.

"What do you mean, move to another rental? We've been looking at places to buy for three years. You were so gung-ho about making a bid on the Central Park West apartment we saw. Why do you suddenly want to rent?" I asked, alarm bells ringing. I sat upright and pulled off my mask.

"I just told you. It's a quick fix. To get you out of the noise, if you want," he said. "It's not realistic to think we're going to buy something now."

I jumped up and stood in front of him. "Why is that not realistic anymore?" I asked, but felt out of place, as if I couldn't challenge Jonathan in this condition.

He looked at my twisted face silently. At least thirty seconds passed.

"Tell me," I asked, again.

"I think we should focus on your recovery right now. This is not a time to be making big decisions," he said in a tone as delicate as a hand icing a cake.

"You just finished telling me that I was being, quote, ridiculous, because this would pass. But here are your true colors. You have no intention of staying married. I knew it. You're counting down the days until it won't be bad form to walk. Just say it, don't give me this crap," I said, spit flying.

"Is that what you want, to buy an apartment right now?" he asked incredulously.

I shook my head, thinking that I just wanted him to say that he'd stay with me no matter what. But I also knew he deserved more than a masked monster. I was nothing more than a dirty secret hiding out in our apartment.

"You won't even leave the house to go to the grocery store. You're ready for brokers, board interviews, architects? We have no idea what the future holds. Of course, this is ninety-nine percent likely to pass. But it could take six months, a year, two, who knows? You may not want to be in the city. I'm thinking of *you*," he said.

"Well, don't. I'm thinking about me." I paused, took a breath. "Jonathan, I need you to look out for yourself right now. I'm consumed with this. But you shouldn't be. You have to not let this, me, drag you down. Just be honest with me, and with yourself," I told him.

"Of course I have to be consumed with this. This is happening to both of us," he said, brushing away my drama. "*You* be honest. You just shot venom at me about plotting to abandon you because I suggested a rental, and then told me I shouldn't be thinking about myself." Jonathan fixed his collar in the full-length mirror, stretching it as if he felt strangled.

"You realize you just accused me of talking out of both sides of my mouth?" I laughed, unable to resist.

"If you're up to it, make a bid on the apartment. Maybe it'll be a good distraction for you," he said, softening a bit.

"And if I don't get better, then what?" I asked. "Then, I'll take the kids and move out to the suburbs and hide. Forever. And you can stay in the city," I said, answering my own question.

Jonathan turned to face me. "Nobody is leaving anybody... for now. Whatever our issues were before this, we're just agreeing to put them on hold. Just put in a bid on that apartment, please," he said.

How could he not qualify it though? Just weeks ago, I'd ranted in therapy about whether I wanted to stay married. Now, the air had been let out of my balloon threats. Still, he was ready to uproot our lives and plunk down millions of dollars to buy an apartment just to make me comfortable and assuage my fears.

"You must be really regretting your choice in leaving Olivia," I said with a laugh. How different his life would have been if he had stayed with the woman he'd lived with years before meeting me. She was sweet, an administrative assistant, asked nothing of him. She never complained. He had told me she was simple. She fell asleep when her head hit the pillow. It had always puzzled me that Jonathan, the straight-shooter, the man who never strayed too far from the trajectory of his lineage, whose ivy-leagued acquaintances bragged of their wives' successes as much as their own, had stayed with her so long.

Jonathan didn't gratify my comment with a response. "You'll be stuck with it forever if we buy that apartment. Even if I never recover," I said, referring to my face and the apartment.

"Just do it," he said. "We do need to have a discussion about our finances though," he said becoming slightly pale.

I figured he wanted to drag me through some tedious details about transferring money between accounts. "No, we don't. I checked—the apartment is off the market now," I said. Some color returned to his face. Then he frowned, realizing I'd been testing him.

"I really have to get to work. I can't spend all day dealing with your insecurities," he said.

His phone rang and he rejected the call. "My mother. What did you decide about Charlie's birthday party next week? That's probably why she's calling. My parents said you shouldn't feel any pressure to entertain in this condition. They think you should be resting. I agree," he said. His parents, unlike mine, would never advocate entertaining if it made me uncomfortable. Like Jonathan, their chief concern was the well-being of immediate family.

"Is it fair to cancel his first birthday party?" I asked.

"Like he'll know the difference? Tomorrow is his real birthday. Get a cake. Call it a day," he said.

I followed him to the door. "Have a good day. And by the way, I hope you realize that fucking me would have cost you a lot less time." I closed the door behind him.

I ran, showered, and set off to the ENT doctor. As I waited for the elevator in the hall, I heard my neighbor, Lara, and her daughter leaving their apartment. I knew she'd be wearing sheer black pants that deliberately permitted the outline of her g-string to show through, with a tight black tank top to show off her small, perky breasts and stick-thin figure. Her bleached-blonde hair would be pulled back in a tight ponytail with her slightly too long bangs stopping at the midpoint of her brightly made up eyelids. That was her outfit at 6:00 a.m. and at 9:00 p.m. She was a few years younger than I and married to a short, stout man. I had never, to my sister's dismay, seen the Housewives of anything, but I imagined she could be one.

I heard the elevator car stop on the floor above me. There was no way to avoid them. I pulled my hood up, adjusted my hair to cover most of my face, and stood as close as physically possible to the elevator doors.

"Hey, Alix. I haven't seen you in a while," Lara said, in her usual monotonous tone. Lara spoke about milestone events in the same voice she used to speak about the weather, her anniversary, or to offer to help me organize Ella's toys. Months after they moved in, our girls began playing together. I'd flattered Lara about how clean her daughter's room was. Indeed her whole apartment was spotless. There was no clutter, no spills, or half-finished drawings. There was perfectly polished furniture, an original Botero hanging above the fireplace, and a grand piano that no one played. She insisted I see her master bedroom closet—room, actually—when she gave me a tour of her apartment. Cavalli, Herve Leger, Pucci, spaced inches apart. I invited her over to help me get my apartment in the same order simply to rile up Jonathan, tease him, by developing a relationship with her. She prided herself on cleanliness and order. I knew she would accept.

"This is an organized mess," Lara said, examining Ella's room.

"It's a microcosm," I said.

"What's a microcosm?" she asked.

"Never mind. I'm happy you moved to the building. The kids should have regular play dates," I told her.

"Yeah, and we should do something. Lia is in school all day. I have so much free time and nothing to do," she said.

"You can come with me to a matinee Wednesday. I get cheap tickets on TDF. I think I have Phantom for next week," I offered.

"No, the seats are dirty. Why don't we just walk over to Bergdorf?" she asked.

Now, with my face practically plastered to the elevator doors, I answered, "That's because I've been isolating in my prison. Half my face is paralyzed. Bell's Palsy... it's supposedly temporary." I turned to show her.

"That's awful. Lia's teacher had that last year," she said flatly. "You can hardly tell anymore. Go to my acupuncturist. Lia's teacher did. She said Barbara is known as a miracle worker for Bell's."

Covering the left side of my face with my hand, I said, "I don't really believe in acupuncture."

Lara dug into her bag. "In case you change your mind," she said, handing me Barbara's card. "Feel better. It'll be okay. You're lucky you have a good husband," she said, without a hint of personality. I wondered, but didn't ask, on what she based her observation. That he spent his free time with the kids? That he was polite? That he didn't beat me? That he had a job and a dick? Who, but I, could say if he was a good husband? And even if he was, why would that be any consolation? "I" was—or once was—separate from "us," though it occurred to me that there was nothing in my current life that would suggest that to my fairly new neighbor.

A half-hour later, I was face to face with Dr. Magan, the ENT.

"I want you to try to blink, harder than that, like you really, really mean it," he told me. I'd given it my all the first three times, but he was clearly disappointed. I tried again. Dr. Magan made some notes.

"Most people see improvement by now, right?" I asked, deliberately disguising my angst so that he'd give it to me straight.

"Well, with such a dense paralysis, it takes time," he said.

"But you obviously expected to see some movement," I said. "What are you looking for exactly?"

"I'm looking for slight muscular movements in your eye and mouth. I don't see any yet. But that doesn't necessarily mean you won't heal," he told me. "The earlier you show signs of recovery, the more likely you are to recover. But, this is going to be like watching grass grow. The muscles have to rebuild. Let's see where you are in eight weeks."

"Eight?" I asked, certain I'd misheard. A lump began forming in my throat. Tears welled up in my eyes and I forced them back. As if by reflex, I calculated that I wasn't supposed to meet Evan for another nine weeks. "I haven't worked. I haven't gone out. I was about to start a business! Well, what can I do? More steroids? Does acupuncture or electrical stimulation help? Is there another doctor I should see?" I asked, desperately.

"There's no evidence that acupuncture really does anything, but it doesn't hurt. There's really nothing you can do, but give it time."

"I can't live like this," I told him. A tear released itself. I scolded myself that I should be crying, not about my ugliness, but that I was so lacking in depth that I couldn't find an ounce of gratitude within myself despite the graver predicaments possible than the one I was in.

"I know this is hard. Devastating. When you go out socially, just don't fully smile," he told me. "It's the asymmetry that throws people off."

I knew that he was minimizing decades of research showing that facial symmetry was universally a sign of beauty, that smiling is critical to appearing trustworthy, approachable, and feminine.

"Not an issue. I'm not going anywhere like this," I told him, wiping my tears. There were at least another eight weeks ahead of me like this. Never mind the spasms, twitching, and pain. Never mind that I couldn't sip coffee, brush my teeth normally, kiss my children, blow on their food, or handle loud noises. It was the isolation that I couldn't swallow. I wouldn't be able to socialize, eat in restaurants, go to Ella's school activities, go to the gym, or do anything professional. Correction. Those were activities I would *choose* not to do in this condition.

"Excuse me," Dr. Magan said, taking a call from his receptionist. I took the opportunity to send a reply to Dan's last email. "Hope you're enjoying Greece. I'm planning to stay out East for the summer. Let's regroup in August."

"Do you need a work note?" Dr. Magan asked.

"No, I can schedule my mediation cases whenever I like."

"I can see why you'd be uncomfortable mediating. Find something else to occupy your time for now, just to get out of yourself," he said.

I left the office and walked aimlessly for a few blocks.

My phone rang.

"Hi, Mom," I said.

"What did the doctor say?" she asked.

"That it'll be like watching grass grow."

"So, it'll take time. It's a terrible thing. The rabbi is praying for you."

"What rabbi?"

"The rabbi at shul."

"How does he know?"

"I told him and he asked the congregation to say a prayer."

"Jonathan and I haven't even told our closest friends," I said.

"It's beautiful that he said a prayer for you," she said.

"It is," I said.

"Are you crying?" she asked. I knew it'd be uncomfortable for her if I were. Her mother's emotional capacity was singed bare by the fumes of the gas chambers. My mother learned to cry without comfort or affection from her mother. I did too.

"No," I lied.

"How's my grandson doing the day before his birthday?"

"I don't know. I've been at the doctor."

"I'm playing mahjong. Just checking in. Can I call you later?" she asked.

"Yes. By the way, I'm canceling Charlie's party."

"Oh, that's a shame. Well, suit yourself," she said in the same obnoxious tone she'd used to say that a hundred times before. "Your grandparents will be disappointed."

What the hell did Bell's Palsy mean to my ninety-three-year-old grandparents? They wanted to see their great grandchildren. Bell's Palsy in the context of their withering lives, the concentration camps, their losses. This was nothing. I was alive, and had no right to complain.

I passed an antique store and studied my reflection in the window. Even the glassy image prominently showed my eye fused with my cheek and dissolving into my mouth.

Am *I* still there?

Who the fuck are *you* anyway?

My two faces reflected a consciously divided reality: that which I had allowed myself to be—a bored wife and mother, and that which I had passively disavowed—an independent woman with a penchant for adventure; that which embraced the rational and the practical, and that which was based in emotion and fantasy.

Ex-lawyer, volunteer mediator, mother, wife—didn't support my sense of self. My own business would have given me that emotional charge, but like Evan, that dream was deflating with my face.

I watched my reflection lift her hand to cover the afflicted side.

Even if I could alter my internal perception, I couldn't alter how I was perceived. I could no longer wear my personality. All the objectivity in the world couldn't minimize the importance of a face. My smile, my grimace, my smirk—that was how I connected with the external world.

Jonathan and I had met on an online dating site. A small photo of my face, among hundreds of others, had drawn him in. His perception of my face, in an instant, had changed the course of our lives. And what of Facebook, where photos of my face—happy, playing, posing—became pictures of someone else?

Facebook. Evan. He'd been thankfully quiet while I'd been debating whether to tell him what transpired. I had another nine weeks until day ninety, when he expected to see me, and most people were recovered, or improved, by then. If the Palsy hadn't happened, I might've already seen him, kissed him, slept with him. The thought was absurd now.

Telling Evan the truth would ruin what had quite possibly been my last chance of being seen as I wanted to be seen, known as I wanted to be known. But how could I not reach out to him?

I wondered. He expected me to be following up with Mrs. Springfield this week.

I sent him an email. "I think about you (and Joy) often. I am still committed to helping you. I know you're eager and I'm sorry but I haven't followed-up yet."

Fifteen minutes later, after informing those I had invited that Charlie's party was canceled, I got back two emails from him at the same time.

The first, in response to the one I sent, "Thank you."

The second, "I didn't want to make an unethical proposition in response to your sweet email so I'm writing this separately. I have to be in Florida on business. It would be incredible to run into an old friend there next Monday (even if it won't have been 90 days). I woke up in quite a state after our last night together, and every morning since. But aside from that, I want to spend time with you. If you won't take me up on my proposition, maybe we can at least go for a run together. I've been doing a lot of reflecting on things you asked me. And you can tell me your thoughts on secret life versus desire, what really drove you to leave me on that bench, and how your business is coming. No judgment, no strings, just a deep conversation. That is, unless you want more."

One email, and I was no longer walking down the street with my sorrow. I was my former self, walking through midtown with a beautiful man, imagining a night with him, a life with him. I was at the restaurant contemplating ethics, and plotting future encounters. I was on top of him on a bench in control of my destiny. He was offering escape from my present. I smiled. I thought I felt my eyelid twitch.

But escape is futile, I thought. What would I gain by engaging in escape? I typed out my reply: "You have no idea that your email is like a dagger in my heart right now. I can't see you. I have Bell's Palsy. My face is paralyzed. I'll likely recover, but the possibility exists that I may never get better."

I deleted it.

"Florida is impossible. And a run is out of the question (I prefer to work up a sweat rather than start in one). I'll be in touch"

Send.

***

I decided to take Jonathan's suggestion. I headed to the beach, the kids and Luisa in tow, sweating in the stifling air filling the car because the air conditioner bothered my eye. Traffic was abominable as I neared my parents' exit on the expressway. I could easily get off, leave the kids and Luisa with my parents, and follow-up with Mrs. Springfield. *Maybe if you weren't Sherlock Homely!* But if I didn't follow-up with her, Evan would be disappointed. He'd lose interest in me and I'd lose the fantasy of being with him when I recovered. *What's the big deal if Mrs. Springfield sees your face?* I asked myself. *What's more meaningful—maintaining momentum with Evan or repulsing Mrs. Springfield?*

I got off the highway. "We're stopping at Grandma and Grandpa's," I said, cheerfully. I honked as we pulled up to their house.

"Surprise," I said as my parents came outside to greet us.

My father gasped and covered his mouth when he saw my face. My mother stiffened, but hid any further reaction, like I did when Ella was bleeding and I wanted her to stay calm.

"We're taking a traffic break," I said. "And I have an errand to run. I'll be back shortly."

Then I remembered that I'd promised Mrs. Springfield that I'd bring her 'the best' horseradish pickles from the flea market. Not knowing what else to do, I asked my mother for one of the plastic quart-sized Chinese takeout containers I knew she saved, bought jarred pickles from the grocery store, and then transferred them into the container in the parking lot.

A half an hour later, I was parked in front of Mrs. Springfield's house. I tied my hood around my face, pulled a chunk of hair in front of it, and put on my oversized sunglasses. I looked at myself in the rearview mirror. I felt like a bounty hunter. *Ridiculous.* I was about to drive away. But I saw the blinds open in the house and I knew Mrs. Springfield had spotted me.

"What the devil?" she asked, when I got to the front door. "You stroked from smoking, didn't you?"

I explained the Bell's Palsy. I imagined that the terror on her face now must be the same as when she'd looked out her window and saw Joy sprawled out on the street.

"It's a good thing you didn't show up like this last time. I'd have been scared out of my wits," she said. I offered her the container of pickles.

"You didn't have to bring these," she said. "Shouldn't you be in bed? I'd stay in bed. I really give you people credit." I assumed she was referring to the collective whole of the disabled population who left their houses. Then she eyed me suspiciously, nodding. "You didn't come here just to bring me pickles, eh?" I couldn't help but laugh. *What was my tell—the eye that didn't blink or my sagging mouth?*

"I was hoping you might want to talk more about what you saw," I admitted.

"Oh, what the hell, come in," she said, and this time we sat beneath the window in her living room. "How can I say no to you now? Frankly, I've been hoping you'd come back."

"You know who was driving, don't you?" I asked.

She nodded. My whole body relaxed.

"Talk to me," I urged.

"I was sitting right here that night. Like I told you, when I looked out the window, he'd already hit her and was backing up. Right there," she said, pointing diagonally towards the corner. She shook off a chill, rolled up her sleeves to check for goose pimples.

"I knew the car, even from the back. When you're street smart, like me, you keep your eyes open. You know to leave the lights on in your house when you go away, not to carry all your money in your purse, and to keep tabs on the neighborhood, especially the teenagers—who the hooligans are and the cars they drive. Now that blue car was always cruising down our street, except usually he was making a racket with that awful heavy metal music."

"He?" I asked, hoping to get beyond her "street smarts" to the crux of the matter.

"The O'Rourke kid," she said.

I flinched. Paul—my sister's boyfriend then, her husband now.

"*Paul* O'Rourke?" I asked, swallowing hard.

"Right. Your brother-in-law." I wished there were a pause button to give me a moment to digest what she'd told me.

"Did you tell the police?" I asked, my mouth drying.

"No," she said to the floor. "I called my husband—now my ex-husband, that fucking dirt-bag—up from the basement. I told him what I saw, that he needed to call the police." She was silent, as if that was the end of the story.

"Then what happened?"

"He told me I'd better 'shut the fuck up' and listen to him. He said the police would be here any minute, and 'god-help-me,' I'd better not mention Paul." She explained that the "fucking dirt-bag" was in the final round of getting onto the police force. Paul's uncle was the chief of police. If she ratted, and jeopardized his chances of making the force, he'd 'break her pretty face.'

"I begged him. Joy was just a little girl—that poor family. All these years not knowing. When I heard she died, I said, 'Eddie, you gotta tell the police!' He picked up a bat, held it right over my Lulu, my dog. 'I'll kill him,' he told me. What was I going to do?" she asked, folding her hands in her lap. "He turned into a rotten cop. Would have been doing everyone a favor if I kept that bastard off the force. You live, you learn."

She started down memory lane; the divorce, the straw that broke the camel's back, the other woman. I tuned out, processing the information.

Thank goodness Evan hadn't spoken to her himself, I thought. I knew I couldn't tell Evan what I'd learned, or for that matter, Sabrina. Surely she hadn't known back then. She'd have told me, as she had about her cheat notes, the birthmark on her labia, that my parents had tapped my phone, that they'd taken out a second mortgage to pay for my rehab. If she'd learned about it later on, she'd have lost all respect for Paul and left him. Though she hung around unsavory characters, she'd never shed the strong moral code we were raised with. Hit and runs: unambiguously immoral. I remembered when Paul had accidentally run over a cat. She was so upset with him that she'd slept at my parents' house for a week. I couldn't destroy her life. It would wreck her, and probably the marriage she was always threatening to end, but so obviously depended on.

Beyond Sabrina's emotional state, though, I wondered if there could possibly be legal consequences. The statute of limitations would have definitely barred a criminal claim. The charge would've been vehicular manslaughter, aggravated if he'd been drinking. Maybe a Class C felony. At most, there'd have been a six-year statute of limitations. The only way it could've been tolled is if Paul had left afterwards and lived out of New York—but those two never left Queens. What about a civil suit for wrongful death? The two-year time to file suit would've long expired, even if the clock hadn't started ticking until Evan had turned eighteen. But, I thought back to my law school days, there were exceptions, like in cases of fraudulent concealment, where someone was prevented from learning that they had a claim sooner. Couldn't Evan argue that Paul had fraudulently concealed his identity all this time? Even if he couldn't win, he could drag Sabrina and Paul through legal hell trying. Wasn't that what I always told my mediation clients to encourage them to settle out of court? I'd have to protect Sabrina from this, and prevent Evan from learning the truth.

Chapter 10

I drove two-and-a-half hours to the beach. This house was the eyesore of the beachfront properties. Jonathan's mother, Caroline, had the sense to purchase it before the town of East Hampton had become a commercial haven for glamour, where ladies lunched in Lilly Pulitzer resort wear in trendy restaurants, while their husbands sweated in their suits in the city. A mother of three, with no understanding of financial markets, real estate, or the hedge fund Jonathan's father ran, Caroline had invested in sentiment, a retreat for her children and future generations. His two sisters and their families had worn out the mattresses and sofas. Their children had colored in many of the books that lined the bookshelves. The house hadn't been updated in decades. There were none of the amenities that people would assume they'd find in a house on this beach. Its value was intrinsic. The house was on stilts. Though it had good bones, it could easily be destroyed by a powerful storm.

"Pick whichever bedroom you like," I told Luisa as if she, too, were on vacation. "Settle in. I'll take the kids to the beach."

During winter, Jonathan's parents told us they were planning to sell the house because it'd become too much of a practical burden for them to maintain. So Jonathan, for the sake of keeping it in the family bought it from them at market value. They agreed not to tell his sisters, so that they'd feel comfortable using it as they always had.

Jonathan's father, Carl had remarked, "Never mind the beach. Now that you own this place, you two should be getting to know the neighbors. You never know what opportunities will come by talking to these people. You wasted time traveling around the world. You did nothing for years after that. All the opportunities you need are right on your block."

"You assume that the only goal your son has is to accumulate more, more, more. Have you even asked him whether he found two years away from Wall Street fulfilling?" I asked.

"You know that banker, at the end of the block. He can't be much older than you guys. But he is *really* successful..." Carl continued. Jonathan had achieved more success at forty-two than any man I'd known. It infuriated me that his father minimized it. I looked at Jonathan to see if he was insulted. He was not. A part of him held himself to the same standard.

Nature ran amuck on the path leading to the beach. Ella wouldn't walk barefoot, fearful of getting pricked by the sharp weeds poking through the sand and the pinecones dotting the path, so I carried her on and off the beach. Days passed. Thoughts of Evan and Paul bobbed around like buoys in the ocean. I kept them at bay.

I showered and prepared to pick up Jonathan from the train. I wanted to look as nice as possible. I thought I'd been feeling a twitch near my eye since Evan's last email. I couldn't tell if there'd actually been improvement, but I was inspired to wear a summer dress. Its bright colors and lightness seemed out of place under my disfigured face. I picked up a scone from Jonathan's favorite place in the next town. Jonathan was buried in his phone as he walked off the train and through the parking lot. He glanced up only to find me.

"Hi," I said, when he reached me, but he didn't look up.

"Hey," he replied and finally did. He took the scone, without a thank you. He didn't notice the twitch, or the dress, but I was secretly filled with hope that I was improving. When we got to the house, Jonathan told Ella that he liked the baseball cap she was wearing and he planted endless kisses on Charlie's face.

A half hour later, we changed into bathing suits, and walked down the path behind the house to the beach. Just over the dune, we sat on a plank of washed-up slatted wood that looked like it might once have been part of a boardwalk. Though the portion of beach behind our house was technically private, there were public beaches a quarter mile to the left of us and a half of a mile to the right. Couples, families, and joggers traversing between the public beaches sporadically dotted the shoreline fifty feet from where we were sitting.

"That's my favorite bikini." Jonathan was eyeing me without a trace of disgust.

"Go for it," I told him.

"There are too many people around," he said, but he was hard.

"Just be quick," I urged him.

"This is going to be *really* quick," he warned me. He pulled my bikini bottom to the side. I hadn't planned to have sex with him except from behind, but I forgot my face. He pushed into me, hard and fast. I felt his thighs tighten against mine, his vein started pulsating, his thumb pressed my clit and I gushed around him. I tugged his balls permissively and his come spilled out of me and onto the sand. It reminded me of a jellyfish. If he'd been disturbed by my face, his body gave nothing away. Then Evan entered my mind, unwelcome. I kicked sand over the mess.

"You just banged a Palsy in broad daylight," I said.

"You know doing it outside always gets me," he said, adjusting his trunks.

"We polluted this pristine beach," I said.

"Remember the show we were watching last week about pollution and all the methane that's emitted from cow dung?" he asked.

"From fucking to cow dung. Yes, I remember," I said.

"We really are destroying the planet. I've been thinking about whether I could be vegetarian lately," he said.

I looked at him like it was he who had two faces. I'd saved animals my whole life, from injured crows to stray dogs, and had never considered it.

"Del Frisco's would miss us," I said. "But you did just remind me to call back Madeline Schwartz, head of the animal organization. Now that my business is on hold, I may as well see what she needs help with."

"Your 'business' should be on hold irrespective of your face," he said, immediately extinguishing the endorphins from our quickie. "Your aim should be a part-time job with moderate income and predictable hours."

I lit another cigarette, and called Madeline. She wanted to know if I had any interest in helping out with fundraising efforts for a no-kill shelter she'd opened for special needs dogs. They didn't have enough food, medical supplies, or staff to socialize or walk the animals. I told her about my face and that I couldn't actively help out. She told me that dogs are medically therapeutic, that perhaps seeing these remarkable dogs coping with their problems would help me, so why don't I stop by the facility? Where else could my face matter less? I wondered. I committed to donating a thousand dollars and promised to visit the shelter.

Jonathan left to drop Luisa and the kids at the park. I checked my email. Evan Roth. Just seeing his name in my inbox got my heart racing. Was I imagining it, or had the corner of my mouth just twitched upwards? I opened his email.

"Had a dream last night. We were no place specific. You had your hand on my stomach, just below my belly button. It was erotic and intense. Do we really have to wait until Day 90? By the way, I've been rereading some of our emails. You once asked, with a 'haha' if it was normal that you got turned on looking at yourself in the mirror. I somehow failed to respond. In your case, yes, it's normal. Is it normal that it turns me on thinking of you turning yourself on? - E"

I vaguely remembered that now ironic email. It was like another woman had written it.

I knew I should tell him about the Bell's and shut down this communication, in spite of and because of what I now knew about Paul. But I couldn't. There was no longer any real risk to Jonathan. This was harmless, self-indulgent fantasy. And it was all I had to transport me away from my reality. I replied:

"I'm flattered. But what happened to being a patient man? They say that planning a vacation activates your pleasure center more than actually going on a vacation. I imagine the same could be said for planning our next meeting. p.s. Dreams reveal a lot. Now I know your sensitive spot."

***

"How's the beach?" Sabrina asked once I wrestled my phone out of Charlie's peanut butter-covered hands.

"How did you know I was out here?" I asked.

"The parents told me you went to the *beach house*. You have to hear the way Mom said 'beach house.' So annoying. Like it makes her rich."

I laughed, commiserating. No matter our differences, we shared the same radar to detect the bitterness, flaws, sarcasm, and passive aggressiveness that lingered below my mother's cheery exterior, imperceptible to anyone else. Though others saw her as a down-to-earth, energetic woman, tirelessly helping others, my sister and I knew she only needed constant validation, and was ill-tempered. "Maybe we should put a picture of it on her *chinoiserie*," I said in a dramatic French accent. "It can't just be a china cabinet."

"Don't put a picture on the chinoiserie, put a bowl of cccchummus," she said, imitating my parents, who pronounced humus the Israeli way.

"So, what's up?" I asked.

"When are you heading back to the city? I want you to stop by. I'm itching to see your face first-hand. I want to take pictures and post them." I heard Paul laugh in the background and realized I was on speaker.

"Mean girl," I said. "So come out to the beach."

"Too long a drive to go back and forth," she said.

"No, it's not," Paul chimed in. I pictured him as a teenager, cruising in his car, hitting Joy, and driving away. I wanted to blurt out that I knew he was a murderer. "I'll bring some beers and kielbasa. We'll have a Q."

"Just stay over for a night," I told her.

"Now, we're talking," Paul said. Always up for anything involving beer and food. Always the life of the party. He seemed equally enthusiastic to hear details about my mediations as he was to find out what our kids ate for breakfast. "Scrambled eggs? How many? Salt? Anything on the side?" He paid detailed compliments, could win over anyone. Fitting for a sales man. This year it was mattresses. The prior, cars. Before that he'd been a travel agent. But ever since we were kids, the smiling salesman could turn drunk boxer on very little notice.

"Sleep there? Should I? No. Who would watch Salmon and Maurice?" she asked, referring to her tabby cats.

"Salmon and Maurice," Paul said with irritation. "Just leave them a few cans of food. You never want to go anywhere."

"Yes I do," she protested. "Should we really go?" she asked Paul, and I could imagine the worried expression on her face.

"Stop overthinking it, Sabi," he said, using the nickname he'd given her in high school. "We're not deciding whether to go to Antarctica."

"Okay, sure, we'll definitely come," she told me, confidently, as if she could undo her ambivalence and convince herself, Paul, or me that she was easygoing.

We hung up, but she called back three times over the next hour. Did she need slippers? Should she bring long pants? She couldn't find directions online. She changed her mind, she wasn't coming. No, she was, and should she bring a toy for the kids—how old was Ella again?

I sat across from Jonathan, under a skylight, in a cushioned white wicker chair in the family room. "My sister is coming out at around three and staying for the night," I told him.

"That's great," he said, barely looking up from the document he was reading.

"What are you reading?" I asked.

"Wasserman, the new guy we're hiring to manage marketing, sent over an employment agreement. Atypical that he did, but it looks fine to me. Not going to bother sending it to the lawyers. Want to take a look?"

"Sure," I said. I reviewed it, with Jonathan looking over my shoulder.

"Mostly standard. But I see what he's doing. He wants to make sure he can only be fired for cause. You need to define cause to include negligent acts, not just intentional ones. And..." I flipped through the pages making sure I didn't miss anything, "... add a non-compete clause."

"I'm not asking him to sign a non-compete when I haven't asked anyone else to," he said, as if I were being too rigid. "It's not a great way to start a relationship."

"Stop being so diplomatic. None of your other employees had a lawyer draft up an agreement that contemplates a payment schedule in the event that they are terminated. Wasserman's not low-level. He will be in on your partnership meetings. Do me a favor. Add a two-year non-compete, even one year, if you're more comfortable. Your company is too young to afford the risk."

"You're right, you're right. I'll ask our lawyer to draft it."

"I'll save you two grand and draft it myself. Then just ask him to review."

"Thanks, baby," he said.

I drafted the clauses, showered, dressed, made macaroni salad, and prepared patties out of chopped meat to barbecue later.

"Aunt Sabrina is here!," Ella yelled from the front patio. I heard two car doors slam shut as I went outside.

"Hey Alix," Paul said, waving enthusiastically from behind the open trunk. He was grinning ear to ear, his red hair looking bright orange in the sun. *You're the one who should be incapable of smiling!* I thought, thinking about Joy.

Sabrina came up the stairs, her long fingernails pulling through the blonde ends of her hair to get the kinks out. We didn't kiss or hug hello. We'd inherited that inability from our mother when we were kids. As we got older, we were surprised that it wasn't that way between females in other families, but it was too late to correct it.

"He wouldn't shut the windows. Am I a complete mess?" she asked, nervously and seriously, as if there were a surprise party waiting for her inside the house.

"You look fine," I said.

"You don't," she laughed, "it's *much* worse than I imagined." I shook my head no, looking at Ella, and waved my hand horizontally under my chin, indicating that she shouldn't talk about my face in front of her. "I'm joking, it's not *that* bad. But absolutely worth driving to see," she said. I realized only a sister could make a comment like that, and only mine would.

"Come, Aunt Sabrina, let's got to the beach. I want to show you what I made. Come on," Ella urged, jumping up and down.

"Hello, Ella. You look very pretty. And you're so big. I like the flowers on your bathing suit. Where's your brother?" Sabrina asked, sweetly.

"Come on, come on, let's go to the beach," Ella continued, now pulling at Sabrina's shoulder bag which fell heavily to the crease of her elbow.

"Uh, on second thought, actually, where's your babysitter?" Sabrina asked, elbowing Paul, who was now at her side, in the rib, for an acknowledgement that she was incredibly funny, and looking at me for the same, as if she weren't insulting my child.

"You don't want to play with me?" Ella asked, looking hurt. I watched Sabrina register that Ella was too old for jokes to be made above her head.

"Awww," Sabrina said, sitting on a patio chair, her blue eyes genuinely apologetic. I remembered how she'd bite me as a child and then spend the rest of the day making amends. "Look what I brought you." She opened her bag and pulled out a make-your-own bracelet kit. "Can I help you make one?"

We passed a couple of hours playing on the beach. Paul and Jonathan were tending the grill, holding up giant sausages with tongs, making phallic jokes.

"These are going to be tasty," Paul said. "I got them from Nicky's. Best prosciutto, sausages, and cheeses anywhere in New York. Guarantee you've never had better sausage than this. I'd bet my left ball on it."

"In fact, we're so sure you're gonna love it that we're offering you a hundred percent refund if you aren't completely satisfied, and we'll even pay for shipping," Jonathan joked.

"Are you making fun of my job?" Paul asked, no longer smiling.

"What?" Jonathan asked. "No." He continued laughing.

Sabrina looked at Paul as if to make sure his top wasn't about to blow.

"Kids?" I called into the house, really meaning Luisa. "Go upstairs and have a bath, please, before dinner."

"Got it," Luisa called from somewhere.

"Can we talk about your face now?" Paul shout-whispered. I nodded.

"Tell me the whole story, beginning from the minute you noticed something was off."

I did, pausing to answer his strange questions—what was I wearing that day, what street was Charlie's gymnastics class on, did I put ham in the pea soup that I went home to turn off?

"Does it hurt?" Paul asked. "Looks painful. What's it called again, what you have?"

"Bell's Palsy."

"Crazy. Never heard of it before."

"Yes you have," Sabrina said. What's the last name of that kid Tom that lived on Utopia? He had it in high school. Remember, it was like three weeks. Everyone made fun of him. I was telling Alix."

"Oh, Tom Moretti? Yeah, I do remember that." Paul said.

"Whatever happened to him?" Sabrina asked.

"Moretti?" Paul said. "That kid overdosed like a decade ago. Really sad. Had a wife, kids." He shook his head. "Be right back. I'm going to the John."

"So, how is it being back to work, Jonathan?" Sabrina asked.

"Not bad," Jonathan said. "Some interesting things happening."

"What do you do again?" Sabrina asked. She'd asked him half a dozen times.

"In a word, we either invest in companies or match them up with investors who will."

"What kind of companies? Like if I opened my own salon and needed a loan?"

"Not exactly. We focus on environment-related technologies. So, we just closed a financing deal for a massive desalination project. Did you know that there are only a handful of cogeneration plants in all of North America?"

"Oh, I didn't know that," Sabrina said, looking thoughtful. I knew she had no idea what desalination or cogeneration meant. I didn't when Jonathan explained it to me. But she wouldn't ask. She'd always allowed her fear of appearing unintelligent to trump natural curiosity.

"Hey Sabrina, do you happen to have an extra Ambien?" I asked. Sabrina's sleeping issues predated my own. In our later teen years, she'd frequently wake in the middle night, drenched in sweat, asking if she could sleep on the floor of my room. Our father, who also woke multiple times during the night, told her it was genetic. "I doubled up last month. The pharmacy won't refill it early, so I'll be short this month."

"It will cost you two hundred," she joked. "Yeah, no problem."

"These girls," Paul said to Jonathan returning from the bathroom, "complete opposites in every way. Alix, brown hair, brown eyes, short, outgoing. Sabi, blonde, blue eyes, tall, shy. The only thing they have in common is insomnia." He paused. "And their big racks. Am I right?"

Jonathan forced a laugh, finding nothing related to my sleeping problems funny.

"You know, they actually look smaller since you went under the knife. Anyway, how'd you even get started with those pills?" Paul asked me, trying to get a tortilla chip into his mouth before the guacamole spilled off.

"The same way I got started with cigarettes, pot, everything else... your wife. When I was stressed about exams back in law school, Sabrina gave me one to try."

"You never told me that," Paul said to Sabrina.

"She's my sister. I don't tell you her business," she said. But she told me all of his. How he drank to the point of blacking out, roughed up a neighbor for continually leaving his car in their driveway, had lied on a job application. She trusted me, and was loyal to me. I thought about how she'd react if the shoe were on the other foot. There was no way she'd ever disclose something terrible Jonathan had done to someone she was infatuated with, and risk hurting me, even if what he'd done had involved something immoral. I remembered when our parents told us about where babies came from as kids. We doubled over laughing because "we came out of the same vagina!"—it was understood, that bond trumped all.

"I guess we all have secrets," I said, glaring at Paul.

"Why can't you girls just go to sleep normally? I can fall asleep eating this chip if I let myself," Paul said, stuffing another in his mouth, aloof to my angry stare.

Jonathan nodded in solidarity.

"Oh, Paul, surely you can relate. There must be *something* that has the potential to keep you up at night... we all have skeletons," I said. Jonathan looked at me confused and everyone was quiet for an uncomfortable moment. What am I doing? I wondered. Like he was going to confess that he hit Joy? And why did I even want him to? So I could tell Evan? So it didn't come to me ever having to tell Sabrina myself? So she could finally see Paul for what he really was?

"Well, I told you that Maurice needs to have a cyst removed from his tail?" Sabrina asked, turning to me, as if the conversation had naturally transitioned to her cat. "Can you imagine? It's going to cost thousands."

"Those annoying cats," Paul said. I heard Charlie crying from the open window upstairs and knew Luisa was struggling to get all the sand out of his creases. If he cried another thirty seconds, I wouldn't be able to fend off the urge to go upstairs.

"You closed the window in our bedroom, right, Paul?" Sabrina asked.

"Yeah," he said. "This is good guacamole. Tell me how you made it, Alix. Cilantro, tomatoes, onion. Tell me everything. Did you chop the onions or grate them?"

"They'll jump out if you didn't," Sabrina said. "Are you sure you did?"

"Yes," Paul snapped.

"I should have checked before we left."

"I closed it," Paul said. "Calm down."

"No, I need to get back," Sabrina said, standing, tight-lipped, her chest rising and falling rapidly beneath her tank top. "I have to get home. I knew this was a bad idea." Rather than going back into the house, Sabrina followed the terrace that wrapped around the side of the house and I heard her rapidly climbing the steps down to ground level. Paul clucked with irritation and followed her.

Jonathan and I looked at each other, realizing she was in panic mode. We heard their muffled voices.

"I'm going to listen from the front porch," I told Jonathan.

"Give them privacy," he said. I ignored him, tiptoeing through the house, out the front door, where I could hear them and see them in the driveway through the cracks of the deck.

"Sabi, don't be weak. Don't ruin the whole weekend with another panic attack," he said.

"I'm sorry, I'm sorry, I can't help it, please don't get mad," she begged, gasping between apologies. I saw through the crack that she'd put her head against his chest. I saw that his arms remained at his side.

"Come on, get it together," he said.

"Why don't you feel bad for me?" she asked, now with an accusatory tone. "Every other night you go for a beer with George to comfort him because you feel *sooo* bad for him. You never seem to tire of that."

"George spent the last few years watching his unit get killed in Afghanistan. He bangs his head against the wall when he hears loud noises. He has good reason for traumatic post disorder."

"Post-traumatic stress disorder."

"You can't compare yourself to him," Paul said.

"Yes, I can."

"Why would you want to? You're pathetic and you're ruining my life," he said.

"Well, you've ruined mine too," she said. I air-punched, rooting for my sister, whether she was pathetic or not. Paul slammed his hand against the house.

"I swear to God, you are going to make me lose it," Paul said.

"I'm sorry," she said. She sounded scared. "I don't mean that. Let's go home. Some eggplant parm and a movie and I'll put on the pink thing you like? Please, don't be angry with me. I need you," she said in a baby voice. It made me ill to hear her grovel for this blow face. The woman who regularly, and casually, told me she was fed up with him and was going to leave him, was clearly the decoy.

"Whatever. Let's go say goodbye," he said, and I prepared to go back inside.

"I can't," she said. "I really can't breathe. I'll wait in the car."

Paul headed back around the side patio. I tiptoed into the house and got to the back patio, just before him. He was smiling ear-to-ear, just like when he'd arrived. Jonathan was scraping the grill, a plate of burgers and kielbasas resting on aluminum foil on the shelf of the barbecue.

"We're heading home to save the cats. She's a little nervous and just wants me to say goodbye for her. Sorry, guys."

He gave me a hug, lifting me off the ground and pressing me to him. "Good luck with your face."

"Hey, easy guy," Jonathan kidded as Paul put me down.

"Be well," Paul said, gripping Jonathan's shoulder. "Can't be hard in a place like this," he added, then reached for a kielbasa, bit into it and groaned with satisfaction.

"Take some for Sabrina," I told him.

"The only thing she'd eat in this state is a valium."

I watched him go into the house to grab their bag, disgust for him coursing through me.

Chapter 11

Three hours in traffic on the Long Island Expressway, and we were nowhere close to the 59th Street Bridge. Jonathan hadn't spoken a word in an hour, although the kids had been sleeping for longer, since we'd dropped Luisa off at the train station. I'd managed to hold my tongue about him staying in the slow lane on the already slow highway. I'd done my facial exercises in the passenger seat mirror ten times.

Ella yawned loudly. "Guys? Are we still at the beach?" she asked, then fell back asleep.

When we finally reached 57th Street, I stared out the window to avoid looking at Jonathan. He'd given me what I'd wanted at the beach, but all it did, I thought, was clear the way for me to focus on what was really lacking between us—we had nothing to say to each other—we were just two warm bodies sharing a car and offspring. A magazine-stand prominently displayed Self, Glamour, Playboy, Vogue. Every face, every image, every advertisement was suffocating.

I searched my pocketbook for the number Lara had given me for Barbara, the acupuncturist. As we pulled into the parking garage, I dialed the cell phone number on the card expecting to leave a voicemail. I was shocked that Barbara picked up the phone so late, and more shocked that she could see me at 11:30 a.m. tomorrow.

"She only takes cash. Did you put more money in the top drawer?" I asked.

"There should be at least five hundred," he said. "What kind of place is it that they only take cash?"

"I don't know," I said. "She also said I should use the entrance to her private office on 83rd Street, not the main entrance to the Clinic on Madison. Maybe it's just her side gig."

"Shady," he said.

"Maybe, but she's supposedly very helpful with Bell's," I said, fighting my own skepticism.

I turned the card over to study it more carefully. In small print, I read, "Affiliated with Dr. Chang and ERoth Wellness and Physical Therapy Clinic."

'ERoth'? Could it possibly stand for Evan Roth, I wondered? There was no way I'd go to an office he was affiliated with. I googled the clinic while Jonathan stood outside the car smoking, waiting for me to take control of waking and unloading the children.

"What are you doing?" he mouthed impatiently, as the page loaded.

I clicked "About Us." There he was, the same photo from Facebook. "Founding partner, Evan Roth is a NYS licensed Physical Therapist. He holds a Master's Degree from Binghamton University. In addition to his work at the Clinic, Mr. Roth is heavily involved in philanthropic activities, most notably, Upstate Golistano's Children's Medical Center where he serves as President of the Board..."

That was the hospital where his sister had died. Fresh guilt weighed on me for not telling him about Paul. As I transferred Charlie from his car seat to the stroller without waking him, I entertained letting Evan see my face. The flirting would cease and he'd understand why I couldn't help him. I could avoid the proactive deception. No, I thought, you can tell him without the shame of showing him!

When we got home, I was prepared to cancel my appointment. But then I remembered that Evan had planned to be in Florida tomorrow anyway. I needed to confirm. I sent him a text:

"Are you heading to Florida tomorrow?"

"Already here. Have you decided to hop on a plane after all?" he texted back.

"I'm imagining hopping on something else."

"Call me right now," he requested.

"Can't," I replied. "And I think it's safer if we stick to texts and email."

The next morning I took a cab to 83rd and Madison. I walked past ERoth Wellness, around the corner, and rang the buzzer for "Barbara."

"I sense you must be Alix," a smiling Caucasian woman with long gray hay-like hair said, as if my face didn't explain itself. She wore a long flowing skirt, and I knew, without seeing, that she had hairy armpits.

"Ah, very intuitive," I said sarcastically.

"I'm Barbara. I'm so pleased to meet you. I want you to know that I let you come in right away because of who you are," she said, tenderly touching my hair. We hadn't discussed the price of the "treatment" but based on her silly comment, the fact that she was touching me, that she managed to fit me right in, and that there was no medical paperwork—she didn't even know my last name—I suspected it would be pricey.

Barbara led me past a number of closed doors to a room, took my pulse, said it was faint, removed my shoes, and asked me to lie back on what was essentially a massage table.

"I don't believe in this stuff," I said, as she dug ten sewing needles into the left side of my face, hands, and right foot. "Will that affect the treatment?"

"No, it's going to help whether you believe it will or not," she said. "Okay, that's it. I'm done. I'm going to turn the lights down, set the timer, and leave you in here for the next twenty minutes." Smart move, I thought. I'd rather not see the needle sticking out vertically above my brow and the one horizontally stretching across my eye. The two needles in my visual path looked like the hands of a clock set to 9 o'clock. That, coupled with the ticking of the timer, made me feel like a human time bomb.

"I want you to relax. I'll be back in twenty," she said, dimming the light.

But it wasn't relaxing, particularly with her chatting it up in the next room with another patient.

"I'm also a firm believer in reincarnation," Barbara was saying. "I just finished reading Born as a Bird."

"Oh, I think I read that one. You should read Against the Grain," the patient said. "That's a good one."

"I was just thinking about that book! You must have picked up on the energy of my thoughts," Barbara said.

Had I heard this conversation prior to the needles being placed in my face, I wouldn't have gone through with it because it only confirmed that she was a quack. As I lay there, my mind wandered back to Jonathan's rejection in the car last night and countless times before. I didn't need needles in my face. I just needed to be free of negativity. How could my nerves be reawakened when my life, my husband, fatigued me? The ENT said improving would be like watching grass grow. The same could be said for getting my marriage back on track. I didn't need to watch grass grow. What I needed was a lawn transplant. And now it was too late.

Barbara returned. "How do you feel?" she asked.

"Tense," I answered, as she slowly removed the needles.

"What were you doing before this happened?" she asked.

I thought back to the dinner party, couples therapy. "Fighting with my husband," I said.

"Stress is often linked to Bell's Palsy. It's an important part of your recovery too. That's why we take a holistic approach. We offer a medical massage after the acupuncture treatment. You can just undress and lay face down on the table when I finish with you," she said.

"Yeah, thanks, but I really don't think..."

A door opened and closed loudly outside the room.

"Oh, the new owner is here. He's a physical therapist, and well trained in homeopathy and massage. He'll be administering your treatment," she said. *What?*

"Hi Barbara," Evan's familiar voice called out through the crack in the door. I searched the room, instinctively, for an escape exit.

"Welcome back. I'm in with a new patient. I'll be done with her in a few minutes if you're available for the medical massage," she said.

"Okay," he replied, from somewhere farther away.

The unfrozen part of my face froze, and the rest of my body with it. How could I have walked into the lion's den? I had to get out of the office. I had to run. It would've been humiliating for him to see me like this, but possibly worse that I'd been flirting with him—just last night—without disclosing it. Panic set in, adrenaline coursed through me. But behind my fear, I flashed back to our last night together and my body begged me to stay. *Oh geez, his hands.* The idea of Evan touching, rubbing, caressing my back, my thighs, my ass... oh my goodness... how could I be getting so turned on in this disturbing situation? It was sick, demented, perfect. He wouldn't have to know it was me. Not if he didn't see my face. There were hundreds of Alix's in the city. Barbara didn't have my last name. I was just 'Alix', a woman with Bell's Palsy. He would never have suspected I had Bell's Palsy. I couldn't have dreamed up a more palatable, hotter, situation. Maybe I could have this.

"What kind of massage did you say this is?" I asked.

"It's a medical massage, a lot like deep tissue," Barbara said.

"My face is sore from the needles," I said.

"You should massage your face daily on your own. This is for the rest of your body. We aim to balance the whole body," she said. *Maybe...*

"I don't feel comfortable having my face seen by a man," I said.

"I understand. You can put a warm towel over your face when it's time to turn over," she said.

"I'd rather not turn over," I said.

"That's fine. I'll let him know to just do your back this time," she said. *That works.* "Okay, then?" she said leaving a folded towel on the edge of the table and making a hole in the paper of the facial piece of the massage table.

"Umm..." For the first time since the Palsy began, I thought about the appearance of the rest of my body. I was tan from the beach. I'd shaved my legs. I moisturized well this morning. I worked out. No scars were visible from the back. My hair was curly today, not straight like when I'd met him. I could do this. It was just a medical treatment. He wouldn't have to see my face. I wouldn't have to say a word. I quickly weighed the risk of him realizing this was me, the risk of this getting sexual, and the risk of Jonathan finding out against the benefit of Evan touching me, getting away with it, living the moment. "Okay!"

"Let me just take your pulse again post-acupuncture," she said, holding my wrist. "It's definitely not faint anymore. You responded very well to the acupuncture." I don't think it's the acupuncture, lady!

I undressed quickly, laid face down on the table, and unfolded the towel enough to cover my butt, leaving the rest of my body exposed. I placed my face in the paper hole of the headpiece and pulled my hair down around it. No part of my face was visible. I laid like that for what felt like twenty minutes but was probably only two before there were two quick knocks on the door.

"Ready?" Evan asked through the door.

Damn. I couldn't talk. He'd know my voice. I'd just pretend I didn't hear. He just had to get started. I'd had many massages. I wouldn't have to say a word once he started.

He waited a few more minutes before cracking the door open. Oh, how I wanted to see him.

"I see you're all set," he said. I could feel my heart pounding on the table under me. Please don't sweat. "Would you like me to put on music?" he asked.

Idiot! How did you expect to get away without speaking? I tried to nod, but the movement was undetectable. I lifted my right arm and gave him a thumbs-up feeling remarkably stupid. Something along the lines of Enya started playing in the background.

Evan briefly lifted the towel covering my butt, unfolded it, and after a delay, during which I thought I could feel him peeking, placed it back down so that it was covering my whole body. Too bad. I felt less feminine with my body covered and hoped a "medical massage" didn't mean the towel stayed on. He lifted my feet, placing a foam cylinder underneath my ankles. I'd forgotten about my toes. I hadn't gone for my weekly manicure-pedicure since the day I'd seen him, five weeks before. I'd chosen a pale pink for my toes, thankfully nothing memorable.

He began rubbing my shoulders, digging his thumbs into my back. *Such strong hands.* Then downward, to my lower back. Based on his pace, I knew, and was relieved, that he was just marking the territory he'd cover when he removed the towel. His thumbs pressed into the base of my spine, causing me to instinctually arch my back to narrow my waist and flaunt the roundness of my ass, his hands firmly holding my hips in position. As his thumbs made small circles on the base of my spine, my pelvis pushed rhythmically against the table. *Oh boy.* I couldn't help but imagine him circling my clit, instead. I knew how sexual this man was. He knew exactly what he was doing. I let out an audible sigh as the delicious moisture collected between my legs. He'd barely begun and I already wanted him to molest me, manhandle me, fuck me. Then he pressed his palms into my ass, parting it, ever so briefly, before gripping me just underneath it, simultaneously working my inner thighs. The towel dried some of the wet mess that had escaped to my inner thighs but more was already replacing it. If I couldn't take this how would I handle his hands touching my bare skin? I wondered. He quickly gave my thighs and calves a squeeze before snapping the towel off of me, folding it up, and replacing it to cover just my ass.

I heard him walk towards the counter. I heard the sound of liquid, then his hands rubbing together. I felt his presence near my head. I opened my eyes. Through the hole in the massage table, I saw his shoes, the same perfectly polished shoes he'd worn the first time we met. The top of my head was against him as he rubbed my back. He was so tall. I tried to estimate what part of his body my head was against. It must have been the top of his thighs. If only I could have lifted my face up and pressed it against his cock. He *must* have been thinking the same thing. He pressed down, firmly dragging his hands from my shoulders to the small of my back, his fingers sliding under the towel to the top of my ass, and back up again, over and over again, each time pushing the towel a little lower, teasing my ass, until it was barely covered. He was testing to see if I'd object to being uncovered. He had no idea how far he could go. I felt sexy, like movie sexy. I raised my hands from the sides of my body to either side of my face, holding the edge of the table in front of me. I knew he could see the round sides of my breasts spilling out from under me and I was silently asking him to touch them.

On cue, he spread his hands wider, lingering at the sides of my breasts, pulling upwards so that more was exposed, then tracing the curve of my waist to my hips, and ass, and back up again. The motion of his hands forced my head to bump softly against him. I wanted to reach up to his ass and pull him harder against my head. Better yet, I wanted his cock lodged in my throat right through the hole of the paper my face was resting on. My breathing became shallow. I held it. He was leaning over me, fully working my ass. This gorgeous man who had dominated my fantasies for months was all over my ass, and he didn't even know it was me. *Or did he?* I suddenly wondered, but didn't permit the horrifying thought to fester. I moaned and instinctively widened my legs so that they were no longer on the foam cushion under my feet.

"Is the pressure alright?" he asked.

"Mmm hmm..." I managed.

Then he stopped. *Damn.* He was no longer standing in front of me. I couldn't feel where he was, but he was dripping oil all over my back. He began rubbing it in, his hands sensually squeezing the area of my back directly opposite my breasts, forcing me to imagine his hands on them. My nipples were rocks. *Oh, this is good, too.* I moaned deeply. Was he doing that deliberately?

"You're very tight," he said.

I'd lost all sense of time. I was aware of nothing except how turned on I was, how I was burning with need, and how desperately I wanted to come.

He moved down to my lower back again. *Oh good.* I raised my ass in unashamed anticipation. Answering my plea, he placed both his hands on my ass. The towel had now slid down to the back of my thighs. "Very tight," he said again, rubbing, squeezing, feeling me. He was spreading me, top to bottom, so that both my ass and lips opened a bit. I was exposed. I moved my ass in tandem with his rhythm, pressing against his hands. The front of me was rubbing against the table. I didn't want him to stop. This was torture. I wanted his fingers inside of me, in any opening. "Mmm," I groaned to encourage him. I was certain he could see everything, all of me. I didn't think I could get any wetter. I was slightly embarrassed. Then he stopped abruptly, and moved his hands to the back of my knees, leaving my ass wanting, leaving me grinding my own body against the table. I exhaled deeply, almost thankful for the respite. Did he skip my thighs because I was ridiculously soaked? Was he repulsed that a Palsy was taking advantage of him?

But then his hands began an upwards path, rubbing the back of my thighs, up and down. Now, I was certain he could feel how excited I was, the heat and moisture emanating from me were apparent. I opened my legs wider as if to consent. His hands settled at the top of my inner thighs, squeezing them, then he softly tapped the wetness, creating a light splashing sound. He was letting me know that he knew, and that he was okay with it. With deliberation, he stroked ever, ever so close to my lips, but only grazed them. I moaned, squirming, my body begging.

Was this how he massaged everyone? Or did he figure out it was me? I wondered, again, in a panicked moment. Or is it just my perverted mind imagining that this has become erotic? If he just slid a finger in me, I knew I'd lose it. *Please, please.* But then his hands were off me. A small breeze came over my body. He must have been switching sides. I took a deep breath, but that demon between my legs was literally pulsing and swelling.

Ahhh, he's back. I dropped my hands down to either side of my body, purposefully letting my hands hang off the table, palms up, inviting him to make contact with me. I had no idea if this was all in my head. I must know, I thought. I must feel that he is tortured too. He was delicately rubbing my thigh with one hand. I heard friction and felt the fabric of his pants moving a bit by my hand. *Nooo. Is he adjusting himself?* I should've been outraged, but instead, I was pleased that he read my invitation. He leaned into the table as if it were necessary for the massage. *Oh my lord.* He was stiff and pressing himself into my palm. I'd forgotten how thick he was. I wanted to stroke him so badly. Don't move your fingers, I told myself. Don't grip him. Pretend not to notice. But a groan escaped me and he deliberately pressed himself harder into my palm. My body stiffened. I closed my eye tight and bit the half of my lip that I could. I told myself he hadn't really crossed the line. That I hadn't either. Then he pulled back so that my palm was empty. I curled my fingers, searching. *Oh no.* Was he insulted that I froze? Did he think he went too far?

"You certainly carry a lot of stress in your lower back and glutes. I'm going to fix that," he said in a very low voice, no longer touching me with anything except the oil he was dripping onto my body. I said nothing but was relieved there'd be more. I felt him get on the table. He straddled over me, his knees on either side of my thighs and some of his weight on my legs. *Okay, this officially crosses the line. I have never had a masseur do this.* He slid his hands into my inner thighs and pushed against my lips, squeezing what felt like gallons of liquid out of me. He rested the heavy bottle of oil on the slit of my ass. *No. Wait. No way.* That's not the oil bottle. I thought, but couldn't be sure, was that his bare cock resting on my ass? *He wouldn't dare.*

He pushed my ass together as if to get it around him, pushing down on me, erasing any possibility that it was an oil bottle that was on me. That was surely and unmistakably his heavy, stiff cock. I grabbed the sides of the table to prevent myself from reaching back to stroke him. I moaned, once, twice, and again, suddenly yearning to feel him come on my back. Despite my eager body, I still couldn't believe he had the audacity to... "Ohhhh," he was really rubbing into me now. This was bad. I realized this was the moment, my last chance to stop what was about to unfold. I truly should. It was wrong to tease him, I certainly couldn't fuck him, and I knew I shouldn't let him spill himself onto my back. Right? But I couldn't say no without giving myself away. I didn't want to anyway. Did he really think I was going to just let this happen? Would I? I had to stop this... *oh god...* right now. "NNN... nnn," I said like I was scolding a child, but I didn't move. He stopped pressing into me and released my ass. He was accepting my protest. But my own body was not. I lifted up onto my elbows and knees, forcing his cock to slide against my pussy lengthwise, and pushed back against him, rotating my hips. This time he groaned and grabbed my now accessible tits. One small move and he'd be inside me. *What are you doing?*

He suddenly raised himself off of me. I exhaled heavily. I was slightly relieved. I'd still done nothing wrong. Well, not that wrong. But then with one hand he reached between my legs, cupping me. For heaven's sake, I could bear no more. He slid his middle finger into me, his index and ring finger squeezing the flesh together around my clit. It was impossible to stop. I groaned in submission. My body tensed up, my clit throbbed, my insides began to convulse, then my extremities, and I came, uncontrollably, fiercely, for what felt like minutes. I was breathless and dizzy. My heart was palpitating. But I wasn't finished. There'd been too much build up. As if he knew, Evan put two more fingers into me and started pushing into me hard, the palm of his hand pounding my ass, in and out, the tips of his fingers pushing down on one wall of my pussy with each stroke, and his knuckles pressing into the opposite. *Oh no*, I hadn't felt this in a while... I could feel the old familiar pocket of pressure forming in me, like a bubble. If he didn't stop, I was going to squirt. He wasn't prepared for this. He'd think I peed. I couldn't warn him. He must stop. But it was too late, and like a whale shooting water out of its blowhole, I squirted and gushed in bursts.

"Wow," I heard him whisper. Something like remorse immediately set in but was overpowered by an intense need to now be filled, for my still spasming insides to be appreciated. I was putty. He could do as he willed with me. I was ready...

"I think our time is up," Evan said. With nothing more he slid his fingers out of me, got off of the table, covered me with a towel, gripped the back of my scalp, pulled my hair slightly, lightly karate chopped my back and clapped his hands. "Feel free to relax for a bit here before getting dressed." My mouth, the half of it that moved, gaped in the privacy of the little hole in the table as I heard the door open and close.

I jumped up from the table to get dressed as quickly as possible. I was deliciously light-headed and felt almost giddy.

"Alix?" Barbara called, knocking on the door.

I spread the towel over the massage table to cover the huge wet spot. "Come in," I said.

"How was your massage?" she asked.

"Very pleasant," I said, certain that my face was flushed.

"Excellent. You can just go to the reception area to pay and schedule your next visit," she said. I was no longer giddy. What if he was out there?

"Do you mind if I just pay you here? I have to get going. How much is it?" I asked, reaching for my bag.

"Two hundred and fifty for the acupuncture and a hundred for the massage," she said.

"Thanks," I said, handing her four hundred dollars.

"Let me get you change," she said.

"That's okay, keep it," I said.

"I don't take gratuities. I am a doctor of eastern medicine," she said, possibly insulted.

"Give it to the masseur," I said, rushing past her with my head down and hair in my face straight out of the office.

Once I was safely outside, I laughed, intoxicated at what had transpired. How had I gotten away with it? A rush of euphoria washed over me. In my pathetic condition I'd just lived out my massage porn fantasy and my fantasies about being with Evan. I wished I could tell Jonathan all about it. He'd have appreciated this... if I weren't his wife! I laughed at the absurdity, and felt slightly sentimental that my instinct was to share things with Jonathan. I laughed at Evan too and no longer believed that he'd only had two affairs. I thought about how disturbed another woman would be, rightfully outraged that he'd taken advantage of a client, and how I wasn't.

I couldn't bear to kill this feeling. I was happy. I was smiling, even if my face didn't mirror it. I didn't want to go home.

Chapter 12

I searched online for the address of Madeline Schwartz's no kill shelter. It was only a ten-minute walk north. Madeline wasn't there, but I asked her young assistant, Dennis, if there were any dogs that needed a walk or play time. He guided me past a blind beagle, a half-shaven German shepherd, a lab mix with both his paws bandaged, to Milton, a four-year-old pit bull with only three legs. Milton circled his cage excitedly, as Dennis unlocked it. I sat on the concrete floor and let him come to me, licking my face, and leaning his whole body into me, without hesitation, without any regard to my deformity, or his own. I took him for a stroll around the block, told him he was a perfect boy when he did his business, amazed by his seeming ignorance of his missing leg. "Don't tell Dennis," I told him, feeding him a skewer of chicken from a street vendor. When we got back to the shelter, he sat in front of me, and sweetly rested his forehead against my knee. "What? I can't take you home. I'll come back to visit. Promise." He put his head down on his front paws when I returned him to his kennel, silently accepting that his redemption was only temporary.

I walked through Central Park, back to the West Side. I'd been sending Luisa to pick up frozen yogurt for me for five weeks so that I wouldn't have to show my face, answer questions, or be stared at. But I was in the neighborhood and I suddenly felt like my face was no big deal.

"Hi Kumar," I said walking into the store, as I'd done daily for fifteen years.

"Oh my god, Ella's mommy," he said, staring at me wide eyed above the deep black circles under his eyes. That's what he'd called me since she was born. "What happened, Ella's mommy?" he asked, horrified, holding both of his hands to his cheeks.

"Bell's Palsy," I said knowing that between his limited English and the rarity of the condition that he would have absolutely no idea what I was saying. I raised my hand to cover the bad side, feeling my high wearing off like Novocaine.

"No, no, no, Ella's mommy," he said deeply disturbed. "It gets better?" he asked.

"Maybe. Probably." He looked like he might cry. "It's okay, Kumar. It's definitely going to get better. A few weeks," I said, developing the new skill of comforting someone about my face as I spoke.

He just continued to stare.

"Why this happen to you? Why? So young. So nice. Two little babies. So many years I know you. Why?" he asked, and I was fully back to reality. He was reducing me. Instead of being high from my rendezvous with Evan, I saw it for what it really was: a grotesque, disfigured, desperate, overly excited woman, who now needed to manipulate and pay someone to get her off.

"I don't know. It is what it is. Just an extra large, half peanut butter, half vanilla," I told him.

He couldn't bring himself to turn away. He rustled through some paper by the register and pulled out the family photo holiday card I'd given him six months before. He held it to his heart, came out from behind the counter, and sat on a plastic glittery stool, burying his face in his hands. "I'll pray for you," he said. He didn't have the social discipline to be polite about this. His honesty was sobering. I was a tragedy.

"Come on, Kums," I said lightheartedly. "Make me my cream. I have to go," I said.

"This is problem. But this okay because you are a beautiful family," he said looking at me with a seriousness that bored into me. "You have a good husband. This man, he loves you so much. This is all what matters." He finally got up to make me my extra large. I felt like I was at my own wake.

By the time I got home, my session with Evan seemed like a dream. I had to relive it. I didn't bother to undress. I washed my hands, locked the door to my bedroom, reached into my underwear and replayed the whole scenario until I returned to a state of bliss.

"How did it go?" Jonathan asked when he got home from work.

"How did what go?" Ella piped up.

"I went to a doctor for the cold in my face today," I told her. Her eyes lit up, always curious about medical details, because they made her nervous.

"Oh, well, what did he do?" she asked. I thought back. *Ohhh, what he did.*

"It was a woman. She gave me a lot of shots," I said, half smiling at her. Jonathan frowned at me for scaring her.

"What?!" she asked, putting her fork down to focus on what I was saying.

"I'm just kidding. No shots," I told her.

"Well, you look a little better, Mommy," she said.

"Do I?" I asked. She was back to the television.

"Did it help?" Jonathan asked, then sneezed, and sneezed again. He was allergic to dogs.

"I really think it might have," I said.

Moments later, my phone blinked a red light. I had an email. It was Evan. The subject line said: "Wondering." I half-smirked, knowing his mood would be colored by the day he'd had. The massage had wet his appetite and he was seeking an outlet. He was wondering, I was sure, if we could meet up. Amused, I clicked on his email.

"Just wondering... Did you really think I wouldn't know it was you, Alix?" My hand shook so much that I dropped the phone.

***

My fairy godmother had vanished and I was transformed back into the despicable creature that I was instead of the memory of myself I had revived. My face had been nothing more than a vessel on that massage table, skin with openings for my heavy breaths to escape. Now, I was diminished, disempowered, stripped again of all that I was, raped of my dignity, jerked forcefully back to lucidity. And my guilt was undeniable. I'd done a lot less wrong five hours ago when I thought my indiscretion was anonymous. Nobody had knowingly touched Jonathan's wife. Somehow I hadn't disrespected him. Now, I'd officially cheated and given Evan one up on Jonathan.

I waited until the kids were asleep and Jonathan was working at the computer to get back to him. I checked to see if he was online on Facebook. He was. I sent him an instant message.

"How did you know?" The computer showed that he was typing a response for what felt like minutes before his words appeared on the screen.

"Don't you want to apologize before interrogating me?"

Was he upset that I teased him? Lied to him? Tipped him like a whore? I quickly typed back:

"Me, apologize? For what? You should be apologizing."

"Oh really? What should I be apologizing for?"

I could feel him smiling. I racked my brain. Why should he apologize? Oh yes, because as usual, I couldn't take responsibility for my actions.

"I don't know! For being irresistible." *Oh, my head pressing against his thighs.*

"You provoked the whole thing. There was nothing to resist."

"Are you to tell me that in my condition, which you are now keenly aware of, you think I provoked the situation?" I hoped to communicate outrage, but we both knew he was right, that I was nowhere near being the victim of the all too disturbing and familiar scenario of a man in an authoritative position taking advantage of a woman.

"Alix, do you think most women stick their asses—beautiful, I might add—up in the air the minute a massage begins? Do you do that in all your massages?"

"Do YOU do that in all your massages? You could get sued! SHOULD get sued!"

"Oh, you've got me wrong. I'm still much the prude I was when we were twelve. It's not even just consent I need to feel secure. It's enthusiastic consent. Otherwise I wouldn't be interested. So, of course I've never done that. I've also never done THAT to a woman. Nor have I witnessed a woman doing THAT."

I blushed.

"I'm humiliated!"

"I loved it."

I blushed again. If it weren't for my face, I'd have asked him to elaborate. I'd ask him to relive the minute details, turn him on all over again. But I couldn't, even through the protection of the computer screen. He knew I was deformed. That part of me was stifled, quashed, didn't fit.

"How did you know it was me?" I asked, again.

"It wasn't hard, particularly with the butterfly tattoo on your behind (did u forget we talked about that the first night?)"

"So you knew the truth the whole time and you were just observing my behavior. Sneaky man," I typed.

"You must have wanted me to know."

"No, that's why I checked that you were in Florida," I typed, but wondered if he was right.

"I wondered what that text was about. The conference was yesterday. I took a 7:00 flight back this morning. Now, much as I enjoyed the massage, it doesn't excuse your attempting to take advantage of me."

"My face excuses me!"

"I'm genuinely sorry about what you're dealing with. But no, that's no excuse. Why didn't you just tell me?"

"I was hoping I'd never have to." Just as I'm hoping I won't have to tell you about Paul, I thought.

"It took every effort not to screw you on that table."

"What stopped you?"

"Unlike YOU, I have the respect not to do something like that under false pretenses." He was typing really fast.

"Interesting where you draw the lines of morality."

"Interesting that you didn't draw any. For all your wavering on the bench that night, I have to admit I'm a little surprised. What happened to not cheating?" he asked.

"I don't know... Anonymity lends itself well to disassociation," I said but shook my head. What was it about this Bell's Palsy that was shifting my entire code? I wondered. The opportunity to feel whimsically desired and beautiful had been unlimited before the Palsy. Perhaps opportunity itself had provided me with the strength not to indulge in it. Now I regretted that I'd resisted my temptation to be with Evan pre-Palsy. With my future robbed, I'd have valued that past.

"I'm just so far removed from society now that I no longer feel bound by it. I'm subhuman. Like an animal. Animals don't contemplate right and wrong. They act on impulse. Desperate times, Mr. Roth :/ p.s. that's my half smile."

"Funny emoticon. But are you okay?"

"About what happened today? I haven't felt like myself in five weeks. Today, I did. I'm not really thinking beyond that." But I was.

Since I was thirteen, I added a sexual layer to the most innocuous interactions. My expressions made it clear that it was not only okay, but hot, that you wanted to be my daddy, my boss, my son, that you wanted your asshole tickled. But any whore could do that. I cloaked my sexuality in respectable robes, mastering the plane where intellect met sex. Now my sex appeal, my trusted companion, ever faithful and comforting, had abandoned me, leaving me in a solitude at thirty-seven, that I couldn't even envisage at seventy-five.

"I mean about the Palsy. I'd be losing my mind."

"Losing my mind would be easier."

"You'll get through this, and it'll get to the point where unless you tell someone you had this, they won't know."

"It's funny that you kept pushing me about why I've always been so sexual. I didn't realize I'd be forced to resolve that issue. It's like someone has axed my pussy off!"

"Have you?" he asked.

"Axed it?"

"Resolved it?"

"It's not that tricky! Wielding control over men feels good, always has. I certainly don't get off on or feel the need to break people or hurt people. But I've never shed the awareness or lacked appreciation for it. I tamed it. But I still fuck with everyone. Whether it's a job interview, a judge, my husband. It's my crutch."

"Why is it your crutch?"

I'd asked myself that many times, and had no idea. Was it merely a factor of having grown up as an attractive female with big breasts and understanding, internalizing, no, loving its power? Never mind that I was raised by an intellectual father and an egalitarian mother, was growing up as an attractive woman just a portal to the forties, or the garden of Eden, where beauty punctuated womanhood, even for a woman as introspective and psychologically aware as I was? Why not? Psychological mutations are inherited and it takes generations for the kinks to be worked out.

Or was it all from my narcissistic mother, telling me I'd be just like her, that I'd be a "late bloomer," confining me to little girl status, denying me a sexual self, convincing me womanhood was out of reach, condemning me to be flat-chested, like she was, until I was, god, no, sixteen! And wasn't that the real reason I'd starved myself at thirteen. So that I'd have an explanation for why I didn't menstruate, other than that I was just like my mother, believing that psychological complexity, fucked-upness, was more interesting than a girl with a Barbie doll.

"Why, why, why? Does it matter? What matters is my internal world, my inner life, whatever the cause or origin. What matters is where I am now."

"Alix, please let me see you. There's beauty in this. You don't realize it, but there is. These are one of the few chances—they're so infrequent—where if you stand close enough to someone, you witness something extraordinary and transformative, first in them, and then, necessarily, in yourself."

"THERES NOTHING BEAUTIFUL IN THIS!" my fingers shouted at the keyboard. Though I should have felt somewhat annoyed that he seemingly wanted to exploit my condition to learn something from it, the hope that there was something transformative to be gained from all this resonated more.

"Have you ever studied art history?"

"No," I typed.

"You know the Mona Lisa, though, right?"

"Yes."

"What makes that portrait so interesting?"

"I'm not sure it is very interesting."

"Da Vinci bores you? Ha! That makes you either a liar, a snob, or artistically challenged. Well, I'll enlighten you. It's her peculiar smile. It's the asymmetry of her smile. She may well have had Bell's Palsy."

"I'm not interested in looking interesting. I want to look like ME."

"It could be worse. It's better than getting hit by a car and dying, or being unable to save it from happening to your sister."

I knew it'd be insensitive to point out that he'd once again made the situation about him, and that I was likely being hypersensitive because he was only trying to help me. He must try to play hero to everyone, or at least women, now, I thought. Perhaps that was why he was pretending my situation wasn't repulsive.

"You're absolutely right. I've lost perspective."

"So, this is why you haven't been able to follow-up with my old neighbors?"

I felt awful. I owed him the truth based on this brewing intimacy. It was almost painful to lie, especially on behalf of Paul, for whom I had no respect. *It's for Sabrina, not Paul!* I reminded myself.

"Yes."

"I get it now. Anyway, I didn't mean to change topics. If the Bell's doesn't go away, it'll give you character," he typed. "The character of a woman who knows there is more to life than a symmetrical face."

"I have to go."

"Wait."

I did.

"Do you remember what you told me before we met? You were pretending to be all concerned that you weren't back to your pre-pregnancy shape, but you were still so obviously comfortable in your skin. You said, and I quote, *I'm old enough to know that I'm hot enough to not be hot enough.* Where's that woman, Alix?"

"Gone."

"Find her and ask her when can I see her."

"When this resolves."

"I'm sure you're aware that a physical therapist, such as myself, can be helpful with facial exercises. I also suggest more acupuncture."

"And regular massages no doubt? Goodnight."

Chapter 13

Jonathan was in the bathroom clipping his fingernails as I signed off from the computer. He clipped compulsively. I'd asked him to do it when I wasn't home, but he persisted.

The silly words of my email to Evan repeated in my mind. *Hot enough to not be hot enough.* What I would have given to feel that confidence again.

Click. Click. Click. There were only five nails on each hand. Why were there twenty clicks! "Are you almost done? Can you at least shut the door?" I asked, with annoyance.

"I didn't know you were here," he said, popping his head out of the bathroom, and scowling at me as if my reaction to his nail clipping represented everything wrong in our marriage. I scowled back, as if the fact that he did it despite my objections, did as well. He finally stopped and walked over to his desk where his computer was open to a page of real estate listings.

"Our apartment—the one we liked—is back on the market, listed with a different broker," he told me. "I reached out to them and told them we want to make an offer."

"I like that you are calling it 'our' apartment already. Wow. Are you sure about this?" I asked. "Remind me why you want to buy it."

"We've talked about why. It's by the right schools, it's right on the park, and it doesn't make economic sense to rent in perpetuity. And it's quiet. They asked me to submit our bid with a statement of assets and liabilities. I left a draft on the dining room table. Can you add in the balance on your accounts?" he asked, with a peculiar look on his face, one he usually reserved for airplane turbulence. He was nervous.

"What about us?" I asked.

"This is what we need to do," he said with a shrug. He was shrugging off my question, shrugging off making a romantic statement about our future, shrugging off his doubts, shrugging off the sorry state of my face.

"Wouldn't it feel better to make a move like this under better circumstances? Not on the heels of a steep dip in our marriage, or my face? I know this is messed up to say, but you do realize that you are in essence giving away six million dollars if we fall apart. That house will end up mine, and you'll be living in a studio while I live it up in a five bedroom on Central Park. Do you really want to do this?" I asked.

"Yes," he said, with a look of consternation. I took a deep breath, as if I'd been previously holding it in and could suddenly breathe.

"You sound so sure, but look so nervous," I said.

He began lap number one of what I could tell would be a lengthy pace.

"Just put in your account balances. Don't forget stocks and retirement accounts," he said.

"Fine. There's no harm in making a lowball offer. There will be plenty of time to reconsider after we get their first counter," I said.

"We're not going to risk losing this one. I'm going in a hundred thousand over ask, so we don't end up in a bidding war like last time," he said.

I wanted to blink hard to calm myself, but my left eye wouldn't budge. I would have negotiated with Duane Reade for the price of a shampoo bottle if it didn't make Jonathan so miserable. But since I'd blown a couple of deals trying to save a couple hundred thousand in the past, I sensed that I should relinquish control. I glanced at the financial statement. I had no idea what the passwords were for any of my accounts, except the account I occasionally withdrew from. I hadn't checked the balances in over two years. It took me a few minutes to remember where I had a retirement account and another five to retrieve account information and reset passwords.

I jotted down the information on the sheet and scanned what Jonathan had already filled in. "Babe, I think you forgot something..."

"No, it's right," he said, picking up the pace of his pacing and staring at the ground.

"No, there's nothing in the liabilities column. I don't see my student loan on here. You know, I still have an automatic payment of two hundred ninety four dollars a month on that," I said. "And turn on the AC. You're literally working up a sweat with that pacing," I said noticing the beads of sweat on his forehead.

"Your student loan? I told you to write a lump sum check for that when we got married..."

"I know, I just never wanted to deal with changing the auto pay."

"Okay, add the loan in," he said, looking ill.

"Don't look so sickly, it can't be more than twenty thousand or so at this point," I said, frowning.

I added twenty grand to the liability column and reviewed the numbers Jonathan had filled in.

"And the bond portfolio is off," I said. "There's no reason to understate it." Jonathan, modest, private, reserved in all matters, but particularly in financial matters. Only I got an occasional glimpse of arrogance in private. We lived on "59th Street," not "Central Park South," my engagement ring had a flawless diamond, but there was no need for it to be over two carats, we'd buy an apartment for under six and a half million, though we could afford much more, gifts came from the heart without regard to cost. But as with his parents, gifts were never expected and rarely given. His parents, wealthy by any standard, hadn't spent more than a hundred dollars on a few trinkets for our children since they were born. I didn't get it. In my family, grandchildren were to be spoiled, all your money went into buying your house, and asking someone their salary was an acceptable line of conversation. While Jonathan disapproved of the oftentimes, inappropriate way I carried myself in public—I was too opinionated, flirtatious, and blunt, he would tell me privately—he didn't ask me to change. But he had corrected me about how I spoke about anything related to wealth. I was not to discuss the "Hamptons," only "the beach," the price he had sold companies for, even though the Wall Street Journal made them public, and we "made donations" rather than "created a foundation."

"I didn't understate it," he said.

"You did. This is at least thirty million dollars less than where we were two years ago," I said.

"It's right," he said, and I turned to him to find the face of a little boy who wetted his bed.

"Alix, I have to tell you something," he said facing me and stilling himself. "I blew myself up."

"What do you mean?" I asked.

"The options I was trading... I was over-leveraged. I lost it all," he said and sat down in his lazy boy so that I was looking down on him.

"So what?" I asked, not quite sure what he was saying but realizing his ego was in delicate form. "That account was only funded with, what, six or seven million? And you were up something like forty? You were playing with surplus. Easy come, easy go. We knew that couldn't last. That doesn't affect the twenty-five million or so in bonds, the nest egg. I think you left out the bonds."

"No," he said, tears welling up in his eyes. "I blew up."

"Jonathan, I don't understand. Your trading account has nothing to do with the bonds. Whatever has happened, it's okay. It was just winnings."

"I was over-leveraged. I had to cover my positions," he said. "I blew up," he said again, and an actual tear rolled down his cheek. I'd never seen him cry before. I couldn't believe that this, and not my face, was what he was crying over.

"Stop saying you 'blew up.' I don't know what that means. Whatever it is, it's okay," I said kneeling before him and wiping his tear. "What happened? In English."

"You know what I was doing, I was betting against the stocks. I sold call options, meaning if the underlying stocks went down, I could buy the contracts back at a profit. The broker requires a certain amount of capital, cash, to be in the account to take on the risks I was taking. As the price of the stocks go up, I have to put more money in the account to hold the positions. I, I," he stammered, "I liquidated some bonds to fund the account. They were good positions, not expiring for years. I thought it was the right thing to do. I thought I'd only need that cash in there for a short time, but the market kept climbing, and it was insane, every position I had skyrocketed and then skyrocketed again. It got to the point that unless I liquidated more bonds, I had to start closing positions, good positions that by now would have tripled what was in the account," he said. "If only I had liquidated more..." his voice trailed off and he was clearly thinking back to the flashing greens and reds that I'd seen on his multiple computer screens for years.

"Whoa," I said, finally understanding that he'd unwound some of the bonds and lost the money.

I thought back to the day I gave notice to my law firm that I was quitting. Ella was five months old and I'd just returned to work after maternity leave. Jonathan had already stopped working indefinitely. We'd both been stay-at-home parents, enjoying long lunches, the theater, and strolling through the park with our new baby. I called him from the office.

"Hey, where are you?" I'd asked.

"With my parents and the baby in the park. How's work?" he asked.

"I just got a document review assignment. A financial fraud case. Sixteen million pages," I told him.

"Which bank?" he asked.

"I can't say. It's not public, yet. What am I doing here?" I asked him, fingering the picture of him and Ella on my desk, not yet aware that the desire to be home with her would wear off quickly, when my hormones went back to normal. That I would soon feel her umbilical cord wrapped around my neck.

"I don't know. I told you not to go back," he said.

"Should I give notice?" I asked, aware of the privilege to make such a massive decision on a whim.

"Give notice," he said, without hesitation.

"Would you be miserable supporting me? You married a successful, independent, attorney."

"I don't care what you do. We have plenty of money. Just do anything you are passionate about and I'll be happy."

"I'm passionate about you. Do we really have enough money to not work... *forever*?" I'd asked. I grew up on hand-me-downs from my sister, defrosted bread, and a quota on how much toilet paper I should allocate to pee. My parents' lessons about money predated hitting puberty: save money, have a job with benefits, put away for retirement, and never rely on a man for financial security. The prospect of giving up my job made me uneasy, but Jonathan had opened my eyes enough to realize that the lessons bred from the middle class mentality of my parents did not translate across economic classes. Official accounts earmarked for college or bills were unnecessary. Eating out or cooking was a matter of preference, not cost. One lost bet at the craps table, even if it cost more than our total vacation presented no mood shifts that a good fuck couldn't lighten. Though I'd been slowly getting used to it, giving up a paycheck, I feared, would make me tolerate things I otherwise wouldn't, belittle me, and make me indebted to Jonathan.

"We really do," he said.

"What if you decide to put everything into new businesses or trade it all away in those options you're doing?" I asked, but knew he was too stable a man to do that.

"I'm sure I'll make some money and lose some money at whatever endeavors I pursue in the future, but I would never risk the bond portfolio. That's our nest egg. It's enough that we'd never have to work again, either of us, unless we wanted to. You have nothing to worry about."

"Promise?" I asked.

"I promise, Alix."

I gave notice that day. The head of the litigation department asked me to reconsider, reminded me that I was a "super star," up for promotion to partner the following year, and the only associate at my level that had made three hundred fifty thousand dollars the prior year. "You'll go crazy not working. You're addicted to working," he said. "Your kind needs a place like this." I questioned his motives, thought he was just grieving the loss of his highest billing associate. I wasn't addicted to work. I had no emotional investment in helping huge corporations become wealthier, but I had a genuine passion for the game itself, of using my talent of tinkering with words and meanings and ambiguities to my advantage. But he turned out to be wiser than I thought. Without that outlet, I now used that talent relentlessly on Jonathan instead.

Now Jonathan was pale, hunched, and his lips looked dry, clearly grief-stricken. One part, I presumed, was the realization that he had defied my trust and let me down. But another part was the relentless burden of twenty-twenty hindsight that he should have put more money into the account rather than close his positions at a loss. But mainly, he'd lost a ton of money. For him, it must have felt like castration. How could I make a man who defined self-worth with net worth understand that this was okay? I didn't give a crap about the money he'd lost, but he was a fallen man in my eyes. He'd broken a trust and a promise and a confidence that I'd had in him. But this was not the time to address that, or the hint that today's massage hadn't been the only stain of deception in our marriage. Right now, I needed to comfort him. Nothing was worth the anguish I saw in his eyes.

"Jonathan, you look at me right now. You're a great man and you've done nothing that you should be ashamed of. You're not a failure. This doesn't change the fact that you're a self-made millionaire, a brilliant entrepreneur, a leader in the financial sector. Is CNN no longer going to ask you to speak about Wall Street? No. Does your father have to know any of this? No. Does anybody beyond me need to know that you lost some money? No. Will it make your children love your silly faces less? No. What's your legacy? Is it that you lost money nobody will ever miss? I don't think so. Think about what you've done with yourself until now. You began in a basement and developed multiple killer, publicly traded companies employing, what in total? Two hundred fifty people? You changed two hundred fifty lives, made two hundred fifty people rich. You changed Wall Street once, and you're building to that again, now. That's your legacy."

"I fucked up. I fucked us up," he said.

"Can I still afford diner take-out?" I asked with a smile, and rested my head in his lap.

"Yes," he laughed, and wiped his cheeks.

"Then, I'm good. Don't worry about me, or us. I just want you to fuck me regularly. That's all I need," I said.

"I couldn't bring myself to tell you," he said.

"When did this go down?" I asked.

"It's been a little over a year," he said, and he took my hands in his. "I'm sorry." I was soaking up the affection and the fact that he genuinely needed me to make him feel better, that he still valued my opinion of him, and almost wished he'd lose money more often. But the realization that he'd kept this from me, that perhaps I wasn't so far off when I joked in the therapist's office about a gambling addiction, that he knew what he'd done at the time I'd said that, and that he'd kept it to himself then and for over a year made me throw up a bit in my mouth, and wonder what else he'd hidden from me.

"Why didn't you tell me?" I asked, not letting on that I felt deeply betrayed. "Why would you go through this alone?"

"You were at the end of the pregnancy with Charlie. I didn't want you to get stressed, then you had a new baby, then you found out you needed surgery, then the Palsy. It never seemed like a good time," he said, "to stress you out more." I was speechless and disgusted that he was hiding behind protecting me, as if I were a child, or his mother, but I had to find the words to comfort him. He was in pain.

"It's okay. I get it. Please stop beating yourself up so that I can get the opportunity to do it for you," I said trying to make light of the situation.

"I'm a loser," he said.

"If anything, you should be proud of yourself..."

He looked slightly entertained for a moment and gave me a look as if he were waiting for the punch line.

"Seriously, how many men in all of New York have the balls to risk that much money? That depth of passion—not the monetary consequence of it—is what made me love you. To just not give a crap about losing that much money says a lot about a man... maybe you're less greedy than I thought!" I gave him the biggest, brightest eyes I could, though my left eye wouldn't cooperate in moving. "Are we still rich enough to buy this apartment and provide a good life for these kids?" I asked.

"Yes," he said.

"So, can you remember that, forgive yourself, and just move on?" I asked.

"I really do love you," he said.

"I love you, too. But please stop clipping your nails when I'm around."

With Jonathan comforted, I could take a moment to focus on my disappointment. It didn't matter that we'd gone from filthy rich to rich. What mattered was that he was capable of lying to my face, that he had a secret life I knew nothing about, and that he'd been willing to sacrifice the stability of his family to satisfy whatever hunger, craving, need, was brewing in his psyche. Far from being the completely stable and reserved rock I thought I married, he'd become a loose cannon. He was becoming me. His stocks were my massage. My sexuality, his trading options, tools that could be used in a sophisticated and sensible manner. But one wrong mental turn could easily turn either into instruments of destruction, rolls of the dice.

I didn't want to know what drove him there. I didn't want to hear it was me. How different were we really from one another? I wondered. I was as obsessed with sex as he was with money. Irrational though it was, it was integral to my character, to being able to look in the mirror. I sympathized with Jonathan. This entire last year that I'd been secretly tallying how many times he'd approached me for sex, he'd been feeling like less of a man, a complete loss of face.

Chapter 14

I was at the dog shelter, sitting on a bench next to Madeline Schwartz, scratching Milton's belly with one hand and playing tug of war with a Maltese scarred from first-degree burns. I started visiting the shelter regularly the day after the massage. I walked the dogs, fed them, played with them. Distracting, heart-warming, outside myself. It gave me a viable reason for isolating. Jonathan had no idea how much time I'd been spending at the shelter. He would have scoffed at it. He didn't understand that I needed purpose outside the family, and right now, this was all I seemed fit for.

My phone rang.

"Dan," I said. "Sorry I haven't been in touch…"

"No problem. I'd spend my entire summer out East too if I could. I have good news. I spoke to Rappaport, and McAllister. They're both interested. And I have a few others in mind as well. It seems like we can all get certified on the firms' dime, like you did, since it's considered Continuing Legal Ed by year-end. There's a thirty-two-hour training course being offered in October. Let's meet at Le Bernardin next Friday so we can do some bonding and bat around some ideas as a team."

I thought back to my time at the firm, all the fancy corporate morale and bonding events—the musicals, the restaurants, the golf—the ones I loathed, that the other young associates relished, feeling like the spoils made them whole beings. The partners, Dan included, were always desperate to have a drink with me after work, have lunch, impress me with the tickets their clients gave them. I was unaffected. They were annoyances. I preferred being home, doing nothing with Jonathan, over the pretentious bullshit. "Why would you want to go out after working twelve hours, rather than home to your wife?," I'd once asked Dan, turning him down for drinks. The fat wife who didn't want sex was to blame. "Why not divorce, then? I'd sooner leave my husband before having an affair or living in a sexless marriage," I told Dan, ignorantly, because that was before I was married, before I understood domestic dysfunction.

"I couldn't handpick better partners," I said. "Among the four of us, we'd have experts in business torts, malpractice and personal injury, entertainment, and labor. Not bad. But I'm not quite ready to move forward yet. And I honestly can't say when I will be." I explained the Bell's Palsy and that I planned to get the website together, reach out to PR people, and take care of paperwork while I was out of commission. He told me how sorry he was, and to let him know when I was good to go.

"While I have you on the phone," I said, "have you ever heard of New York tolling statutes of limitations for fraudulent concealment other than in professional negligence cases, say in a hit and run, where the driver is later identified?" I'd been worrying myself since my own spot research over the last few weeks had uncovered cases like that in other states.

"Interesting. Hmm. No, I've only seen tolling in med-mal cases, or where there's some fiduciary duty involved."

"Thanks. I'll be in touch when I rejoin the living," I said, hanging up.

"I don't know what that was about, and it's not my business, but I think it might be good for you to start putting things on the calendar, looking past all this," Madeline said. She was wearing cargo pants, a red plaid flannel button down, and the wisps of her short white hair were deliberately pointing in different directions. "You've been coming here every couple of days for about eight weeks now."

"And?" I asked.

"And, much as I appreciate the help, I do think you ought not use us as a hideout. I reached out to you to for your fundraising connections, not to have you working here. If you wanted to come on board as counsel, or as part of the board, that's one thing... but you're a bit overqualified for dog-sitting, no? You have to get back out there. Live your life! Chase your dreams!" she said.

"I like coming here," I said, touched by her concern. "See you soon." She shook her head.

At home with the kids, I saw an email from Evan.

"Happy 90 days," was the subject line. It'd been three months since Evan and I dared to imagine having an affair every ninety days, and eighty-eight since the Palsy began. I knew that with both kids under my watch and an hour until Jonathan came home I wouldn't savor the words in Evan's email if I read it now. I stowed it away in my mind. I would return to it later tonight, like a squirrel unburying an acorn, when I could read and reread each of his words, with the pace it deserved. I'd grown accustomed to the drill.

"Okay, try to whistle, Mommy," Ella told me, taking a break from jumping on my back as I lay on the hardwood floor of our den.

I attempted to whistle, hoping to surprise both of us. I couldn't. There'd been slight improvement every few days since the acupuncture—or the massage. Was I improving from acupuncture, which I'd been doing twice a week at a new place, or because I'd been kinder to Jonathan out of guilt, or had the massage nourished my right brain? Although my mouth still drooped, and I had chronic pain at my temple and jawline, I could force my eye to blink, drink beverages without a straw, and no longer had to tape my eye shut to sleep. I could grin symmetrically, and smile, asymmetrically. I could raise both eyebrows, but when I did, I heard the sound of strain, like the vibrations of a rubber band being pulled taut and then flicked. I was less of a spectacle. I'd been estimating a full recovery in two weeks for the last seven.

"I think I hear something if I really try to listen," Ella said in a whisper, like if she were quiet enough she'd hear something. "Charlie, Charlie, look, Mommy can almost whistle," she told her fourteen-month old brother.

"Momma, Momma," Charlie said, nuzzling his face with affection into the back of my neck, biting it with his only two teeth.

"Momma, momma," Ella said, imitating him, pressing her forehead tenderly against mine. "I love you so much" she said, gritting her teeth as if she were controlling herself from eating me. A warmth crept through me and I told myself that there was nothing more fulfilling than this love. There was no place more secure, insulating, or comfortable than this. If I were dying in a movie, this would surely make the cut for a flashback to happy times as I passed through to the gates of heaven. This, was my purpose. I wanted to be nowhere but here.

"Now really, really try," Ella said staring intently at me. "You just have to try your best."

"I can't. I have to go turn the chicken cutlets over," I told her, sad to part from the affection.

"I don't want chicken cutlets. I want pizza," Ella said abruptly, with an irritating whine.

"No pizza tonight," I told her lightly, feeling the moment turning.

Ella pouted. "Then I'm not eating anything and I'll never be your best friend again." Charlie pulled Ella's hair and she yanked herself free, banging her arm on the corner of the television console. "Owwwwweeeee," she yelled. Charlie's equilibrium was thrown off and he rolled off of me, banging the back of his head on the hardwood floor. He started wailing.

"I need ice," she screamed at the top of her lungs, as I lifted Charlie, who was still crying, trying to determine the severity of the bang.

The phone started ringing. I assumed the doorman was calling to tell me that the delivery from Diapers.com arrived. I made my way over to the phone with Charlie on my hip, but before I could answer, the smoke detector went off.

"I can't listen to that noise. Make it stop! Where's my ice? You love Charlie more than me," Ella shrieked at my heels as I carried Charlie, and a broom to the smoke detector. I tried to put Charlie on the floor but the corners of his mouth turned down, he grabbed my hair so I couldn't release him, and panic filled his eyes. I lifted him up again. My arm was wet and warm. *Of course.* Charlie had a blow out and it was seeping out of his diaper onto my arm. He was wailing. I was poking the fire alarm with crap on my arm when the door slammed. Jonathan was home from work.

With accusation in his eyes, he glared at me while both kids cried and smoke rolled out of the kitchen. Whatever warmth had washed over me had been extinguished by an imminent desire to be anywhere but here. I suddenly imagined the cameraman in my flashback from minutes earlier panning in on the smear on my arm. The children were mind-numbing. My marriage was body-numbing. My face was literally numb. A coffin, a coffin would be more insulating than this.

"How is your face?" Jonathan asked when they were finally asleep.

"I can see teeth," I said, forcing a smile and pointing out my left cuspid. He didn't look.

"Tell me about your day," I said, sitting on the armrest of his chair. "Details."

"I have a hundred things going on. I'd rather not," he said, dismissing me. He sneezed, loudly, and then annoyingly, twice more. "I can tell where you were today," he said. "The shelter, right?"

"I have a hundred things going on. I'd rather not discuss where I was," I said, with a hint of spite. He sneezed again.

"See, I accept that," he said. *Yes, your acquiescence is a weakness, not a strength.*

"So, we have to send our board package over tomorrow with all the letters of recommendation. I don't know how they will view our tax return with all those losses," he said nervously. "And I'm not giving myself a raise this year."

"They'll see it for what it is. You're an entrepreneur with plenty of liquid assets. They all have money. They understand that investments can go sour. They're concerned with the bottom line. You have plenty of money. And you know what? If what we have isn't enough for them, they can go fuck themselves," I said. "Are you concerned about losing the apartment or your ego?"

"Both," he said.

"You've got to let go of this deflated ego. They may reject us because of my hideous face. These coops can do whatever they want, and without explanation. I think the package is ready. We have our personal letter sucking up to them, two personal reference letters each, two professional reference letters each, and two letters that speak to us as a couple."

"These couples letters are absurd. What did Craig and Sarah say?" he asked.

I took the letter out and pretended to read, "Dear Board, We attended Jonathan and Alix Beck's beautiful wedding eight years ago and have since gotten to know them as a married couple. They're the perfect American couple. When they married, they were the most dynamic, energetic, happy, cultured, exciting, social couple to know. Now, they are flat, never go out, sleep apart, their sex lives have dwindled, and they speak badly about one another to my wife and me. We're pretty sure that they'll fit right in with the other miserable rich folk in your building. Love, Sarah and Craig. p.s. we think Jonathan might have gotten crushed in the market and that Alix may have been crushed under a cement paver—her face is busted."

"Very funny," Jonathan said.

He glanced at the clock, then his phone.

"Let's try to have you stay in the bed tonight," I said. "You don't have to put your mouth guard in. I'll just wear earplugs," I told him.

"If I'm not on the couch, how will we hear Charlie from the bedroom? I'll put on the monitor," he said cautiously. We both knew this topic could erupt into a brawl. When Ella was born, I'd made rules. We wouldn't let her sleep in our bed, we'd keep the monitor on once she was sleeping through the night, or go to her if she cried in the middle of the night. Other mothers, parenting books, and pediatricians dubbed it "sleep training" and advocated that following those rules was better for the child, would make them more independent. Whether that was true or not, my hope had been to preserve the marital bed as a place to be intimate.

"There's no need for a baby monitor," I told him. "He sleeps until seven every day. If he wakes up, he'll put himself back to sleep. How many times has he cried in the middle of the night in the last eight months?"

"He whimpers sometimes and then goes back to sleep," Jonathan told me, with resentment in his voice because he was reporting to me about something that he believed I should know, something he only knew because he slept on the couch, in earshot of Charlie's room.

"Exactly. And that's exactly why their pediatrician insists on no baby monitors after six months. There's no point being disturbed by whimpers. If he's in dire need, we'd hear it," I said.

Jonathan shrugged. He'd never bought into my philosophy. He was raised in a family where children came first and wholly defined their mothers. Children were to be coddled, but not the marriage. "Don't tell Ella you have Bell's Palsy. Children don't notice anything if you don't tell them," his mother had said. Caroline felt children were to be sheltered from anything that might cause emotional damage. Carl had had an affair when Jonathan was a teenager and unilaterally decided to spend millions on the woman who then blackmailed him. Caroline mistakenly believed the children didn't know. She thought she had protected them from the grim truth that their father was dishonest and selfish. She'd only taught them that it was acceptable to live miserably with secrets, and that breadwinning men could do so with impunity.

"Fine. What will you do if you wake from my snoring and can't go back to sleep?" he asked. When we were dating, I would stare at him in his sleep, his statuesque face, happy to be near him, dreading going home the next day. It didn't matter that I would be sleep deprived. It was worth it. Now, I stared at his face, and had to restrain myself from smothering him with the pillow.

"I'll deal," I told him. "You've been dealing with my face, the couch, everything... give yourself a break already. And I made an appointment for us to see Dr. Stearns again. We can talk through the sleep issues," I told him.

"Really? What prompted that?" he asked.

"Well, that's where we were before this all happened. And though we've been fighting less since the Palsy started, it has definitely taken a toll on our lives. It's probably a good idea to resume," I said.

"Probably. By the way, I spoke to my sisters today... I don't even want to tell you... They said there are things missing from the beach house."

"What things?" I asked.

"Someone's goggles, a beach towel, and a pair of sneakers," he said, rolling his eyes. "They think Luisa stole..."

"Are you serious?" I asked.

"I told them they were out of line, that we've trusted her with our children, our loose cash, that they're crazy for thinking anyone would want their old sneakers and that it was all probably misplaced. Told them how you accidentally put Ella's stuffed animal in the freezer and couldn't find it for a day. But, you know how they are..." I did. The sisters had never worked a day in their lives. Though they could afford it, they never had nannies, and were proud of themselves for it. The help, our help, and anyone else who wasn't part of their family unit were nothing more to them than a pair of socks, easily discarded and replaced, and not to be trusted. That we had taken Luisa with us to the family beach house was disdainful to them.

"So, what did they say about their possibly misplacing that stuff?" I asked.

"You're going to be annoyed..." I nodded to signal that he should continue.

"They said not all women are scatterbrained," he said.

He was right. I was annoyed. Like Caroline, they felt that motherhood and keeping the house somehow put them on intellectually equal footing with their professional husbands and they resented their men, all men, for making them feel insignificant. It didn't occur to them that by leaving it up to a man to give them validation as to their significance, they were doing it to themselves. Or perhaps I just needed to justify my own lack of ability to find the significance they did from motherhood.

"Did you tell them that the fact that they pride themselves on their ability to keep track of their children's socks is setting women back fifty years? Did you mention that it's not something to be proud of that they have no interests outside raising their children?"

"Okay, no need to get nasty. They had a right to ask. They don't know Luisa," he said.

"You're right," I said. I knew to shut up.

"Anyway, imagine if it were true. We'd have to let her go. I've said this before. If we had to let her go for some other reason or if she quit, we'd really be in jam. The point is, we should have someone else lined up. We can't be so dependent on one person to meet all our needs."

"We should have someone else. It's not good to be so dependent on one person," I repeated his words, reminded of the acorn I'd stowed away. "It's not realistic to think one person can give you everything, and frankly it's not healthy, or humanly possible. It shouldn't even be expected..."

"What are you talking about?" he asked, looking confused.

"Oh, um, I'm just saying, you don't have to worry... it's not like I'm going to be working for a while, not with my face like this. If we ever had to let Luisa go, I would get by just fine." He looked at me like I looked at Ella when she told me she thought she was old enough to drive. "I'm going to the roof to chain-smoke. I'll be back in half an hour."

On the roof, I pawed the dirt off my acorn.

"So, it's been 90 days. You've been dodging my emails. I know you aren't a hundred percent. But what's really going on? It's been a long time to be so self-conscious. I've been writing, exploring dark places. Can I send my draft for your feedback? If I seem intense and dramatic, it's because you make me so. Not to get biblical, but I'm consumed with lust, envy, and a desire to covet. Your husband gets your mind on a regular basis and then gets to sleep with you. What a lucky man.

-E"

I reread his email, wondering if my brain was under surveillance. He was an air pump for my flattened self-esteem. I forgave him for minimizing the impact of the Palsy because he hadn't seen it. Though I'd resumed going out on an as-needed basis and to visit the shelter, I hadn't entertained the thought of seeing him. I wrote back to him:

"Is this your all—on intense and dramatic? Be prepared to step it up a bit when I recover. I wouldn't say I'm self-conscious. I would say, self-aware. But, as you have so insightfully suggested, there probably is more to my not seeing you. I think I have newfound guilt with respect to that lucky man you speak of because, objectively, he's been so good about all this. Momentum is sometimes the only thing that propels situations forward (in marriage or extramaritally). As for your writing, I'm honored to review it."

He responded immediately:

"I know you want to see me. You're scared. I won't push. Maybe after you read this piece, you'll change your mind."

I read the attachment. He'd written more about that summer we were thirteen:

"Alix was pushing me out of my comfort zone, pushing me to experiment, to break rules, to embrace danger, to take what I needed from her without regard. I thought I loved her..."

How the tables had turned, I thought, smiling.

I kept reading, but my smile faded. He'd described the accident and its aftermath. He'd been playing ball with Joy for half an hour in the street. They'd almost gone inside thirty seconds before the accident but Joy had begged for one last throw. The car sped into her, threw her eight feet up, and then sped away around her broken body. Evan ran to her, thinking she might be dead, but then she looked up at him, and simply asked, "Did I catch the ball?" He was sure she'd be fine.

The police came quickly. He told them he'd only seen a blue Sedan—it'd all happened so fast. When his parents returned from the hospital that night, his mother kept screaming, "Who did this? Why?"

Though it was for my eyes only, I couldn't help but type, "PAUL O'ROURKE" right into the document. Then I continued reading.

His father accused him of not protecting Joy and said it should have been him, the irresponsible one, instead. Joy was stable by the next morning, but needed to remain hospitalized for observation and rehabilitation. His mother wanted nothing more to do with "godforsaken Queens." She wanted Joy moved out of the city hospital she was in, and into one by their house upstate where her cousin was a doctor, as soon as possible. "The hell with your commute," she told his father, "we're moving back." Three days later, Joy was transferred to an upstate hospital where she received physical therapy and rehabilitation. But weeks later, just before she was to be released, she suffered a brain contusion and died. His parents said they were too grief-stricken to care for him and sent him to boarding school. Soon after, Evan's appendix burst. He needed emergency surgery.

"My parents were so overwhelmed with Joy's death that they never visited me in the hospital. But Mr. Carolson, the cool, young gym teacher with spiked hair at boarding school ("Please Evan, call me Pete") did. After the surgery, Pete started sneaking me weed, then painkillers, 'to help me feel better,' he'd said. I'm still not quite sure why Pete took some special interest in getting me high. (Or maybe I was quite sure and kept doing drugs to forget his nasty intentions!)." Just after graduating high school, Evan spent three months in rehab for opiate addiction and started college a semester late. The therapists chalked his problems up to "survivor's guilt."

I thought back to his dream about my hand on his stomach, right by the appendix incision, I figured.

I felt anguish for what Evan had been through at my brother-in-law's hands, and now, filled with fresh images of Joy, I was almost certain that the right thing to do, eventually, was to tell Evan what I knew. Immediately, I needed to confront Paul. It disgusted me that he'd driven away and gotten away with it. I needed him to know that I knew. I needed to hear it from him, hear his remorse.

I called Sabrina's house, hoping Paul would pick up. Sabrina did instead.

"Hey, Alix. Maurice is fine. He made it through the surgery," she said.

"Good. Listen, I have a consumer fraud mediation and I think Paul might be able to help me understand something about sales warranties. Is he around?"

"So does that mean your ugly face is back to normal?" she asked.

"No, I scheduled this one months ago, and they just sent me the briefs. Obviously I'll delay it if I'm not better soon."

"I really don't understand why you work at all, if you don't have to. If I were you, I'd..."

"Is Paul there?"

"Hang on," she said and Paul came to the phone.

I took a deep breath.

"Hey, Paul, I don't have a sales question, but I don't want Sabrina to know what I'm saying. I want you to say 'implied warranties' out loud, okay?" I could picture Sabrina watching television, and knew she'd tune out.

"Sure. Implied warranties," he said, and laughed a little.

"This is serious. It's about Joy, Joy Roth." I paused, deciding on a question. *Just be direct. This isn't the witness stand.*

"Were you driving the car that hit her that night?" I asked.

"I have absolutely no idea what you are talking about," he said quickly and dismissively. I wished I'd waited to talk to him in person so I could scan his face for evidence of a lie.

"Yes, you do," I said. "Look, I know it was an accident. I just want to..."

"I can't help you with that." Then he whispered, "And for Sabi's sake, lay off. She just started a new anti-depressant. She cannot deal with this." He hung up. I was enraged that he was lying to me and using my sister as the reason why. But I was even more enraged that it was true—that my sister, who I could still remember as a relatively carefree, six-year-old, in pigtails, was in fact, incapable of handling such a disruption.

I had no idea what to do, but I knew that I needed to maintain control of the situation. I had to let Evan believe I would still help him to prevent him from poking around on his own while I figured it out. I emailed Evan again: "I'm sorry I've dropped the ball on helping you find the driver. It's only temporary."

He wrote back: "Don't worry about it—seriously. While I still hope that we find the driver, your "other" method to get the pain out of me would be equally, if not, more, helpful. It's almost magical how having you in my life—even indirectly—has shifted my focus. I've been inspired to write, and the writing is cathartic. Just don't drop the ball on seeing me when you're better. Next week or next year, I'll be patiently awaiting it."

Jonathan was already asleep, already snoring, when I got back downstairs. I stuffed my ears with earplugs and drank extra wine. I slept like a person with fever, waking in fits to the sound of his snores until 5:45 a.m. when my body finally forfeited to REM.

Chapter 15

"Alix, get up. Now!" Jonathan yelled frantically into the doorway of our bedroom. Then he ran off. It was 6:30 a.m.

I slid on a tank top and rushed down the hall. I heard Charlie crying. When I turned the corner into the short hallway to his room, the smell was overwhelming. There was poop all over the crib, his pajamas, and his forehead. Jonathan was standing over him but Charlie was calling for me. Jonathan shot venom at me with his eyes.

I tossed my hair up into a quick bun and scooped Charlie up to pacify him. Jonathan disappeared into the shower without a word.

"What? This is all my fault?" I asked, when Jonathan returned in his suit, staring at me with hatred while I bathed Charlie. This was my reward for making an effort to have Jonathan back in bed. I almost wondered if Jonathan had given Charlie a laxative to prove his point.

"This should not have happened," he said, his voice slightly raised. I thought back to the time I'd let Ella try a big kid swing, despite his protest, and she'd fallen off. He wouldn't make eye contact with me for the rest of that day.

"It's a one-off thing. He's already forgotten. He's okay," I said, now trying to pacify Jonathan.

"That's not the point!" he barked. "This is why I *have* to sleep on the couch. I can't rely on you to take care of these children. *This*, just so your precious Ambien sleep wouldn't be disturbed by the monitor."

"You think you're doing Charlie a service right now speaking like this to me? Look at his face. You're scaring him. I'm his mother."

"Some mother," he said, with contempt. "You do nothing."

Here we go! The mother attacks! I thought. I tried not to become enraged. He must have felt guilty. He couldn't be there for Charlie the way he'd been for Ella now that he was working. Ella had been just as dependent on him as she'd been on me at Charlie's age. It made him cringe that Charlie only wanted me. At bottom, he didn't see me as deserving of Charlie's affection, or his.

"Get out of my way, please," I brushed past him with Charlie wrapped in a towel. "I need to go make Ella her lunch, get these kids dressed, change Charlie's sheets, clean his crib, and get Ella to camp... or as you put it... do nothing."

"Oh, poor Alix, and then what are you going to do? Work out for two hours? Maybe meet a friend for lunch? See a show? Walk some dogs? Maybe waste a few hundred dollars on something you're *so* insightful for knowing the kids' need?" he asked, with the hostility I knew so well before the Palsy, but was no longer accustomed to.

I was seething, but I didn't want the fight to escalate. The afflicted side of my face was already tightening from the tension, my emotions filling each pore. Even though I didn't feel sorry for him anymore, I knew if I fed this fight, I'd suffer.

"Then I'm going to a hearing specialist to see if this ear thing is permanent hearing loss..."

"Let me guess, the only one in New York who doesn't take insurance?" he spat. I didn't show the wound he'd inflicted.

"Then the acupuncturist, and then to the grocery store so I can make this family dinner," I answered.

"What a rough life," he spewed.

But it is, I thought to myself. I had no idea how my life could be this easy and this hard at the same time, how Jonathan could give me both so much and so little. Now I was having a hard time containing myself. He knew I couldn't deal with tension right now.

We passed like strangers when he returned from work, spoke only as needed, and went to sleep in our respective wings of the apartment. Though we'd had dozens of nights like this, this was the nastiest he'd been since the Palsy began and we both knew it. His pity was wearing thin, I thought. I was glad our appointment with Dr. Stearns was coming up.

The next morning was Saturday. I woke naturally at 8:00 a.m., not surprised that Jonathan had let me sleep in. I wished I could be grateful. But I knew he wasn't doing it from the goodness of his heart, but only to prove that he could handle the kids without me and ramp up ammunition for his next passive aggressive attack that he did more than I did for the family on weekends. I took the opportunity to stay in bed. I thought about the drama at the beach house, his sisters, and then fantasized about their husbands. It was 8:30 a.m. Jonathan had been with the kids himself for an hour. I knew I had to get out of bed. He was pacing in the den, staring at his phone, when I stumbled in to kiss the kids. I could tell he'd been with them, but not present, for the last hour. Jonathan didn't say hello. He grabbed his jacket and headed downstairs for a cigarette and coffee.

We went to brunch with his parents at a stuffy, twenty-seven-dollars-an-entrée, kids-not-really-welcome, restaurant. Charlie was miserable in the high chair. I'd forgotten to bring toys to distract him. Between his parents bickering and lecturing us, Ella was being ignored. It'd been forty-five minutes and the oysters Carl ordered had yet to arrive. I imagined it would be another twenty minutes before Ella's "frites" made their way to the table. Caroline, next to me, quietly asked how I was feeling. I told her I was doing better. She pushed for details about my recovery. I told her it was a slow process and not easy. She felt victorious that I complained and told me I shouldn't focus so much on it. I told her I wasn't, but she'd asked. I excused myself to go to the bathroom. When I returned, Caroline turned in her seat so that only her back faced me, to whisper in Jonathan's ear. Ella's frites still hadn't arrived.

"Mommy, I want a dollar to give that man," Ella said pointing to a homeless man on the sidewalk once we'd left Jonathan's parents and were walking home.

"Absolutely not," Jonathan barked. "We're only a block away from our building."

I looked at him with scorn. "That's very nice of you," I told her fishing for a bill.

"Great, teach her to approach people like that without caution. That's a great lesson. Encourage him to bring his friends to linger near our building and approach her too, why don't you?" he said. Ever practical, ever safe, ever discerning, even in the details of compassion. I gave her a dollar.

"Let's go to the park," Ella said when she returned.

"Later, after I go for a run," I said.

Jonathan laughed obnoxiously to himself. I felt my blood vessels constricting.

"What's so funny?" Ella asked.

"Your mother," he said, nastily. Now I was gritting my teeth and adrenaline had kicked in. I looked at the kids and reminded myself that flight wasn't an option.

"You'd better change your tone," I warned him.

Again, he laughed obnoxiously, louder this time. I felt like punching him.

I grabbed his wrist, digging in hard, as he pushed the stroller. "I love when you treat me like this," I whispered. "Makes it so easy," I added, thinking about what I could do with Evan and not feeling an ounce of regret for the massage, my flirtations, or the connection I had with him.

"Makes what easy?" he asked. He was no longer laughing. He was eager to know.

This time I smiled—half-smiled—obnoxiously, and said nothing.

"You make me sick," he told me.

"Mom, why is daddy talking like that?" Ella asked.

We didn't answer.

"Someone answer me!" she demanded.

"He's kidding."

I looked at Jonathan to establish that we both knew that we must stop this. He refused eye contact.

"It doesn't sound like he's kidding," she said. I looked at him for help. He said nothing.

"He's just tired," I said.

"Why am I tired? Because of your mother I'm tired. Ask mom what time she slept until today." I knew I'd pay for fantasizing about my brothers-in-law.

"He's being silly," I told Ella.

She laughed maniacally to comfort herself. This I couldn't take.

Jonathan and I avoided eye contact for the remainder of the day. When the kids went to sleep, I told him that the broker had sent an email asking for some clarification. "Write back, please," I said, without a hint of hostility.

"Okay," he said, completely normal.

"A new cleaning lady is coming tomorrow," I said.

"Okay, I'll leave money," he said.

"Are you coming in for Homeland and fro-yo?" I asked.

"Yes, just a small portion please," he said.

I scooped his usual large portion and we went to our respective sides of the bed. Tomorrow would be a normal day without a trace of tonight's fight, except for the slightly deeper dent, an imperceptible etching made by the hammering of our souls in the neck of the sculpture of our marriage, inconsequential in its isolation, unless it culminated in the heads rolling off.

Chapter 16

"It's nice to see you two again," Dr. Stearns said. "I saw you in May. It's been over three months. How are things?"

"We didn't come back sooner because I have Bell's Palsy," I said.

"Aha," he said. "But I see you've made quite a recovery."

I looked at him quizzically. "Not really." I flashed my full smile.

"I wouldn't have noticed if you didn't do that," he said.

"I'm surprised you said that, you know, as a shrink. That's the number one comment I get from people, 'unless you move your face, I wouldn't know.' So I guess I'm supposed to be happy that if I just walk around like a Stepford wife, nobody will know?" I asked, addressing both my face and our marital discord. Dr. Stearns looked momentarily uncomfortable.

"I didn't mean to underplay the emotions you must be feeling," he said. "Studies have shown that disfigurement or disability affects people the same way psychologically whether it's total, partial, minor, or severe. How have you been coping?"

I thought about my secret world with Evan, the fact that I hadn't gone out with Jen, only felt comfortable around three-legged dogs, my fear that I'd never be a productive member of society again, possibly never work again because who would hire this face, that I was scared of a relapse, that I felt like fucking the handyman just to know I was desirable.

"I'm just trying to be patient. Know what the number two comment I get is? That I'm lucky I have such a good husband."

"How does that make you feel?" Dr. Stearns asked.

"Like maybe the phrase "good husband" is outdated. I expect, maybe unfairly, a whole lot more than someone to share daily woes with. And ungrateful."

"Why?"

"Because I don't think it would otherwise occur to me to feel lucky for Jonathan not leaving just because I'm ugly. You know... in sickness and in health," I said.

"Maybe the idea isn't so much that he hasn't left you because of it but that you have a support system in place," Dr. Stearns suggested.

"It's ridiculous to assume that being married necessarily helps things. A bad marriage can negatively affect the prognosis of a sick spouse, right?"

"That's true. And a health crisis can break marriages apart or bring you closer together. How have you been coping?" Dr. Stearns asked Jonathan.

"I don't matter," he said, with an obnoxious smile.

"How many dozen times have you said that in this relationship?" I demanded.

He looked at me as though he'd made his point.

"Don't you realize that in order for you to answer that you don't matter, I've had to ask how you are?" I asked.

"It's very typical for the well spouse to begin to feel insignificant in a situation like this because much of the marital attention is focused on the unwell spouse," Dr. Stearns said, validating Jonathan. "But it's important that you communicate how you're feeling."

"Fine. I feel like my entire life is dictated by Alix's health," Jonathan said. "Right now it's the Palsy. But there's always something. Emergency c-sections, gestational diabetes, breastfeeding, stomach separation, plastic surgery..." *Holy crap.* He'd just characterized pregnancy and breastfeeding as afflictions and everything that stemmed from them as impositions. I controlled myself from gasping.

He paused, but for once, he seemed to want to say more. "You're always worse off than I am, relatively, so I sacrifice for you, but that doesn't mean I'm not also doing badly, and you don't acknowledge the toll it takes on me." I knew it was true. His existence was always a side dish to my entrée of drama. I wanted to soothe him, tell him I understood. I also wanted to poke his eyes out with a skewer. *I'm sorry. I'll try for you.* I was preparing the words, but then he went on.

"Not only am I the one working full-time, I do a lot more to help with the kids when I'm home so that she can be rested and relaxed to recover."

"That's not a favor! You're a father. It's as much your job as mine to take care of these kids," I said.

"How have the children reacted to the changes at home?" Dr. Stearns asked.

"Not well," I said, at the same time that Jonathan said, "Well." Jonathan looked at me.

"The children feel the tension," I said. "Last week, Ella asked me why I'm so different when I'm alone with her and Charlie than when Daddy is there. I asked what she meant, and she said, 'you play more and you're sillier and happier when he's not here. When Daddy comes home, you both seem mad.'"

"Oh, come on," Jonathan said.

"'Come on?' What do you think we're teaching her about what relationships should be like? How can our kids feel emotionally secure with Mommy and Daddy acting like strangers toward each other half the time?"

"Parents fight all the time. There's nothing to worry about. Ella thinks the world of me," Jonathan said.

"You're missing the point. It's not about how she perceives you. It's about how she perceives us."

"It can be healthy for children to see parents fight and make-up because they learn how to handle conflict," Dr. Stearns jumped in. "But it's harmful for children to see parents persistently withdrawn and nasty towards one another. It often shows up in behavioral problems or sleeping difficulties."

"Alix is the one with sleeping difficulties," Jonathan said.

"Oh, for Pete's sake," I said rolling my eyes at Dr. Stearns. I'd told Jonathan we could work through our sleep issues in therapy today. Now, I just wanted him to shut up.

"What is it exactly about me taking this damned sleeping pill that gets you so up in arms? I don't understand!," I said.

"It's not normal to take pills every night. Who knows what they're doing to you. Maybe your pills caused the Palsy! You're out of your mind for fifteen minutes after you take them, or longer if you don't go right to sleep, and remember nothing," Jonathan said.

"What do you care if I'm out of my mind for fifteen minutes?" I asked. I was back to the skewer.

"Why don't you tell him some of the things that have happened in those fifteen minutes?" he urged me.

"You mean how nine times out of ten nothing happens?" I asked. "Generally, I take my pill, a sort of euphoria washes over me, and then I go to sleep."

"No, I mean, like the time you decided to run to Duane Reade to buy frozen chocolate muffins in a jacket, no shirt underneath, flannel pajama pants, and snow boots and came back with a stick of beef jerky stuffed in your boot that you said you shoplifted. Or the time you sent an invitation to all of our friends setting up a party, for no reason, and didn't remember you had done it until you got the RSVPs the next day. Never mind the dozens of times you ordered from the diner or ate through our cupboard and found empty cans of beans, egg cartons, and pasta boxes all over the floor and remembered nothing until you saw the evidence. How about when you posted a picture of yourself in a g-string on Facebook and forgot until the first person commented?" he asked.

I couldn't help myself. I started laughing out loud.

"Do you think what Jonathan said is funny?" Dr. Stearns asked.

"I'm sorry, but it's hysterical. And it doesn't happen very often anymore," I said. "It's an unwelcome side effect."

"Maybe you just like to get high," Jonathan said.

"Do you like the high from the Ambien?" Dr. Stearns asked me.

Did you not just hear me say I feel euphoric from it?

"I'm not disputing that I'm an addict. I'm saying, so what if I am? If it prevents me from being a sleep-deprived human being, I think it's worth it... and you used to also," I said to Jonathan.

"How do you not see this as a problem?" Jonathan asked.

"I told *you* it's a problem when we started dating. I'm the one who explained it to you. And what did you say? That you would change it. *You* minimized it."

"What did you think about Alix's addiction to Ambien at that time?" Dr. Stearns asked.

"I thought she was just a high energy, anxiety stricken, oversexed, overworked woman and we could fix it," he said.

He had tried. I remembered the endless arm-tickling, the sheets he'd bought me, the sound machines. It wasn't my insomnia that had become intolerable for him—it was his failure to transform me.

"Well, guess what? I'm still a high energy, hypersexual woman, and it can't get fixed. I'm not a company you can buy up and reorganize and expect to fall in line with your parameters. What'd you think you were going to do to change me?"

"You're thirty-seven now. You're certainly not overworked. You'd think that in eight years, now that you have a family, that you would have matured a bit and be less..." his voice trailed off as if he were searching for words.

"Well I'm not."

"You've never tried to change," he said.

"When should I have tried to stop the pills? When I was working fourteen-hour billable days? When I had infants? Now that I have Palsy? And what have you done about *my* complaints? Nothing! You weren't screwing me when I wasn't maimed. You withheld to punish me. And what, because we took a vow I'm supposed to live in a sexless marriage? You get my fidelity even though you haven't kept your end of the bargain?" I asked.

"Yes," he said, sternly.

I rolled my eyes. I looked at Dr. Stearns as if I could will him to do his job.

"Look, fear underlies most things. What is your big fear underlying this sleeping issue?" I asked.

I thought I was asking Jonathan to really take a moment to be introspective and was surprised that he answered right away. "Well, what if I am not around?"

"Why wouldn't you be around?" I asked. "Oh, I get it, you set me up with this new apartment so you know our kids are cared for, and then you're leaving me?"

"No, if I kick the bucket," he said. God damned practical mind, planning for the future, I thought. You're worried about maybe dying, when I'm already dead. We are dead.

"What is it that you want Alix to do?" Dr. Stearns asked.

"Go to sleep without a dependency and be there for me, as a wife," he said. Sleeping with you is sleeping with a dependency, I thought to myself. You created me, or you killed me, and now you're staring at the bloody knife in horror and I can see my sickening reflection in the polished mirror on it, and slipping on the blood you've siphoned out of me. The Palsy could last forever. I was unhealthy, hardly the evolutionary representation of someone to mate with. I was wearing on him. The weight of me was crushing him, even when he was lying on top of me. My mental health was a full-time job for both of us. I was a cancer. Cancer. This was uncomfortable. Time to redirect.

"Dependency. Kicking the bucket. You are going to kick the bucket. How many cigarettes did you smoke today?" I asked.

"This isn't going anywhere. My wife has deep-seated issues related to being threatened into giving up her addictions," Jonathan said, dismissively.

"You sound like a moron complaining about my addictions as if you don't have your own vices," I said gazing at Dr. Stearns. "It's not just smoking." Jonathan shifted uncomfortably in his seat. I cocked my head to one side and lifted my shoulders as if to ask Jonathan's permission.

Jonathan shook his head, but said, "Go ahead."

"So Jonathan has recently disclosed that he lost a chunk of our nest egg in the market, over a year ago, and kept it from me," I said.

Dr. Stearns sat up straighter in his chair. Jonathan explained his trading losses while I relaxed into the back of my chair.

"How do you feel about this, Alix?" he asked.

"I was surprised," I said. "You don't know this man. Anyone who does lauds him for being so principled, calculated, honest. It concerns me that, in order for him to act so out of character, he's mentally in a really bad place. I mean, I guess it's pretty clear based on all he is saying that he has hit a breaking point. And obviously, it's hard that he lied to me, and breached a trust. Maybe he's depressed. Maybe that's why his libido has decreased."

"So what I hear you saying is that you're rightfully extremely concerned about his stability," Dr. Stearns said.

Had I said that? I didn't think so but was grateful that we'd shifted away from the Ambien.

"I guess stability is one way to put it," I said.

"Financial stability is a valid concern," he offered.

"I think it's more about mental stability," I said.

"I think the two, mental and financial stability, are intertwined here," Dr. Stearns said. "I think Jonathan and I should have an individual session this week as it might be easier to work through it that way," he said eyeing Jonathan. "I have a lot of experience and success treating gambling addiction." *Don't gloat!* I told myself.

"My concern is really where your head was. If it wasn't, quote, gambling, then why did you do it? What brought you to the point of losing control?" I asked.

"I didn't lose control. It was a calculated risk," he said.

"If it wasn't a loss of control, or compulsive, and it was calculated, why didn't I play in, your promise to me?" I asked.

Blank.

"I wasn't thinking about it in terms of breaking a promise to you. It was necessary at that moment in time," he said, perfectly convinced by his logic.

"For now, our job is to find a temporary agreement to make Alix feel comfortable while you regain her trust. The first thing I'd recommend is setting up your bank, bond, and trading accounts so that all activity is transparent and requires Alix's authorization," Dr. Stearns said.

Jonathan looked at him like he'd said the earth was flat. I felt for him. He was running a huge company, managing five hundred million dollars, and was now being treated like a derelict when he couldn't have been farther from it. I could taste what he felt and it sickened me. I remembered being sixteen. I was being sent to rehab because my parents knew I'd experimented with hard drugs. *She's out of control. No, mother,*

I'm just lost in my sister's shadow. She will die or kill us if we don't take her in the morning. *No, father, I just wanted my life to reflect the complexity I feel inside.* The signs are all there. *No, both of you, throw out your checklist. I am not an addict, I just want to scream something.* I find a bar. I find men. I'll be locked away in the morning. I should do what's expected of me. I'm such a novice that the white powder is wasted on the seats of my car, under the emergency brake. I'm sniffing it off of a key the man I am riding in the passenger seat is holding. His friend is rubbing his gums in the back seat. What's visible to him but my bouncing head and fingers gripping the back of the passenger seat, maybe a nipple. The drugs just happened to be there, props, merely, for the play I was performing for myself, to distance myself from the middle, from the expected, the masses, the herd, those on autopilot.

"Who did this to you," is all that my father could speak, when he found the condoms and traces of powder in the morning.

I forgot, forgot, how sick I'd been, how sick I still was, not from addiction, not drugs anyway, not the sort you got better from, recovered from. The kind you camouflaged, the kind I camouflaged, no, that Jonathan camouflaged, with this better life. The dark paths I had walked away from. How sick you are for loving me, husband, I thought. I forgive you. I was outside the norm to you. You wanted me to pull you out, and instead you dragged me in. You must despise the middle, too. You have reacted, and you are only just a man, I know.

"Dr. Stearns, with all due respect, there's no need for such restrictions," I said. I was laying the net for Jonathan as he fell from his tightrope. How had I pushed him to the ground and arrived timely enough to catch him before he hit it? Sneaky, disgusting, mauled girl.

Chapter 17

Jonathan and I hadn't had sex in the four weeks that had passed since therapy. We might have broken a record. But Evan and I had continued flirting by email, sharing fragments of thought, goodnights, impressions, his book—everything unrelated to our spouses and children, and thankfully, nothing related to picking up the investigation of the driver.

Jonathan was dressed in an almost sheer white linen button down with black pants. We were going to a fortieth birthday party for one of the men Jonathan had made rich in his employ, our first social event since the Palsy began. I stood naked, overwhelmed by my closet. Every dress was too good for me, all my heels an inch too high, remnants of a confident woman who worked rooms, the life of the party. At least this would distract attention away from my face, I thought, stepping into a short, low-cut, silk print accentuating the curve of my breasts and cleavage. *I would feel so much better going out if we had had sex.* The thought kept repeating in my head. I'd have felt less ugly. I'd have been less anxious. Jonathan might be right that such a simple thing—sex—shouldn't hold so much psychological value. But I had allowed it to, and so it did.

I'd wrapped myself as best I could. I was practicing my smile in the mirror, memorizing the one that looked the most normal, not too wide, part my mouth only slightly, don't show teeth. I'd have to remind myself not to laugh. I saw Jonathan approaching me, already wearing his jacket, in the reflection. "My god, you look stunning. I'm as proud as ever to have you on my arm," I imagined him saying before gently placing a kiss on my shoulder and gripping my ass firmly, as if to show desire and restraint. Instead, I saw him register that I was still in front of the mirror, not quite ready to leave, and he clucked with irritation and turned back around. I knew he'd say nothing about how I looked, and think nothing about the angst I might have been feeling.

I was tempted to back out of this event rather than push through the discomfort as we hailed a taxi, as we sat in traffic in Times Square, and again as we approached the meat-packing district. But Jonathan had made it clear that he expected me to go, to adapt to my face, to continue with our life. "You can't just watch life go by waiting to be a hundred percent," he had told me. If he was not ashamed, I had no right to be ashamed. The scent of leftover perfume in the taxi had been threatening my nose. I succumbed, sneezing twice. It was too confusing for my face. My eye started to spasm uncontrollably. I looked in the rearview mirror, expecting it to stop the moment I tried to get a glimpse of it. It didn't. There appeared to be an epileptic worm under my eyelid. Jonathan looked at me looking at myself, then turned his head out the window without inquiring.

The party was in a private, members-only club in a six-story brownstone. The trance-like techno music got louder as we ascended the dimly lit mahogany staircases. I could feel Jonathan's eyes not watching my behind just as strongly as I used to feel it when they were. At the landing of the third floor, I absorbed the sound of shot glasses hitting the bar, the glistening foreheads of people swaying to the music, heads reeled back in laughter, someone's pet monkey just stole foie gras from a waiter's tray, snow-rimmed nostrils being rubbed clean. I heard whispers of "Jonathan and Alix." People were strategically maneuvering through the room to greet us. Unreturned kisses to my face. My practiced smile. No thanks, I said, to the martini I couldn't sip. I'd have a cocktail with a straw. Yes, it has been awhile since we've seen you. The kids are great. No, we haven't been away. Jonathan had been ushered into another room. Sarah and Craig, the only ones we'd told about my face, spotted me from across the room. Sarah walked away from whatever conversation she was in the middle of as if she'd seen a ghost.

Where was she going? She was coming to me. She had seen a ghost.

"Surprised you came," she said.

"I see that you are," I said.

"If I didn't know, I wouldn't know," she said. "How are you feeling?"

"Like someone else," I said.

"You're not yourself," she said.

"No, I'm not," I answered.

"You aren't even standing the same way," she said.

"It's the heels," I said.

"When I heard, it was impossible to conceive. Of all people..."

"I know."

"What you represented to me, to all of us," she said, waving her arm. "You're the one who had it all, no issues with yourself, the envy of all women..."

"Thanks for the letter to the coop board," I said, changing the subject.

I felt strange. The alcohol must have been getting to me already. I'd rather not eat in public, so I'd better slow down or I'll get completely inebriated, I thought.

"You haven't written back to my texts," she said.

"Forgive me."

"No, I get it," she said. She was a depressed woman. She'd been on antidepressants for years. It was a shame to identify with her. "Have you spoken to someone, I hope? I can put you in touch with Susan, my therapist. She's a saint. We've been exploring a new technique involving music to..." Sarah injected her therapist into all conversations in an unconvincing attempt to make herself comfortable with her reliance on one. It would have validated her somehow if I were as dependent on a therapist as she. She'd have frothed at the mouth to know that Jonathan and I were in couple's therapy. "Are you even listening to me? Yeah, you're definitely not yourself," she said again.

"Yes, I know. My sparkle is gone. People need their facial muscles to be themselves," I said. "Do you think I am not myself, or is it that you are no longer perceiving me as me?" I asked realizing the depth of my question would be lost on her.

"What do you mean?" she asked, looking confused.

"You know the song, when you smile, the whole world smiles with you?" I asked.

She nodded and abruptly said, "Oh, that reminds me, I wanted to download that app that recognizes songs in case I hear something really good here," she said. She began tinkering with her phone and I was jealous of all the faces she made in frustration at the task.

"Well, imagine you couldn't smile... then the world around you might not feel like it, either, right? Basically, would the effect you have on others be the same?" I asked as she continued tinkering.

"Oh, come on, you can smile," she said. I felt my forced, fake, practiced, half-smile. This was not the smile that I normally flashed at social events. "The difference is subtle, really," she said.

I looked beyond Sarah to the groups of socially animated animals around us unconsciously mimicking each other's laughter and wide smiles. I couldn't participate. Putting all my energy into keeping a neutral face that wouldn't appear freakish, I felt like an outsider. There was no point in joining conversations. I'd either appear bored and disinterested, perhaps too dumb to get the jokes others were laughing at, or I could draw attention to my lameness to excuse my awkward flat affect. Jonathan was just another of these animals. He hadn't asked me how I was before we went out because he couldn't see what I was feeling. The only clue would have been my face, and it was devoid of emotion. I'm less human like this, I thought. I'm a fish with no emotion, demanding apathy instead of empathy.

I saw Jonathan flitting around, and wondered if that Grey Goose and tonic was his first. He used to attach himself to my hip at parties, or watch me intently if we were separated. Now his eyes were everywhere but on me. I felt myself sinking into the floor, into the moldings, into the paintings on the wall, into the beautiful dent of the burlesque dancer's shoulder blade. She was standing in the doorway connecting to a neighboring room, watching the peculiar crowd of about eighty, waiting for her cue. A white statue with feathered angel wings, she took her position in the middle of the floor waiting for her song to start. She had long, curled, auburn hair, voluptuous, hippy. A better part of the guests seemed not to notice her yet. Some of the men did, but didn't want to seem overly enthused under the watchful eyes of their wives. The look in her eyes turned down to the floor had more sex in them than... Jonathan, there you are.

I caught his eye and nodded towards the angel. We shamelessly occupied two tufted leather armchairs three feet from where she stood. She was still, waiting for the music, waiting for her audience to gather. Her chin was on her chest, arms outstretched above her, spreading the wings of her costume, her pink nipples cooperatively at attention through the cut out holes of her corset, distinguishing her from Jesus. When she raised her eyes, I wanted to convey an expression of appreciation. I couldn't. I sat before her, upright and fixed, instead.

She became the music with her dancing. I was mesmerized, captivated, ensnared by this human representation of the pieces of my shredded self. I genuinely loved her deeply, for a second. Jonathan was transfixed, too, moved by this womanly creature, unattached to dirty kitchen counters, toy-cluttered rooms, sleepless nights, and the burden of the future. No costume wings could have elevated me there. To be just a thing, an object, to be this dancer for him, to be an escape, a holiday, a relief, a point of pleasure, a night, rather than a dentist appointment. I envied her, I loved her, I loathed her. I wanted Jonathan to fuck her, to love her, to loathe her. I wanted to fuck her.

She had finished one song. She sat on a chair. I wanted to flirt. I'd been forced to relinquish that. At best I could grow on her, breed on friendship or utility. I wanted to buy her a yacht, I wanted to take her to a show, I wanted to find a necklace that would complement her eyes. I asked her if she wanted a drink instead. I was a disfigured freak and I'd just offered her a drink when she already had one in her hand. *What are you doing? Fool!* She thanked me with a Russian accent but looked confused and showed me her full glass. I had nothing else to say. I had nothing more to entice her. I returned to my seat next to Jonathan, but my eyes didn't leave her.

"She's so hot," I whispered to Jonathan, pleased that we were enjoying her together.

He rubbed his hands together, like a praying mantis, letting a playful smile unfold on his lips.

"You're such a dyke at heart," he said.

"You really think so, don't you? If I were going to cheat on you, do you think it would be with a man with a giant cock or a woman like this?" I asked.

He looked at me like I'd asked a no-brainer. "A woman like this," he said, as if he were proud he didn't fall for a trick question.

"You really think I'd prefer a woman over a man?" I asked and was genuinely amazed that he really didn't get how cock-deprived I felt.

"Yes," he said, even surer of himself.

"Why?" I asked.

"You told me before we moved in, even, that you'd always want to be with women," he said.

"And what was your response?" I asked.

"That I understood," he said and I was surprised he remembered.

"So what happened to letting me?" I asked.

"I changed my mind," he said.

"And you still wouldn't be interested in watching?" I asked, marveling that I was married to the only man who didn't want to watch his wife with another woman. He was that possessive.

"Just watching, no," he said.

"Ah, well, that's an improvement! Are you implying that you'd want a threesome?" I asked.

"Not if it meant you'd get as jealous as you did—when was it, at my thirty-sixth birthday party—when you seduced that girl you invited from work, encouraged me to fool around with her as my birthday present and then complained that I kissed her more passionately than you," he said.

"We've grown since then," I said. Grown apart, grown bored. "But there's no way I'd let you have sex with another woman. And, you should know that if I were going to cheat, it'd definitely be a man," I said.

"Uh-huh," he said. "Did the babysitter put the kids to sleep yet?"

I checked my phone. "Yes."

The music started again. I was back in the angel's palm. She was still wearing her white corset and feathered wings. I fidgeted with my pocketbook to put away the phone. I dropped it and the battery slid across the floor.

Jonathan pursed his lips, then muttered, "Goddamit, Alix!" as if I'd just dropped an urn carrying the ashes of his mother. "How many damned phones are you going to break?" he barked. I couldn't sit next to him. I couldn't be near his hostility. The angel was now working the other side of the room, completely out of our view. I picked up my phone battery and prepared to leave.

"Where are you going?" Jonathan asked, shortly.

I sat back down.

"Do you not realize I've been downgraded in life to mere spectator?" I asked. "Spectator," I repeated.

He stared at me.

"Why would you get so intensely angry about something so *meaningless*?" I asked. "You'll excuse me," I said. "I'm going to find the ladies room."

I wandered up the stairs, exploring the empty sixth floor of the brownstone, until I found a small terrace to smoke on and ruminate. I was on my second cigarette with no desire to go back to the party, peering through the window at an empty great room when the angel walked into it, wingless, and sat at an iron vanity. She was reaching both arms around her back, struggling to unhook the finely laced corset. I felt like a small boy watching his mother undress. She caught me and gestured me inside, a look of relief on her beautiful face.

"Could you possibly help me with this ridiculous thing?" she asked when I went inside.

"Of course," I said, standing behind her. I saw her reflection in the vanity and mine behind her from the neck down.

I moved the auburn curls off her back and onto one shoulder and unhooked the first of some twenty hooks. I could smell her, vanilla and fruit, possibly strawberries. My hand, so petite, suddenly felt manly, intimidated by the task, and her skin.

"Why do you bother to smoke out there?" she asked, pulling a cigarette out from a metal case in the drawer that looked straight out of the forties. I stopped unhooking to light her cigarette. "Thank you, love," she said. Being called "love" by a stranger would've normally been annoying. But she managed it. I felt like a ragamuffin servant helping a glamorous movie star, admiring her, feeling privileged to help her, basking in her appreciation. Her milky white back was flawless, sculpted, smooth, and soft. There was a beauty mark under the second hook. I had the odd urge to pull the one blonde hair out of it with my teeth and plant kisses down her back. I wanted her to stand and bend over the vanity so I could see her folds and creases, so I could lap her from front to back with my nose pressed into her ass. I wanted to crawl in front of her. I wanted her thighs tightly pressed against my ears to muffle the sound of the party and to numb my mind with the task of her clitoris, where my face, mashed up, scrunched up and uncomfortably stretched, as it was, would be inevitable and welcome. She must have felt what I was thinking because she turned over her shoulder to look at me. I smiled, crooked, unpracticed, and shyly, feeling like a pervert. I'd undone enough hooks that the bra portion of the corset had fallen beneath her perfect, perky breasts. I saw through the mirror that her skin was a little red where the top of it had pressed into her breast.

"You need to put something on that," I said, gently touching the raw spot, bringing her nipples immediately to attention. *Oh, I want to touch all of you so badly.* I'd have begged her if I thought it would persuade her. I wondered if her failure to move my hand away conveyed something. I opened the last hook and the whole of her corset fell to her lap, leaving her in nothing, but a white garter belt, panties, and white knee-highs. She turned to me in her seat so that she was facing me, crossed her legs, unfastened the garter hook attaching her knee high and rolled it off, her eyes not leaving mine. *Is she teasing me?* She opened her legs slightly too wide as she uncrossed and re-crossed her legs to unfasten the other garter hook. *She is teasing me. Why? To flatter me or mock me?*

"What's your name?" she asked me.

"Alix," I said. "Yours?"

"I am Irena. Why are you so sad, Alix?" she asked me. I watched her full red lips as she spoke.

I didn't answer.

"This is your friend's party, no?" she asked, but based on the look I thought I saw in her eyes, I felt like she'd asked me if I wanted her.

"I'd kiss you," I told her, the ridiculous words escaping my mouth before I could tell myself to shut the fuck up, "but I can't even pucker. I'm paralyzed. I can't even kiss my husband."

She didn't blink. She didn't drop my gaze. She looked neither offended nor surprised. "You don't need to pucker. You don't have to try so hard. You shouldn't have to try so hard. Let him come to you..." *He won't.* My pulse was invading my ears. "Like this..." *You won't!* She stood. *Am I taking this the wrong way?* But then her beautiful little face got closer until it disappeared into the black of my forcefully closed lids. Her lips were smooth and tasted like the vanilla she smelled of, rather than the cigarette she'd just finished. I didn't move my mouth, but panted into hers as she captured mine, aware of her bare breasts almost against me. The heat of her tongue, the softness of her lips, unmistakably a woman's. She must pity me, I thought. *Pity all of me. Please.* I knew she would not. It was just a moment she was giving me. I tried to savor it, but she'd already stopped, stepping into another outfit, refreshing her lipstick, and gone.

I wasn't going back downstairs. I was not wasting the freshness of this desire. I couldn't. I found a bathroom with a small chaise lounge in it and stood against the locked door. I lifted my skirt, slid my hand into my underwear, and closed my eyes. I could still smell her. She took my hand and led me to the chaise lounge. She sat with her back straight up against it, and opened her long legs, positioning them so that one was bent up on the couch, her high heel digging into it, and the other planted on the floor. She was still and staring at me. She grinned, slinked down on the chaise, and curled her finger to indicate I should come. I removed the straps of my dress, letting it fall to my ankles, then went to her, putting my knees between her open legs, my hands on either side of her, lowering my chest to her, like a cat. I brought my mouth to hers, allowing her to grab my lower lip in hers. She extended both legs under me and I straddled mine on either side of her thighs. She ran her hands on the outside of my thighs and over my ass as I slid my hand into her panties. She jerked her hips upwards asking my fingers to go deeper. Instead, I pulled her panties off, then mine, and pressed our bare flesh together into that shared, wet space, smooth skin on smooth skin, not knowing where her wetness began and mine ended. "Mmmmm," I moaned, my cheek turned into the bathroom door. *Quiet!* I was instinctually desperate for cock, to be filled. Jonathan walked in on us. *No.* Reset the fantasy. He wasn't welcome. I didn't want to share her with him. I stopped rubbing myself. I welcomed Evan into my mind. *No.* I didn't want to share him with her. Goodbye, neither of you are needed, I thought. Her small hand was on the back of my head and now she was purring and pushing it down between her legs. She held my head tightly in both her hands so that I could do nothing but leave my lips and tongue available. "You shouldn't have to try so hard," she said, exactly as she had before, and used my face like a pumice stone while I held her thrusting ass, and oh, that was all I could take.

I'd lost sense of time. I had no idea how long I'd been gone. I looked at myself in the bathroom mirror. *You ugly, lame, hag. You're supposed to be down at the party. Who does this?* I was disturbed but amused with myself, and laughed accordingly. My left eye squinted when I did. I didn't mean to wink at myself, but I had. I opened my mouth to form an O. Again, my left eye closed. *How long has this been happening?* For the last few days, there'd been an increase in fluttering in my ear, like a psychotic butterfly was trapped inside. It was as if any movement in my face caused my hearing to go in and out. I thought it foreshadowed muscle regeneration. I thought I was about to witness another marked improvement. But maybe it was related to this squinting issue. I would need to see the ENT first thing Monday morning.

When I found Jonathan, he was clearly looser and more inebriated than when I'd left him. I pulled him to the dance floor so I could avoid talking to anyone and lost myself dancing with my hair in my face until it was reasonable for us to leave.

***

"I'd say you're about eighty percent symmetrical. You've made excellent progress," Dr. Magan said, quickly inspecting my face. "Give me an update."

"I. Can't. Give. Head," I said, making a joke but also being serious. "I mean, it's been over four months now, and there's been no improvement in at least three weeks. I'm still in pain, can't wriggle my nose, my mouth is suddenly higher on the left side. You're saying that I'm about eighty percent better, but I'm still not me. And just the other night, look what I noticed." I smiled, then puckered, pointing to my automatically squinting eye.

"I see," he said calmly. "Looks like you've developed mild synkenesis."

"What is that?" I asked.

"Involuntary movements that accompany voluntary ones. Some wires crossed when the muscles were rebuilding," he said. "Imagine that you're trying to put a circuit breaker together in the dark. If you connect the red wire where the blue wire should go or vice versa, the command gets confused. So, if you turn on the light for the kitchen, the bathroom light might go on instead. Here, when your brain tells your mouth to smile, your eye closes instead. You had a full paralysis. The nerves had to regrow and be retrained, and they didn't retrain properly."

"Are you fucking kidding me? Does this happen a lot?" I asked.

"It happens to maybe two in ten people with Bell's Palsy," he told me.

"Is that related to this odd straining sound I'm hearing in my ear when I move my face?" I asked, annoyed.

"Yes, the muscles are confused. So, when you try to, say blink, your ear drum is receiving a signal to protect itself instead."

"Is this going to correct itself?" I asked, angry now.

"No, but it may improve."

"When?"

"Over the next year," he said.

"Could it get worse?"

"Yes, but we'll see," he said.

"Initially you told me I'd be better in three months..."

"No, I told you most people getter better in three months, but for those that don't, it can take a lot longer, and some never do," he said.

"Do you still think I'll eventually make a full recovery?" I asked, or begged.

"Full? Probably not," he said, "but it may get to the point where only you notice it. It's important that you keep doing the facial exercises, at least a few times a day. And if it gets worse, we'll get you a physical therapist, possibly do botulism injections to help the synkenesis."

"Botox, as a medical treatment? Is that covered?"

He nodded.

"Free botox for life? I hope it gets worse!" I joked.

But, that's it, I thought. I'd been waiting it out for months, clinging to a modicum of faith that I'd eventually get better. There'd been an endpoint. Now there was none. I couldn't continue to rot.

I called Jonathan with the intention of telling him about the synkenesis. But he was in too good spirits. He'd landed fifteen percent and a seat on the board of a new energy company in Boston. He'd fly out there in an hour to meet the executive team and stay over for two nights. He couldn't comfort me anyway. I couldn't change my physical paralysis, but I could discard the emotional and sexual one he'd imposed on me.

I saw the image of his face before my brain processed his name. *Evan.* My intestines informed me before my mind. I felt the most feminine of muscles clench before I could even visualize that I wanted his massive body on top of me, his legs forcing mine wide open, the hardness of his cock plunging through the scar tissue encasing my deconstructed ego, assuring me that I was still a living woman. *No.* There was too much risk. It'd mean that I was out of control. It wasn't normal to have an affair, to abandon my loyalty to Jonathan, in this state, as a means of coping with it. But the need was acute and desperate and as irresistible as the movements of my mis-wired face.

'Out of control', 'risk', 'need,' the words reminded me of Jonathan's. What was it exactly that he'd said about all the risks he'd taken financially? And as if I'd inhaled the fumes of rationalization, I flashed back to our conversation in therapy.

"I wasn't out of control. It was a calculated risk."

"What about your promise to me?"

"I wasn't thinking in terms of breaking a promise to you. It was just necessary at that moment in time."

So was Evan. Necessary at this moment in time.

Fuck it. I sent Evan an email message: "My face has made no progress, but it has been well over 90 days (the initial 90, discounting the massage) and I'm up for meeting, if you can handle it. Tomorrow night? - Alix"

He replied immediately: "See you at 6:15. Same place. - E"

Chapter 18

Preparing for Evan distracted me from my face. I'd eaten nothing all day. I knew I'd be doubly affected by alcohol on an empty stomach. I debated between an elegant, sexy dress that stopped just below the knee and a tight bandage dress that accentuated every curve and barely covered the top quarter of my thigh. I felt like a schoolgirl.

Jonathan rang me as I was getting ready. I told him I was going to dinner with Sabrina, and that Luisa would stay with the children. I asked him which dress he liked best. I was a murderer asking him to dig the hole I planned to bury him in. I should have been wearing blood red lipstick to match my mood, but I could no longer wear lipstick without drawing attention to the asymmetry of my mouth, and I couldn't smack my lips to apply it anyway. He told me to wear tight black pants, and I did.

I called Sabrina to make sure she wasn't doing anything tonight that would end up on Facebook and kill my lie.

"Alix, I can't talk. I'm having a huge brawl with Paul. I might as well tell you the truth...We're getting divorced, for real this time."

"Yeah, I've heard that before," I said.

"Really. We already filed," she said.

"This changes everything," I said, thinking about Evan, trying to disguise the hope in my voice. If I no longer had to fear destroying her marriage—if it were already destroyed, I could tell her the truth. I could tell Evan. But, that was not my agenda tonight. I heard Paul's voice in the background.

"He's telling me to ask you if you can mediate the divorce for free, actually."

"That'd be a conflict even if I did family mediation, which I don't. I can find you someone. I'm so sorry for what you're going through. Maybe you want to meet me for dinner tonight to talk?" I asked, just to hear the reason she couldn't.

"No, my eyes are puffy from crying. I'm not going anywhere." *Great, she's a viable alibi.* "I'll call you tomorrow," she said.

I took a cab to meet Evan. I arrived twenty minutes early and Evan was already seated, waiting, twirling the mixer in his drink, nervously. My thoughts needed outstretched arms to prevent me from tipping. When he sees my face, I thought, I'll have effectively destroyed whatever we'd been creating.

My face was tight, the Palsy exacerbating the chronic tension between what I showed and what I felt, or that tension exacerbating the Palsy. I was entangled in the braid these men had woven down my back, looping the disgust I felt for my new self with the disgust I'd always felt. It was no more about destroying something with Jonathan, than it was about creating something with Evan.

Evan visibly relaxed and smiled broadly when he saw me walking towards him. He'd already ordered a glass of wine for me. I conspired to take sips discreetly so that he wouldn't see how difficult it was for me to drink, or that my left eye would squint uncontrollably when I tried to secure my lips on the glass. A slow sip of wine coupled with eye contact used to be a weapon in my arsenal of seduction, and now it was a fucking challenge.

"You had me prepared for a ghoul. I don't even see it," he said. I could tell he'd prepared that comment well in advance of meeting.

"I see you have a blemish on your forehead, and..." I quickly searched him for another flaw and it was hard to find one, "your hairline might be receding," I laughed.

"That's not funny. I'm really self-conscious about that," he said.

"My point is that it's okay to acknowledge the obvious."

Evan shook his head. "I'm sorry," he laughed, "I know this is huge for you, but this is like my daughter asking me to acknowledge her imaginary friend at the dinner table," he said.

"Would it help you to know that I'd give anything to take you right here, right now, at this table?" he asked.

I grinned.

"This is only my second time out in four months," I said, "and the first time didn't go well." I told him about the party, about Irena, and my conversation with Sarah about the importance of facial muscles. I'd managed to consume the rest of my wine, and half of another glass without him staring in horror at my mouth. "What do you think about it?" I asked.

"I think it's pretty hot," he said.

"No, not about Irena," I said. "About the possibility that I may truly no longer be myself without my facial muscles? The way you normally think about things is that you feel happy and then you smile. But what if it's the reverse... that you smile first and that the smiling is what in turn causes you to be happy?"

"You may have changed because of this whole ordeal. Maybe it's for the better. But I don't believe that any changes are from you not being able to show your emotions. Feelings come before the physical signs," he said with conviction. "Think about it. I feel ecstatic that I'm here with you, and I haven't had a big smile plastered across my face."

"You kind of have actually."

"Okay, but look, now I'm not," he said, forcing his mouth into a straight line. "I'm still ecstatic," he said and then a new smile unfolded. He appeared either overwhelmed or bewildered.

"Ahh, see what you just did?" I asked, pointing at his mouth. "I just saw your emotions change. What are you smiling about right this second?" I asked.

He shook his head again. "I'm just thinking that you've asked me about something I've never thought about." He searched the room and gestured the waiter for another round.

"You need the full gamut of emotional expression to be yourself. I'm living an emotionally diluted life now, like a watered-down drink. It's not just that I can't convey emotion, but I can't feel it," I said, attempting to narrow my brows, and, again, causing commotion in my ear, and a twitch under my eye. "This has flattened me..." My voice trailed off.

"Maybe you were already flat. Maybe you just need to get back to life. I don't mean to before the Palsy. Before you put your husband and your children before your natural intensity and ambition," he said.

I grinned, in undeniable agreement.

"Where do you think physically unexpressed emotions go? You know James' famous line, if you refuse to express a passion it dies," I said.

"Is passion an emotion?" he asked.

"I guess it depends on the context," I said.

"In this context," he said, gesturing back and forth between us.

"An emotion," I said. "An important one."

"Not an emotion that forms on the face," he said, in a low voice.

"True," I said, squirming from how hot his voice sounded.

"Not one that requires a smile..." he said, and I felt his eyes undressing me. "Or a frown..." he continued, and it was as if his face was against my cheek, whispering in my ear. I almost felt his hands searching for my breasts. "Or any facial expression at all..." he added. "Not one you are too numb to experience, I take it," he said. He leaned back, like a trainer giving his sweaty client a break between sets.

"True," I said, and inhaled deeply.

"What do you think?" He reached down and gripped my calf under the table, keeping his eyes locked on mine.

"About what?" I was truly disoriented, rendered speechless by the warmth of his hand on my calf.

"If we refuse to express it, will it die?" he asked.

"I don't think so," I said, pointing my toe so that the calf he was digging his fingers into flexed beneath his hand.

"Do you think expressing it will intensify it?" he asked, loosening his grip and running his thumb gently up my calf.

"Maybe that kind of passion is better left unexpressed. That was the point of the ninety days, wasn't it?"

"Do you want to test the theory?" he asked, standing, the intensity in his eyes making me nervous.

"Yes."

"I'll settle the bill and meet you outside. I know you need a cigarette."

"Actually, the restroom," I said and took a deep breath. "Be right back."

We wandered outside and headed west. The air felt good, dead leaves gracefully alternating their weight against the resistance of their descent, around us. I felt like we were thirteen again. Evan led me by the hand, but I hesitated. He tightened his grip.

We stopped in a narrow gap between buildings. I leaned against the brick wall, and put my palms against it beside me. Even in my heels, he towered over me. "You're unbelievable," he said. "I don't know what you're doing to me." He leaned in and his tongue was in my mouth before I even remembered my incapacity to kiss him. I took his hand and placed it on my breast to give him something to focus on before he remembered I was lame. He was pushing his hardness against me, pushing his tongue deeper into my mouth, pushing me beyond the point of turning back.

"I need to have you, Alix," he said. "All of you."

He rubbed a thumb against my nipple. I wanted to moan, open-mouthed, to show my appreciation, but I knew that if I did, my cheek would pull upwards and my one eye would wink. My body knew nothing of the self-consciousness I felt and was unabashedly preparing itself for use.

I pushed my pelvis into him, and Evan let out a small growl. Suddenly, he lifted me against the wall. "Mmm," I moaned, my legs locking around him, my heart quickening, and my hesitations unraveling. I was supported by one of his arms under my rear, the wall, and the stiffened cock pressing into me. He gripped the back of my head, his fingertips pressed into my scalp, tilting my head back.

A service door opened and a man cleared his throat with a feigned "ahem." We startled, giggling like children as he gently lowered me to ground. I didn't know where we were headed, but undeterred, we walked until we'd crossed the West Side Highway.

Evan stopped walking and looked at me.

"I didn't know we would really end up like this," he said with a worried expression. I didn't want to think too hard about what he was saying. I didn't want the fresh pool of arousal drowning my doubts to be diminished.

"Can you disappear for the night?" he asked.

I shook my head, thinking a part of me already had, and my spine itched to be back at that brick wall. I didn't want to talk, as if the sound of my own voice would remind me that I wasn't supposed to be here. If I attempted to work through the hurdles—the nanny, a call from Jonathan to say goodnight from Boston, the baby waking up without me—I'd just give up and go home.

"This is all I get?" he asked, disappointed. "Fragments of nights?"

"Yes." He furrowed his brows, grabbed my arms, pulled me into him, and kissed me hard.

"I don't want just fragments," he said, looking down at me like a spoiled child that had been offered only half of a cookie, and released me with defeat.

"Is this goodnight, then?" he asked.

I knew not to let this spinning coin hit the edge of anything.

"Sit down," I told him, motioning to a bench facing the Hudson River, the lights of New Jersey reflecting in his surprised eyes. I knelt before him on the concrete, and stared up at him, singularly focused on this dark, carnal, warped need burning in me to feel desired, to be a sexual woman, not a disabled gimp. There was an urgency in me, as if my conscience were an approaching captor.

I pulled his belt through the loop and unbuckled it as disbelief swept over his face. *Your mouth doesn't work! You are disabled, inadequate. Why would you do this to yourself? Why, why, why, would you expose your weakness?* I wondered if I was trying to humiliate myself, out of desperation. Without a complete demolition, I couldn't recreate myself.

I swirled my tongue around his head, my hand and mouth in sync, working him up and down. My cheek scrunched up, palpitated, hurt. It was humiliating, but I was still aroused. It was the rush of taking a risk, feeling vulnerable, feeling passion. My vulnerability was building, and with it, Evan was building too. I wanted him to hold my head steady, but he wouldn't. I was going to drink this man, not wasting a drop of the redemption, spilling into my core, past my mauled face.

I stayed kneeling before him for a few minutes before I got up, sat next to him, and lit a cigarette.

"No words," he said, zipping up, shaking his head. "You have to stay with me for the night. We can go to my clinic," he said, "and dedicate the rest of this evening to you."

"I really shouldn't," someone said. He looked at me strangely, as if he didn't understand why I'd draw a line after I'd already crossed it. Neither did I, but I stood up. "I should go..."

"Your eyes are telling me you aren't sure, but..." He stood, and with surprising dexterity, unbuttoned my pants and reached two fingers down into my panties, "... it doesn't feel like you're unsure at all." He looked down at me with sexy, serious eyes.

As if by some automated force, I moved his hand away. The skies were darkening, my captor was close enough to smell. *What is this overwhelming thing?* It felt like guilt. It felt like remorse. I turned and walked away.

Chapter 19

I was walking home, still worked up, the endorphins and excitement playing hide-and-seek with my mounting self-reproach. *What the fuck were you thinking?*

In my adolescence, acting out sexually had been the only way I'd known to carve out my identity. *How pathetic that it still was!* I stumbled home, through the sobering air, wondering how I could be thirty-seven years old, and still so limited, so lost. *Puberty and Palsy,* I told myself. *Times when I was desperately searching for my identity. Stupid woman! Stupid excuses!*

Being with Evan had confirmed that beneath my paralyzed face, I still had the capacity for passion—and that my marriage did not. Could I blame Jonathan totally? No. The Palsy? No. The bitter disappointment, the pitiful disillusionment, the creeping disenchantment and tedious, factory-like dullness of marriage and motherhood? Perhaps.

I barely nodded to the doorman, as if his eyes were black lights searching for come on my face. Thankfully, Jonathan was in Boston so I wouldn't have to face him with betrayal blistering my face like a fresh sunburn. It was sure to fade, I reassured myself as I prepared to greet Luisa. But the lights were out, and I heard the unmistakable symphony of Jonathan's choking snores. Why was he home? I panicked.

I washed up, and crawled into the pull-out sofa bed. He stirred.

"Ugh," he said. Even in his sleep, his resentment and disgust surfaced. It was an "ugh" so heartfelt and equally heart-piercing, that it would've normally forced me to retreat to my separate bed. But this time I deserved it. I had the sickening feeling that Evan's come could possibly burn through my throat and scorch his skin. My guilt was multiplying like hormones in pregnancy, doubling and tripling. A scarlet letter wouldn't have covered it. I'd have needed the whole alphabet. Adulterer. Bad Mother. Cunt. Degenerate. Exaggerator. Fabricator. Guilty. Guilt. Guilt. It was an unremitting constant, an endless white noise, as predictable as death. I felt guilty leaving the kids. I felt guilty getting my nails done, doing mediation work, going to the shelter. Guilty exercising, guilty spending money on the nanny, guilty for sitting on the toilet thirty seconds longer than I needed to, guilty that Jonathan felt guilty, guilty for having the time to feel guilty. Like a work for hire, I needed to spend my time as Jonathan saw fit. The only time I didn't feel guilt leaving one of the kids was when I was in the hospital having another cut out of me.

I fell into a fitful sleep, up every forty minutes, remembering what I did. I dreamt the recurring dream that I hadn't had in years, of giving birth to multiple snakes. Once they were out of me, they conjoined as one. I used to think that it reflected my fantasy of sleeping with multiple men at once. My old shrink had said it reflected my belief that I was unworthy of motherhood. This time the snake disappeared, but I could feel it in the room, looking for a body to inhabit.

At 5:30 a.m., I searched on my phone for "insomnia addiction therapist New York." I sent an email that I'd like to make an appointment to discuss tapering off sleeping pills.

My shifting woke Jonathan, and although I'd been trained to ignore the morning hard-on pressing into my back as if it were nothing more than the horn of a passing car, I bucked up against him, hoping that making love now could somehow erase what had happened last night. He pulled away, abruptly.

"Good morning," I said, but he was already getting out of bed. "I'm sorry I woke you. Come back to sleep. Kids won't be up for an hour. I promise not to touch you." A twinge of resentment lingered at the serrated edges of my guilt.

"I'm up," he said, pulling on crinkled pants from the floor.

"I'm sorry," I said, again, apologizing for waking him, touching him, polluting our marriage with my toxicity.

"Why aren't you in bed? I came to the couch specifically not to bother you with my snores."

"You're thoughtful to the point of extravagance," I mumbled.

Ninety years since women could vote, fifty years since the hairy armpit epidemic, nine years since the first woman had run for president, but we were still less than a day old in the course of evolution. It was still hard-wired into the primeval feminine brain to seek security, in some form, from a man. Maybe, it was precisely because Jonathan had given me this secure, yet aseptic life, that my carnal needs were amplified.

"I thought you were going to be away for a few days," I said.

"Change of plans. Where did you go with your sister last night? You got home really late for just dinner." He never asked specifics about where I went. Either he was suspicious or I was being paranoid.

"She's finally getting divorced, for real this time. I listened to her whine for hours. Nothing about how my face is, not one inquiry about the kids. I'm not kidding. She's an absolute narcissist, like the whole world revolves around her."

Jonathan snickered. I hoped I'd effectively distracted him by giving him the chance to say I was the pot calling the kettle black. "But you didn't get back until after..."

"So, why did you come back from Boston early? What's the real deal? Did your girlfriend need to go back home to her husband?"

"Why would you say something so ridiculous?"

"I have no idea what you're doing. It's peculiar that your itinerary changed and you didn't let me know."

"You haven't asked for my itinerary in ages. You could care less if my plane went down." When had I stopped asking for his itineraries? Was it after I stopped buying him trinkets on my way to work, leaving romantic post-its on the kitchen cabinets, sharing sentences from books I was reading, leaving notes in the pockets of the pants he took on business trips, and shaving his neck between haircuts, as I'd done daily, unnecessarily, naked, on our honeymoon in Bali? After shopping for groceries and cleaning the apartment became designated chores on one of our lists, rather than joint activities? After I started to pretend I didn't hear his critical voice asking why we were out of diapers, whether the milk in Charlie's bottle was fresh, or whether I had checked to see if the bathtub toys were moldy?

"I don't ask for your itinerary anymore because you don't talk to me about what you're hoping to accomplish, or what you daydream about on the plane. And for the record, I'd rather your plane go down than find out that you were off jet-setting with some younger woman."

"I know," he said, shaking his head. "I remember. How much would it have cost me in the prenup if she was young *and* went to Harvard?" He paused.

"I think the agreement would have expired by now as per your sunset provision," I said, rolling my eyes.

"When do you think I would have the time to be off jet-setting with some woman? Don't you get how busy I am?" He stared at me incredulously. I felt bad that I was putting him through this just to reinforce my alibi. "I was asked to do an interview on MSNBC, so I took a last minute charter back."

"Yeah? Well, I'm glad you don't even think it's worth telling me when you're on the news anymore. It used to be that we didn't go to sleep until we'd downloaded every detail of our day. And now you don't even mention you have a major interview?"

Silence.

"Why don't we talk anymore? Why do you keep everything, everything, in?" I asked. "You say 'ugh' when I get into bed with you!"

He pursed his lips and exhaled.

"Maybe you should try it," he said.

"What?"

"*Not* communicating. It's harder to be dignified, not to spew just because it makes you feel better in the moment. If I said all the things I've thought every time I'm unhappy with something, you'd have run off lifetimes ago," he said.

"And I should be happy to hear that?" I asked.

"That's maturity. Because ten years from now, we'll still be together and those issues won't matter. We don't need to have a discussion about why I might have grunted when you got into bed. Why poison the well with what is only passing hate?"

Hate? "I *did* stop communicating. And all I got for that was confirmation that if I didn't complain, we wouldn't fuck. That, and a paralyzed face." He looked confused. "I think the fact that 'ugh' is your reaction to me getting into bed *is* a major issue."

"It's not a crime that I don't want to have a ten-hour discussion about what I was thinking before going to work at six in the morning. You aren't entitled to hear my every thought. It's a privilege. And so is sex! You don't just get carte blanche access to me because we're married."

I knew he was right but I wanted to shout at him. *Sex is not a privilege in marriage. Men have always seen it as a right. Now women do, too—at least this one. Let me out of this marital tyranny! And just because I agreed to be buried next to you, doesn't mean I agreed to pour gravel in my mouth while we're living.* But I buried my anger and opened up wide for the dump of the shovel, in penance for my own crime.

"Okay."

"Okay?" he repeated, as if he'd never heard the word from me.

"Okay. For as long as I've been complaining to you about sex, you've been complaining about my pills."

His head cocked to the side like a bird. "Go ooon," he said with a feigned English accent, making it difficult not to laugh.

"I thought about what you said in therapy, that you want me to quit. I've made an appointment with a doctor who specializes in sleep disorders," I said.

"Really?"

"He's supposed to be really good," I said with confidence, as if it weren't all of fifteen minutes ago that I'd discovered the guy. "If you're ready to deal with the consequences of me being up all night, I'm ready."

He sat on the bed. He was smiling more broadly than I'd seen in ages. "All this because your sister is getting divorced?" he said.

Not quite. I told him about the synkenesis, that I felt bad that my face was unattractive, but we had to work on the things we could control.

"I'd take twitchiness over bitchiness any day," he said, pleased with his rhyme, minimizing the synkenesis. He genuinely didn't get how devastated I was. *Why haven't you kissed my twisted mouth?* I thought, remembering how Evan had.

"You told Dr. Stearns that you wanted me to be there for you as a wife. What exactly did that mean?" I asked.

He looked at me suspiciously, like I was a suspect fairy godmother who had asked him for his three wishes.

"I just don't want to always feel like you think you're being beaten up by me or the kids. I want you to get as much help as you want. Just don't make me feel like you're overstretched."

But we *are* overstretched, I thought. Overstretched between a generation that prioritizes rearing your children over your own needs and one that smacked their children until it was time to choose a nursing home. Overstretched between what the kids, employees, partners, the house needs and a spouse's seemingly abstract need for intimacy. Between the parts of ourselves we carved out before succumbing to marriage and children, and the role our spouses already carved out for us.

"Okay," I said.

Jonathan was puzzled, but happy.

"I'll do my part to change, too. Starting tonight, I'm gonna hit that," he said comically.

***

I spent my entire run cursing myself, blurting out "What did you do?" every half-mile or so. I took Jonathan's clothes to the cleaners, picked up the baguette he loved from the bakery, made his favorite meal, sautéed shrimp with garlic, Italian chicken cutlets, mashed potatoes, cole slaw. I showered, shaved, and planned to be extra-pleasant. With a half-hour free before the kids or Jonathan came home, I sat down to work on the mediation website. I wrote, "WHORE" over and over, until I noticed that I had two new emails. One from Evan, one from Jonathan.

I didn't want to read Evan's email. I didn't want to hear what last night meant to him, that I was everything he'd ever dreamed of. Like Evan could zealously fuck me forever, like there'd be no in-laws in his family I'd end up fantasizing about. Or worse, that he wanted to stop seeing me now that he'd seen my face and gotten what he wanted.

I opened Jonathan's email first, as if I'd symbolically chosen him over Evan:

"Did the broker call you too? The board approved us! They want to close ASAP! We're supposed to do the final walk-through in five days and then go straight to the closing. I have to get to the bank to get the checks before that. Plan for a celebration dinner after the close."

Could the timing be any worse? Was the universe delivering me a double serving of guilt?

I replied:

"Great news! I'll make a reservation."

Now, for Evan:

"No words for last night. I keep thinking I imagined it. Are you even real? Now that I've sunk my teeth in, I want to see you daily. But at the very least, I'll see you in 90."

I replied:

"Thank you for dinner... though we didn't eat, which is why I was hammered, which is why what happened did. With every step I have taken today, I feel like I'm going to fall through the cracks, and into the earth, which is going to open up and swallow me whole. Forget the 90. Maybe 900 will be enough to convince me that it was my imagination."

Evan responded:

"You say that now, but that's the beauty of 90. Three months is a long time. By the way, being hammered is no longer an excuse at our age."

Jonathan was to arrive home in a few minutes. I sat with both kids on the couch to await him. Ella mushed her stuffed animal into my face while Charlie inadvertently yanked my hair as I hugged him. Both children quickly became bored with our snuggling. I suggested reading to them, but Ella wanted to watch Sponge Bob. I suddenly felt entitled to lock myself in the bathroom and text Evan.

An hour had passed. I'd made six trips to the refrigerator for varying requests, cleaned two spills. Dinner got cold, and the kids were already eating in the den when he arrived. No celebratory kiss, no "hello." I heard his footsteps traipsing to the kitchen, where he lingered, from the hallway. I could see him picking at his dinner plate on the counter. It was like he was in a locker room, psyching himself up for the big game, mentally preparing himself to transition from work to us, his needy family.

Like if he waited long enough, the family obligations would disappear.

"Jonathan? Are you home?" I tried not to let my irritation become apparent in my voice.

No answer, but he'd heard me.

"Why isn't Daddy answering?" Ella asked.

"Wawa?" Charlie said, handing me Ella's cup.

"No, Charlie, that's my cup," Ella said.

"Are you home?" I repeated, louder now.

"You know I'm home." He finally joined us in the den, his eyes still not meeting mine.

"We're all in here."

"Is that *such* a crisis?" he asked.

"I made your favorite dinner," I said.

"Yeah, I saw that." Now I was really annoyed.

"Charlie wants water, in a real cup," I said. "Can you grab it or is that too much to ask?"

"Not before I get a proper hug from my angel," Jonathan said. He hugged Ella with his eyes closed, and I sensed that he wanted me to watch. I suspected he was telling me, "See, I do have the capacity to love."

He muttered something on the way to the kitchen, and again on the way back. I was pretty sure I heard "bitch." Five years ago, I knew he wouldn't think it, let alone utter it.

"You don't need to give him that much water," I said when he returned, and since he clearly didn't intend to 'hit that', I added, "He'll just spill it and make a mess that I'll have to clean."

"I know he doesn't drink that much," he spat as if I'd accused him of not knowing his children's middle names, "I just didn't want him to have to tilt the glass too much. He could choke." I simply rolled my eyes.

Charlie had gone off to play in the bathroom and Ella was engrossed with her Kindle. This was my chance to be civil, correct the moment.

"It's great news about the apartment. Where is the closing going to be? Should we pick a restaurant nearby to celebrate afterwards, or just go to..."

Jonathan wasn't listening to me. He was staring at Charlie in the bathroom flushing the toilet, lifting and closing the seat several times, as he did every day in harmless fascination. Jonathan's eyes were serious, troubled, as though a war had been announced, because there was a possibility that Charlie would slam his fingers in the lid. As if he didn't know how our son lived through the day without his supervision. I'd stopped speaking mid-sentence, but Jonathan didn't notice. He was now forcing a crying Charlie out of the bathroom.

"You know what? I'm going to lie down for five minutes." I'd promised to give up my pills, we had two beautiful kids, were about to close on an apartment—why couldn't I get a fucking "hello" when he walked in the door? My face was so tight, I couldn't let this ball of anxiety roll any larger. Tomorrow would be better, I told myself. I locked the door to the bedroom behind me, popped a half a Xanax, pulled out the dildo from my night table, the one with the suction cup attached to it, stuck it to the full length mirror, hiked up my skirt, got on my knees and reared up against it, remembering last night, only I envisioned me and Evan in the new apartment, in the kitchen, with—god, no, you're disgusting—Jonathan picking at a dinner plate watching us.

Chapter 20

It was a cool mid-September day. I walked towards Fordham University to hear Jonathan's lecture for a business class. He'd been invited to speak about attracting investors, and perhaps in an effort to include me in the 'substance' of what he did, he'd invited me to attend. Afterwards, we planned to do the final walk-through and close on our new apartment.

I'd spent the last couple of days mulling over the implications of Sabrina divorcing Paul. With Sabrina planning to divorce Paul, it wouldn't make any difference to her, I decided, if I gave Evan the peace of mind he'd been seeking. It'd give her decision to divorce him more conviction. Better yet, it might somehow provide leverage in the separation agreement to know Paul's secret.

What it gave me, I knew, was a legitimate reason to meet with Evan again even though I'd convinced myself that I wouldn't be unfaithful to Jonathan again. Surely, I'd have to deliver news like that face-to-face. I was ready to call Sabrina.

"What's up, bro?" she asked.

"I'm planning a surprise thing for Jonathan, and I had to use you as a cover last week. In case it comes up, we had dinner last week."

"Got it," she said, and unsurprisingly didn't question me.

"What's up with you?" I asked.

"Paul got wrecked and had a fistfight with someone last night and who do they call to pick him up from the bar? Me. His knuckles looked like cauliflower, bloody nose, the whole nine yards. I'm so fed up with him. I wish they called the cops instead of me. I can't anymore with him. I can't believe I'm going to be forty, and this is my life. But if I don't have a kid now, I'll probably be childless forever. You think I should have a kid?"

"A kid? With who? You're getting divorced," I said.

"Hold on, Mom's on the other line," she said. She put me on hold. I was anxious to get on with telling her about Paul.

"Mom wants me to ask you what the acupuncturist said about the stiffness in your face and whether you're coming to Aunt Lynn's next week."

"Tell her he said the wind is bad for my face," I said, "and no, I'm not going to Aunt Lynn's just so everyone can inspect my face."

"Hold on, I'll hang up with her." I used the spare moments to do my facial exercises.

"Oh Lordy," Sabrina said, "Mom said she'll mail you a ski mask to wear to protect your face. She's probably already heading to Filene's. Anyway, should I have a kid?"

"You just told me last week that you're really getting divorced," I said.

"That was before... I realized," she said.

"Are you kidding?" It dawned on me that she was pregnant.

"This is probably my last shot... and maybe Paul will stop partying if we have a kid," she said.

"Those are *not* reasons to have a baby or switch your decision about divorce," I said. "Children don't fix a marriage; they make it worse. Believe me."

"I should know better than to look to you for support. You have no idea what it's like to have problems," she said. "You're just as judgmental as the rest of our family. I'm getting off the phone. Don't say anything to the parents."

"Wait," I said, "I'll absolutely be supportive whatever you decide." Telling Evan that her husband killed his sister would fall into the "unsupportive" category.

Sorry, Evan, I thought, walking into Fordham. In her distorted mind, it was my fault she had a sub-par life. It wasn't going to be arguably my fault, too, if she miscarried from stress.

"John C. Maxwell said, 'Leadership is not about title positions or flow charts. It's about one life influencing another.' It can be as a mother, musician, or CEO for the Fortune 500," Jonathan was saying as I sat. *Puh-lease!* Did you think I was a leader, Jonathan, because I encouraged Charlie and Ella to paint with Q-Tips this morning? I wondered.

I was probably the only uninspired person in the room, I thought, scanning it. There weren't many females in attendance, maybe twenty in the hundred and fifty faces. Two sat together in the front row, eight chairs from me, soaking up each of Jonathan's words as if they were directed personally at them, all inspired and bright eyed—the sort of bright eyes that could only be found in the young, attached to supple skin, the kind of eyes that could toss the brain of a married man into a tail spin with a glance, because there wasn't yet a hint of bitterness in them. They were still all heart, beating with possibilities, the disappointments awaiting them too remote to anticipate. Their energy was practically contagious. I could see, I did see, Jonathan through their eyes, fresh eyes—handsome, funny, successful, and young, or young enough. Except for a few strands of gray, he hadn't aged at all since we married. But why would he have? It wasn't as if his body had become a breeding ground or his face a burial ground. He was in his element here. That was probably how he saw himself, how I once did. And that was how he deserved to be seen, rather than through the domesticated magnifying glass I peered through searching for further evidence to justify my settled anger.

I remembered one of the partners I used to work with suggesting, on the morning of one of my cross-examinations, that I should tell Jonathan, whom I'd been dating for a year, to observe me in court. "Believe me, he'll be intimidated, but he'll love seeing you like this." I'd thought asking him to observe me would've made him feel obligated to leave work to make an appearance at what was mundane to me. But now I got it.

Hands shot up around the room and Jonathan started taking questions. My phone vibrated with an email from Evan:

Subject: 85 days

We need a full weekend together. How can we make that happen? You realize this is the second time you've derailed my life and forced me to fixate on you. Just to be clear, next time is going to be ALL about you.

I replied:

Subject: Derailing
A weekend would never be possible even if I were planning to see you again, which I am not (as of now).

I had deleted "(as of now)" and added it back in three times before sending it. He responded right away.

Subject: Excerpt
You will see me again. You can't resist.

I was editing this part of my book this morning:
Back to my cot, I went. The stench of dirty socks filled the room. The other boys had to make do with their magazines. But I had memories of Alix—my choice fantasy. Some irrational part of me hoped that we'd eventually end up together. Then, and only then, would something good have come from living in Queens. Then, and only then, would Joy's death be less meaningless.

I replied:

Subject: Morbid romance
When did you stop?
Within thirty seconds, Evan wrote back:

Subject: Re: Morbid romance
Fantasizing about you has only gotten worse.
I took a deep breath, then replied:

Subject: Irrational part
I mean, when did you stop hoping we'd end up together?

He didn't reply. I hit refresh a few times, and then put my phone away.

"Any other questions?" Jonathan asked, looking around the room.

One of the two girls in the front row raised her hand. She was pretty, straight black hair down her back, chic, wearing a trendy scarf around her neck. I made a mental note to buy something similar to protect my face from the cold, rather than a ski mask. Jonathan called on her.

"My question," she said, standing, "is... Are you married?" Whispers, laughs, and a few dropped jaws spread around the room. The blonde girl next to her giggled. Jonathan was expressionless. If I weren't self-conscious of my face, if it wouldn't have embarrassed Jonathan, I'd have announced that he was married and peed on the hydrant that I was suddenly proud to call my own.

"Ah. Good question. Yes, I am. So, you want to know how a corporate executive balances family and work... I try to..."

"No, you answered my question," she interrupted, and the two girls laughed.

I felt a sudden empathy. He was going through the same crisis I was, trapped like a bird in the airport within the role I'd assigned him. He was as trusting in me as I was in him, and look at what I'd done. Perhaps he, too, had faltered along the way, especially with my deteriorated face. I certainly would've never guessed that he'd have dipped into our nest egg the way he had. How could I be so certain that he hadn't once crawled into bed with me with the aftertaste of deception thickening in his own mouth? If I weren't there, wasn't it possible that he'd have gone for a drink with this young woman? Offered to help her with a mock interview? Given her a special assignment, with her knees pinned to her ears?

And then unwelcome, the thought occurred to me that perhaps I should spy on him. *No.* He's given you no reason, I told myself. It was as if I couldn't stomach that he truly had the integrity I lacked. Would I compromise what was left of mine to prove it?

"Thanks, everyone," he said, packing up his briefcase.

Jonathan looked my way. I gave him a thumbs-up.

He was too smart to leave anything on his desktop, too careful to do anything from his work email, knew I had the passwords to his Facebook account, and unlikely to have used his phone to do anything wrong because he knew I could access detailed phone records. If he'd done anything wrong, it'd be in his personal email account, password protected. My eyebrows rose with an idea. Years back, after losing an entire legal brief when my computer crashed, I'd installed software on my laptop that logged every keystroke. All I'd have to do was get him to log on to his email on my computer and review the log afterwards. That was, *if* I wanted to spy, which I didn't.

He gestured with his head that he was ready to leave and I followed him out.

"Nice job in there. Must feel nice to have a young girl swooning over you," I teased.

He gave a throaty laugh and rolled his eyes.

"I suspect her friend put her up to it. It was sophomoric."

"I thought it was great. I like that she's not afraid to be a woman in a class of men, embracing it, not giving a crap whether she looks like a girl willing to sleep her way to the top. I love it, actually. Made me jealous."

"Good, maybe you'll be nicer to me if you think there are twenty-two-year-olds waiting in the wings," he said.

"Remember when your friend from Wharton had an affair? I asked you why you thought he did it and you told me that the only men who don't cheat are the ones who don't have the opportunity. You have opportunities all the time…"

He rolled his eyes.

"It's not just opportunity. You have to be open to that sort of thing."

"You think it's always a choice?" I asked.

"Absolutely. You don't just fall into it. There are steps along the way." I thought back to the hundreds of emails I'd exchanged with Evan, the massage, the energy I'd expended on him as I'd withdrawn from Jonathan.

"Ten more blocks," he said, "Are you excited?" His expression was the one he wore before transferring large sums of money, the same one he had on our wedding day.

About the idea of you fucking those two young girls? Yes, I thought. About the idea of both of us having secret lives? Yes. About taking another permanent step in our domestic prison? Not really. It was as if we were in a child's relay race each with one ankle tied to the other's ankle, being forced to coordinate our steps toward the goal.

"It's not too late to back out, you know. We'll have to do a lot of renovation to make this place work. There's no quick fix," I said, sure that I'd transparently communicated the metaphor for our marriage.

"The foundation is intact. I could live with it just the way it is," he said. "It's not my first choice. But I could."

Chapter 21

After the close, Jonathan and I were sitting at a restaurant toasting our apartment. If we were going to make a fresh start, we'd need to communicate again, the way we used to do before we became mere roommates.

"In the spirit of fresh starts, and since we're on speaking terms..."

He looked at me in fear.

"Can we just talk—peaceably. Our only interaction when you come home from work is about the kids. You're just as angry as I am at our life. The difference is, you won't admit that caring for children is just fucking tiresome. We should be able to just laugh about it together," I said. I looked at the wines being offered by the glass on the menu as I spoke. Jonathan was looking, intently, at me.

"It's not the kids!" He put his napkin on the table as if his appetite had been ruined.

"It is the kids, with respect to our relationship." I tore off a piece of bread.

"It's you. It's just you!"

"If you're so miserable with me, why haven't you left me?"

He looked annoyed, like a bored student asked to answer something obvious.

"Answer me." *Because I love you. Say it.*

"We have a life together. A history," he said.

"We *used* to have a life together. Now we just survive together."

"Maybe we just need a vacation," he suggested, seeming to have checked his anger.

"We do. We haven't taken a vacation in ages. God, we used to live. We used to play. Travel. Pontificate about art. We were almost cultured back then. Ha!"

"You should book something for December, you know, if you are up to it, with your face. We should go somewhere tropical, just relax."

Yes! "Yes, that's what we need," I said. I pictured us sleeping in, a relaxing breakfast on our terrace, sex in our outdoor shower...

"I can't wait to see Charlie in the pool... he'll have a blast," he said.

"I meant some time off for us without the kids. We're in two different worlds." I shook my head.

"The focus we put in our children isn't natural. Nor is your insistence on repressing everything you feel," I said.

"What's *natural*? Cleaning cages at an animal shelter?" he asked, mockingly.

"Why do you hate that I volunteer there?" I asked.

"I don't hate it, but you have responsibilities in our house." *Responsibilities in our house? Like it's 1942?* "I think it's great for you to help people, or animals. I'm all for hobbies. As long as it doesn't interfere with anything."

"You probably don't even know why you hate it."

"Why do I hate it?" he asked.

"Because it's the opposite of emotional bankruptcy," I said. "What happened to the dreamer I fell in love with? Remember the ideas we had when you sold your company, before trading, before starting Envirex. We thought we might even attempt writing a play together once."

"Things change, Alix. We didn't have a family then. All I'm concerned about now is the future, the job, the well-being of our kids. The basics." It was as if an automatic sunshade just shot up around his eyes, blocking emotion.

"There's more to life than the basics, don't you think?" I asked.

"I am utterly sick of you diminishing what I am doing with my life." He laughed nastily. "Your newfound devotion to the shelter is born only from a place of privilege—one that *I* have given you. You act like you'd be fine, without all the stability I provide in our life. But you'd be crying like a baby without it."

He took a breath.

"You want to know what happened to the dreamer in me? What happened to the lawyer in you? A year ago, we were talking about you going back to the firm again once Charlie starts school next fall. Then you decided to start your own mediation business out of the clear blue sky. Now you've decided your destiny is to walk dogs. It's all on me."

"Was that before or after you threw twenty million dollars in the toilet?" I asked.

"But you were still planning to go back to work because you said you missed having a professional life."

"I do. But why is it that my plans may have changed?" I asked.

He shrugged. "Well, the Palsy I guess."

"I'll start the volunteer mediations again. And I'll plan to move forward with my business, wherever my face is."

"I don't want you to move ahead with that business, regardless. It's not about you earning money. It's about you recognizing that I have to focus on work without worrying that our marriage or that *you* are falling apart!" *You mean you're asking me to be grateful that you haven't walked out on your invalid wife who makes no contribution to the family?*

"First you decided we had enough money that I shouldn't have to work, now you've decided that maybe I should—but only as you see fit. You have kept our money separate but taken digs at what I spend. You've put me down as a mother, a wife, and patronized my starting a business. You say you don't want me to be insecure, that you don't want to worry about me falling apart, but maybe your security hinges on me feeling insecure and undeserving of all this supposed 'privilege.' I've internalized all of it, and I've doubted myself. Now I'm thinking that all that self-doubt is just the response you've been deliberately shooting for."

"Okay, Freud," he said, pulling the cuffs of his shirt out from under his sweater, though they didn't need it. "I'm just asking for you to be considerate and you take that as me wanting you to doubt yourself. Incredible."

"Well, I'm going to schedule one of the cases I adjourned for next week," I said, and it sounded like I was threatening to kill him, rather than threatening to be my own person. Then I thought about acupuncture, doctor appointments, the withdrawal from Ambien, my sister, Evan. "No, six weeks from now."

When we got home, we heard both kids crying from the hallway and exchanged a worried glance.

Ella and Charlie were both sitting on the floor crying when we walked in. Charlie ran over to me, throwing himself against my legs.

"They were fine until just now," Luisa said.

"What happened, Ella?"

"He was trying to take my doggy. He wouldn't stop, so I hit him and he fell." She looked at her feet. "Sorry."

"I know it's frustrating that he takes your things. He doesn't know right and wrong yet. But you do. Hitting is NOT okay," I said.

"I said sorry already," she said, then shrieked, "Sorry!" at the top of her lungs.

"Sometimes sorry isn't enough, baby. If he falls and cracks his head, sorry isn't enough, right?" I asked softly.

She looked so ashamed, so angry with herself.

"Come here. Give me a hug. I love you no matter what. Even when I don't like your behavior, I still love you. Okay?" I asked.

"Okay, Mama," she exhaled deeply. "Thank you," she said. I felt like a failure that she thought she had to thank me for being loved, that she didn't know it was unconditional.

Once the kids were asleep, I prepared our frozen yogurt, and brought it to our bedroom. Jonathan was in the bathroom.

"We should both keep a copy of the Offering Plan for the apartment on our computers," he called out. I knew he was standing in front of the toilet, scratching his lower back with one hand, waiting to urinate. It was just too convenient, just the right timing, just the right opportunity... and just the most unwarranted, inexcusable invasion of privacy that I suddenly had no will to resist.

"I haven't been able to open the attachment the broker sent through my email. Let me get my laptop. Can you log onto your email on my computer so I can open it and save it?"

"Yes."

Bingo. Password obtained!

Chapter 22

It was October, day twenty-two sleeping together. The sleep doctor hadn't gotten back to me, so after a couple of weeks procrastinating, and instead of seeking out another, I decided to go it alone, to give up Ambien, as promised. Jonathan insisted on sleeping in bed with me, subjecting himself to my tossing and turning, to prove that we were in it together. He thought he was helping me, but he wasn't.

I wanted him out of the bed. I was accustomed to sleeping—or not sleeping—alone now. I'd known it would happen. Told him as much. Warned him a thousand times.

I'd averaged two hours of sleep a night. I expected Jonathan to concede that Ambien was the lesser of two evils, but instead he just encouraged me to push through. He'd suggested I buy a new pillow, but since I knew it'd be futile, I bought three silk scarves, like the girl in his class wore instead.

Fortunately I'd had his emails to keep me occupied while he snored soundly in bed. His emails only went back to a year before the Palsy because of a server error that had deleted them. I'd gone through his inbox and there was absolutely nothing scandalous. I was certain that I wasn't going to find anything at this point, but, tonight, for the sake of leaving no stone unturned, I tackled his sent box.

I read through the emails to Craig, and his friend Dave from work. There were no "Es" except for one lone email. "Emmi P," with the subject "coffee," sent two weeks after the onset of the Palsy. She was the ex before his last. I double clicked:

"So random running into you! I'm glad we got to have coffee and catch up, though I must admit it was difficult to focus—you still make me frrrrr (haha). Like you said, it'd be amazing to get together again. But unfortunately, that can't happen. My wife is having a hard time and I can't risk upsetting her further."

"Frrrr?" What the hell was that? Their old code word for being turned on? I felt a wave of jealousy in the pit of my stomach. He'd met an ex and hadn't told me. Bad, but not enough to convince me that he was any less devoted. His devotion was the epitome of invalidation because it only proved his ability to operate from outside the heart. He stood by his blood, as he stood by me, as he stood by his companies, because there was no room for introspection in that conventional, blind devotion.

I moved on to an email to Frank Bertucci, his financial advisor, on the day the Palsy had begun. Jonathan had written, "Thanks." I scrolled down to the bottom of the email chain:

"Frank-

Good afternoon. Quick question: What measures might I take to lessen my exposure to alimony in the event of divorce?"

What? Right after therapy, I realized, and continued reading:

"Jonathan,

We should meet to discuss. In contemplation of alimony/divorce:

Delay increases in salary/income to the extent possible until after terms are agreed;

Reduce household expenses;

Encourage spouse to work and live within her earned means; and

Wait until any temporary physical disabilities/burdens/debts are resolved."

Scoundrel! Was this why he'd told me he wasn't giving himself a raise this year? Was this why he'd been encouraging me to go back to work at the Firm rather than open a business? Was he just waiting out the Palsy to initiate divorce? Maybe he'd made up losing the bond money! No, I told myself, only women fake tears. I felt betrayed, and then I didn't. Surely, I should've expected that he'd plot to protect his assets, rather than plot to win me back after I raised the possibility of divorce. It was a knee-jerk reaction, I knew. It said nothing about his heart.

There was only one email recipient I didn't recognize, lbj1779@gmail.com, also on the day the Palsy began: "Regret canceling our first official meeting tonight. I'm unavailable due to issues at home. I cannot reschedule right now."

I'd seen four other emails canceling meetings and travel on the day the Palsy began. He'd dropped everything to run to the doctor to meet me, put everything aside, to be there for me. I'd given him little credit. But then I wrestled that thought to the mat because I'd put everything aside for him, too, and since well before the Palsy. I lived without a title, without a paycheck, without a professional purpose, as an androgynous second-class citizen in our house next to our children.

There was no point continuing. There was nothing I could find that would justify what I did. And if I found nothing, it still wouldn't transform Jonathan into the man I wanted—it wouldn't make him Evan.

It was 2:30 a.m. I went back to bed.

Like a horse, I kicked him to open his legs so I could slice mine through his. Like a mule, he resisted. At 5:00 a.m., I flushed the toilet hoping the sound would piss him off and make him leave, but he didn't. I knew I wouldn't sleep without an Ambien or an orgasm. At least if we had sex, there'd have been a benefit to the suffering I'd endured. If I bothered him, he'd be pissed. The thought created a building tension. I got more excited knowing that I wasn't supposed to bother him. It struck me that there was no scenario, not a massage, not Evan, nothing else hotter to me than this. The beauty of sensuality is in the longing, not the doing. His constant rejection was a turn on, wasn't it? It was actually genius, his intermittent reinforcement, more so than the ninety-day protocol with Evan, because it created a natural intrinsic longing.

I greased his thigh like a skillet.

"Ella is already up," he said.

"So?" I asked.

"I only have five minutes."

"So?"

Begrudgingly, he fumbled, like an amateur teenager, to get hard. This was unusual. I could turn around, go down on him, give him the opportunity to get his mind where it needed to be, but something in me chose not to, chose to let him squirm, under pressure and discomfort, like I'd done all night attempting to sleep. He tried to ready himself by touching me, but it wasn't for me. I felt like the last bridge connecting us was about to collapse.

If I let this happen, it'd become an ongoing issue. I could break him. Well, he'd broken me. I'll make him impotent, I thought. *You sick fuck*, I caught myself.

I jumped out of bed and stood over our radiator, my hands on the windowsill, my head against the glass pane. I opened myself, touching myself for him to see me clearly, to give him the visual I knew he needed. Now, he had to get out of bed to come to me, and I knew it would subconsciously snap him out of the pressure and make him feel like the aggressor. Within seconds he was inside of me, obscenely hard. He pushed into me, and I stood against the window, my breasts pressed against it, and he whispered something, repeatedly, into my hair. It was so unusual for him to talk during sex, so my arousal intensified. I moaned, then told him, "Say it louder, baby."

"I said, 'move to the bed.'" He sounded pained. "Stop for a minute. My leg. I have a cramp. I can't stand." He started laughing at himself. I moved to the bed, but he'd lost the intensity and was fumbling to get back inside of me.

"Mommy?" Ella called from the hallway. "Mommy, are you up? I need help. I have to make and there are no baby wipes," she said. He collapsed on my back and dropped his head into my neck. Utterly defeated, we both started laughing.

Another week of nearly sleepless nights passed. I spent the nights diminishing my emotions for Evan, enlarging them. I spun possibilities around: Tell Evan about Paul and run off with him; or keep lying about Paul, and run off with him; or tell Evan about Paul, and stay with Jonathan. Only the third option seemed impossible when I drifted off. But only inaction was possible by morning.

The mediation I had scheduled was confirmed for the next morning. By 3:00 a.m., the anxiety that I wouldn't sleep, and that my face and speech would suffer, was at a peak. I swallowed an Ambien, knowing it would hit me hard after having not taken it for so long, and pledged to myself that I would not sleep-eat. I was thinking about the possibilities with Evan as the euphoria hit me.

Jonathan woke me at 6:00 a.m., said the baby was crying. He had to shower. I still felt drugged. It took me a minute to remember having taken the pill last night. I dragged myself out of bed but when I got to Charlie's room, he was sleeping. I fumed towards the bathroom. As I pushed the door open, I saw Jonathan in his typical shower stance, leaning against the marble, neither shampooing or soaping, muttering angrily to himself, "What should I have done, approach Mr. Runtley and just announce that the board forgot to discuss it?"

"Why did you wake me?" I snapped. "Charlie isn't even up yet."

"I thought I heard him. You have some nerve complaining."

"I have work today, too," I said.

"For what? The third time in four years?" he muttered, in case I'd forgotten that I was worthless.

I flung the shower curtain open. Water sprayed the floor.

"What the fuck are you doing?" He shut the curtain. I flung it open again. I took the shampoo bottle out of his hand and threw it to the floor. He looked furious. I would've loved for him to lose it and smack me, like the gratitude I'd felt when my mother would finally hit me after all the emotional energy I'd put into taunting her, the moment she lost control.

"You're psychotic," he said. And I felt it. I imagined smashing his head into the tile.

"I fucking hate you," I said.

"Just divorce me already. You've already gotten everything you want." *Divorce? Everything I want? I don't have anything I want!*

"What does that mean?" I asked.

"The kids, the apartment, you got everything you want." His bitterness coagulated with the shower steam. "All part of your master plan."

"Did you just call me a gold digger?" I asked. I was groggy from Ambien but my rage invigorated me.

Ella swung open the door to her room. "Are you guys having a disagreement?" she asked, pronouncing "disagreement" slowly, practicing her vocabulary. Her tousled hair, mismatched pajamas, innocent, inquisitive eyes, steadied me, as if she were still inside of me, and that my increased heart rate could harm her.

"Good morning, little beauty. We're just talking," I answered. "It's early. Watch TV and I'll get you in twenty minutes."

"It sounds like you're hurting each other's feelings. You should both say sorry." She paused. "Or is this one of those times when saying sorry isn't enough?" She closed the door to her room and I wondered if, at four-and-a-half, she was already onto playing behind that door or if she was clutching her doggy for comfort.

"I've had it," I said to Jonathan. I'd dreamed of this climactic soap opera moment. I pulled the wedding ring off my finger and chucked it into the shower. I stomped down the hall to our bedroom and grabbed armfuls of clothes from my closet, as much as I could hold, and carried them back to bathroom. I dumped them in the tub, at his feet.

"What are you doing, Crazy?" he asked.

I left and returned with the bag of clothes I'd just bought at Bergdorf, the tags still on, two pairs of expensive shoes, and a pair of scissors. I dumped the clothes and shoes in the bath. I picked up a dress, cut through the silk, just a smidge, then savagely tore it apart.

"Do yourself a favor," I spat, "Act like we're divorced, because I certainly intend to."

"You're really fucking crazy," he said, turning off the shower, but I could see that he was impressed, if not amused, by the display.

I rushed back to our room and hid the three silk scarves I'd bought in my briefcase, because I actually needed those.

***

The mediation was in Hoboken, New Jersey. The parties were already waiting in the conference room, as I took my seat at the head of the long oak table.

"Hello, everyone," I said without a hint of personality. Normally, I'd have been smiling broadly to encourage a relaxed atmosphere. "I am Alix Beck, the mediator. We're going to start by going around the room introducing ourselves, then I'll give an introduction, explain how the process works, the rules of mediation, and the benefits of settling rather than going to trial, particularly in a case like this, where some employees who know the facts of the case are no longer with either company and have no incentive to cooperate. The attorneys will then make brief opening statements, we'll talk as a group, and then we'll caucus." My lips felt taut and tired already. I felt like the lawyers, and their clients, were focusing on my disfigured mouth and squinting eye. I was uncomfortable, nervous, a half-assed imposter. After my introduction, I added, "This is my first time mediating since suffering an attack of Bell's Palsy almost six months ago. If you have difficulty understanding me, just ask me to repeat what I've said." I felt like I'd asked the room for a tampon, but also a weight lifted off of me. If I could settle this case, if I could manage this room, if I could function as a professional for the next few hours, I knew I'd be able to rappel off that confidence.

"Ms. Beck, with all due respect, I don't see the point in having to sit through Mr. Clark's opening. We're taking a no-pay position. There's nothing to discuss. We're only here because it's court-mandated."

"A no-pay position!" The plaintiff's attorney, Mr. Feldman, gave a snarky laugh. "We're leaving." He stood, packing his briefcase.

"Gentlemen," I said firmly, "This is a court-ordered mediation. And while everything we discuss here is confidential, I'm required to report to the court that the parties gave the mediation a good-faith effort. So you might as well sit down and enjoy the free hour of mediation. If you don't feel that we've made any progress after an hour, you're free to leave. Now, please, sit down. I'd like to hear openings."

Mr. Feldman explained that his client, Mark, owned a small pharmaceutical company that had patented technology to orally deliver insulin. Mark had entered into a collaborative agreement with Mr. Clark's client, a huge pharmaceutical company to develop and market the technology. "They weren't diligent. Now, we've learned why. All along, they were secretly developing their own similar technology using our confidential information in breach of the agreement. So we terminated it."

Mark interrupted him. "It's not *similar*. It's identical. Look at the patents!"

Mr. Feldman patted his shoulder. "The damages are potentially upwards of sixty million."

Mr. Clark put his pen down, and rubbed his temples. "That *improper* termination is the basis of our counterclaim. We need a judge to declare it. It's that simple. Mediation is pointless."

The parties went back and forth disputing the similarity of the technologies. Patent applications with hexagonal shapes covered the conference table. I asked Mr. Feldman and his client to leave the room.

"Jeff," I said, using Mr. Clark's first name, "What's this counterclaim? You want a judge to say that the company should have, and should still, continue with the collaboration even though they believe your client broke their trust? You know that's not realistic."

"The time and money that has gone into developing this *new* technology is astronomical," he said. "We aren't backing down. We're already in Phase Two trials."

"If a jury finds similarity between their technology and your 'new' technology, you're going to have a hard time proving you didn't use confidential information. Right or wrong, you know the judicial climate right now regarding big pharma exploiting the little guy." I paused. "Have you considered licensing their technology to use in your independent research? Perhaps a small royalty, if it ever goes to market." Jeff looked at his client who didn't reject the idea outright.

"Only if it's exclusive," Jeff said. "They'll never go for it."

"It's worth a shot."

An hour had passed. Neither party opted-out of the mediation. Within the following hour, we'd negotiated the terms of a license agreement.

By the time I got to the garage, it was mid-afternoon. I had no interest in going home. I wandered into the Mandarin Oriental Hotel. I used Jonathan's gold to book a room. Lying on the bed, I checked my phone. There was an email from Evan. "Subject: Re: Driver." *Dammit!* Had I sent him an email on Ambien and forgotten? I checked my sent messages, suspecting what I confirmed: 3:23 a.m. email to Evan:

Subject: Driver
"I know who was driving."

I should've known that after not taking my pill for so long that this would happen, especially with all the spinning I'd been doing!

Evan had responded, only twenty minutes before, "Let's meet."

I hated that it'd come to this, but I knew what I had to do. I emailed him before I'd thought too hard about it: "Meet me at the Mandarin, the main bar, and I'll tell you." I pulled out the three scarves from my briefcase, and wrapped one around my head and neck, like a kerchief, and headed to the bar.

I studied the faces of the people chattering at the bar, mostly well-dressed professionals, and to the casual observer, I fit right in. Not one of their faces was perfectly symmetrical; crooked noses, varying eye widths, unevenly receding hairlines. But they saw themselves as balanced. That's the goal of my generation, I thought, to balance it all, and to disguise that balance as satisfaction.

Evan arrived, handsome as ever, and planted a kiss on my cheek. It didn't matter that we were meeting to discuss his dead sister, or that the face under my scarf was tense; his energy was overpowering. I felt my pupils enlarging, my mouth drying, and my pulse quickening.

"I like you in a suit," he said, standing against the bar, staring me down. "And the scarf makes me feel like I'm meeting with an undercover agent for an exchange of government secrets."

"I can't tell you how I know," I blurted, before I had time to change my mind. "Tom Moretti. That's who was driving. He was older. I doubt you knew him." I deliberately omitted that he was dead. It felt almost sacrilege, like I was defiling both Tom and Joy's tombstones.

He grew serious and mouthed the name to himself as if trying to conjure up the image. He shook his head.

"I see," he said.

He stared at me. Minutes seemed to pass.

"Are you sure? Tom Moretti?" he asked.

I nodded. "What will you do, now that you know?"

"It's never been about *doing* anything or getting revenge. I want an apology. I want to confront the driver for being a real coward, for running away. I think that'd give me some closure." I felt bad that I was sending him on a wild goose chase, that he'd never get that apology. I imagined the scene that would unfold, though, if I told him the truth; my sister in tears, and Paul inevitably throwing a punch. "I want the truth acknowledged, what my family suffered and why. By everyone involved."

"I understand. I've done so many mediations where the parties start out with demands, but as soon as they've confronted each other, had a chance to be heard, get an apology, the numbers become irrelevant. We'll have to track him down." I touched his hand. "Why do you look confused?"

"I'm just processing everything. This is a lot of information." He pulled his hand out, leaving mine on the too polished bar, and touched his temple, as if he had a headache. "Listen, it's been twenty-five years. Are you *certain* your lead is reliable?" he asked.

"Why are you doubting it?" I asked, hiding my concern.

"Why won't you tell me your source?" he asked.

I didn't answer.

"Did you get your information from your sister?" he asked.

I flinched.

"My sister?" I tried to appear bewildered.

"Whom else would you protect, as your source?" he asked.

"That's quite a leap," I said. Too big a leap, I thought. He must've spoken to Mrs. Springfield, or someone else, and learned it was Paul. He must've known Paul and Sabrina were married and now thought Sabrina had given me wrong information to cover for him. If he wanted, he could reach out to them directly. I'd rather she heard it from me. *What a mess!* I'd have to tell her. "Give me a few weeks. Maybe I can disclose my source," I said, buying myself time to talk to Sabrina.

"Okay," he said, skeptically.

"You seem angry with me instead of grateful for my help," I said, with the hint of a nasty tone which Jonathan knew so well.

"I'm not angry," he said.

"Take a deep breath," I said. He did.

"Look, I'm sure your mind is spinning and you want some time to yourself. So, I'm going to leave you here." He raised his eyebrows, clearly surprised. "I'm actually staying here tonight..."

"Trouble at home, is there?" he asked.

"A bit," I said, "Not enough that I would do anything I'd have to feel guilty about *again*, though," I added quickly. I took my jacket off, knowing the straps of my camisole were falling off of my shoulders, and that my nipples were popping through.

He looked at me mischievously.

"I'm very, very, very exhausted. I'll probably pass out the second I lay down... in room four twelve. I'll probably just take those elevators, right out there," I said, gesturing past the bar, "and go straight up to my room. Four twelve," I pronounced very slowly. He grinned wickedly, his whole face lighting up. "I'm so tired, in fact, that I'll probably carelessly leave the door open, and likely wouldn't hear anyone slip in or even wake up if they were to take advantage of me."

"And that's what would have to happen. I'd *have* to be taken advantage of," I said, looking at him intently, hoping to convey what was expected of him, "because I would not, I repeat, I would not cheat on my husband again." I looked away from him, pretending to focus on something across the room. I stood, hooking my jacket by the collar over my shoulder. I breathed deeply, closing my eyes, imagining him holding me down and forcing himself into me. "Fortunately, there's nobody with anger towards me who would do such a thing... and I doubt anyone could possibly get off taking advantage of a woman who is sleeping, and unresponsive."

Evan looked at me, curiously. "Anyway, have a good evening," I said, smoothing the sides of my pencil skirt. I strode away in my heels with an extra swish in my hips, as the elevator closed. I wasn't certain that he'd take my offer seriously, but I didn't lock my door. I freshened up in the bathroom, and lay on the bed, without removing the scarf or my heels.

Ten minutes of hoping he'd come, and hoping he wouldn't, passed, before I heard the creak of the door, and felt light from the hallway filling the room, though my eyes were closed. My heart hammered. He walked across the room. It was difficult to keep my eyes shut.

"You love control," Evan said in a deep, hoarse voice, as he approached the bed. "Even now, just lying there, you know you're controlling me, luring me up here like this." He ran a finger from my shoulder to my wrist, and I felt goose bumps prickling my arm. He tickled the length of my arm with a light, silky fabric, and I realized he'd found my scarves on the desk. Had I pre-planned this, perhaps I'd have taken that ski mask my mother had sent as well. Evan stretched my arm away from my body, towards the night table, and I didn't help him. I was dead weight as he tied the scarf around my wrist, and dead weight as he attached it to what I thought must be the arm of the lamp extending from the wall.

"This is your M.O., isn't it, my sleeping beauty? Not so different from the anonymous massage, eh?" he asked, and he was now on the other side of the bed, tying my other wrist in the same fashion. I was flat on my back and felt my breasts collecting at my collarbone. I didn't know if it was adrenaline or desire, but it pumped wildly through my body now, and it was hard to lay still. I felt the mattress give beneath me. He must've been sitting on the bed now. His finger traced my lips, and I smelled soap on it. "I would gag you right now with this scarf..." he whispered so close to my face that I smelled the fresh scent on his, and the hint of vodka on his breath, "but then I wouldn't be able to kiss your lovely mouth." *Lovely. He called my disfigured mouth lovely.* He lay next to me, pressed his hard cock against my leg, and took my lips in his, gently probing my unresponsive mouth with his tongue. He kept kissing my static mouth—when had Jonathan last kissed me?

"Well, now, I can't very well have you wake up and recognize me," he said, stroking my hair, then my cheek, then my shoulder. He unwrapped the scarf from my face, and I felt more naked than if he'd removed my clothes. He folded it over my eyes, and raising my head with the back of his hand, tied it behind my head, delicately, as if not to wake me. I was perfectly vulnerable and disoriented. His shoes hit the floor with a thump and I startled. He pulled my camisole slowly up over my breasts and pushed the top of them so they were freed from my bra. I felt his tongue and lips slowly sucking one nipple, his thumb and finger delicately pulling at the other. Now he had a hand on my thigh, under my skirt, moving up towards my hip and around to feel my ass. I breathed heavily as he fumbled for the zipper and ever so slightly, so slightly that he couldn't detect I was helping him, I raised my hips, so he could slide my skirt off, down past my knees, and over my heels.

He began rubbing me over my thin white panties. I wanted to spread my legs, but I didn't dare. "You call this unresponsive, sleeping beauty?" he whispered, moving my underwear to the side so that I was completely exposed. He gently rubbed both inner thighs and then forced my legs wide open. I could feel him staring between my legs as he did. *Touch me.* It was almost unbearable. He ran a hand from my thigh to my hip, to my waist, then cupped my breast, so softly, like he was scared to break me, or wake me. "You're stunning," he said, and *yes*, his thumb found my clit. "You want to pretend that this is about me wanting to take out my anger," he said, kissing my belly, moving down on the bed so he could rest his cheek on my thigh, "But you know it's not about that, is it?" he asked softly. *Ahhhh. His open mouth. The heat of it so close.* If my hands hadn't been tied, I'd have pulled his face into me. But I didn't need to. He started kissing my thighs, trailing his way up, the palm of his hand softly resting on my clit, just the slightest pressure, the slightest movement, and then finally, his mouth was on me, licking, gently tugging, and I couldn't help but moan. I was already building. He rhythmically pulsed one thick knuckle just inside of me, and then paused. I wanted to be filled, and come all over him, but I couldn't wait for that. My legs were tensing, and I knew he felt that I was about to let go.

So he stopped, deliberately. "What this is about..." he said, and I wished he were still licking me rather than speaking. "Yes, what this is about..." *Can't we analyze this later?* The bed shook a bit. He was no longer lying between my legs. I felt his knees between mine, he was above me, I heard his belt buckle opening, I heard the belt buckle hit the floor, and now I genuinely wished I could see him, above me, probably shirtless and stiff, "... is you not being honest, not accepting the consequences of your actions, and not owning up to what you want." I wasn't sure what he was talking about and I couldn't focus on his words. He needed to be quiet now, and take me. He needed to get out of my head and into my body. *This is it.* I was ready and I knew he'd be inside of me, fully, in a moment. But instead of pounding into me, as I expected, he hovered over me. The lower half of my body suddenly felt bare, deprived, and unattended to. All that warm wetness just sitting there, cooling like the fat grilled out of meat.

"You said you weren't asking anything from me. But if you want me inside of you, my dear, dear, sleeping beauty, you *will* have to ask for it," he said. "And nicely."

Evan positioned himself on top of me so that his enormous cock was resting between my lips, ever so slightly moving, teasing my pussy, pressing against my clit, against my stomach, his bicep, or maybe it was his forearm, was flexed solidly against the side of my breast, his mouth at my ear. "Just say you want me to take you," he whispered. "Tell me you need it, and I'll give it to you."

But I didn't want to speak. I wanted to be desired just for existing. I wanted to be irresistible by simply breathing. I wanted to be asked nothing, so I could do no wrong, to be desired in spite of, and because of, my neediness. I wanted to be loved in my sleep, in my emotional lifelessness, worshipped as in death.

He pushed his head just barely inside of me, and I held my breath, and my insides began to suction him. I couldn't imagine he could hold out. He'd fuck me. He had to. But then he just rubbed himself lengthwise again between my lips. "Just ask me," he said, again. I was annoyed. *What happened to "Next time is going to be all about you?"* But god, he was so huge. Before I could stop myself, I bent my knees tightly over his solid thighs, lifted my hips, ground up against him, stroked him with my flesh, feeling his hardness against me, and at last, I hopelessly, violently, exploded on him. I gave in and cried out, "Please, Evan! Please give it to me." I heard the sound of a wrapper tearing and before my insides had finished spasming, he was already thrusting deep inside of me.

Chapter 23

Evan and I passed the next few hours cramming in as much sex as we could. I fell more passionately in love with him as each orgasm built, and as each one rippled away, I wondered what I was doing in a hotel room with someone other than my husband. I fell asleep, without a pill, in his arms. I woke at 2:00 a.m. to his kisses on my neck. We had a last round before Evan left to go home to his wife. I imagined, and felt bad, that she had probably cooked him a flaky spanakopita with a side of chickpea salad and posted a photo of the uneaten meal on Facebook in his absence. I had four missed calls from Jonathan and three text messages that asked, "Where are you?" The third one, at midnight, was all capitalized. I texted him back, "Went out after mediation, phone died, be home soon."

I thought back to the first time Jonathan and I had made love—that beautifully unchoreographed, honest exchange—each as vulnerable as the other. It had to be that way. This first time with Evan, equally, had to be this way. What we shared was what we, or I, had left to give—so much less. Neither time was less perfect relative to what I'd needed at the moment.

Jonathan and I didn't talk when I got home, or in the morning, the next few days, the next few weeks. I was back on Ambien. He was back on the couch. How many times could a couple of bad moments turn into a couple of bad months, turn into a couple of bad years, before turning into a couple of bad lives? Nonetheless, I appreciated the lack of opportunity to tell a proactive lie.

I had another follow-up appointment for the Palsy. The doctor and I agreed that there'd been marked improvement—even I could see it—but the upper left quadrant of my mouth still wouldn't budge, and the left side of my smile wouldn't bear as many teeth as the right. It could take up to eighteen months, he told me. Another extended deadline, the frustration of endless moving targets.

"There's nothing I can do for you. It's all up to you at this point," he said. He rattled on about electricians trying to reconnect wires in the dark again. "It's really mind over matter. Only you can interpret or recognize the subtle improvements, through trial and error, trying to move the muscles. You have to work at it. You just have to figure yourself out," he told me. Figure myself out, huh? I'd been at it for thirty-seven years!

"I can't look at this anymore. Isn't there anything you can do cosmetically to even me out?" I asked.

"Stop being so hard on yourself. Nobody is examining you the way you do. I'm telling you, nobody can tell that you're not fully smiling, or that you can't make a fish-face or swish mouthwash. It's quite mild now."

"Then why did you just write 'gross asymmetry' in your notes?" I asked, looking over at the laptop he'd been typing on.

"I'm a medical doctor. I'm trained to see fine differences. The world isn't. Think about how far you've come, not what's left of it."

"You make a fine cheerleader. Back to my cave to hide," I said, getting off the examination table, and hunching over in exaggerated despair.

"You shouldn't hide. Look in the mirror." He held up a handheld mirror, but I turned away.

***

It was the first snowstorm of the season. I stared out the window, Ella and Charlie sharing my lap. Jonathan was on the phone with his father in the other room. "Yes, well, the reason the weather is so unpredictable is because of climate change... No, it's the entire Republican party!... No, dad, you're dead wrong, you're just concerned about your taxes."

"Tell me a story from when you were little. Please. Just one and I'll go to bed. It has to be about snow," Ella told me.

I told her about the first time I'd fallen down skiing. "I wanted to get right up and try again, not to let my fear stop me. But my legs were shaking, and no matter how much I tried mind over matter... oh, mind over matter? It means getting something that you want by really focusing and giving it your all, even when it seems impossible... yes, that's right, like when I say no to candy and you beg and get it... so, my legs, they were shaking and felt just like strawberry Jello. I had to stop and take a deep breath and wait for it to pass." Ella's eyes lit up. "Oh, I know that feeling in the legs," she said excitedly. I looked at her quizzically. "That's exactly how I feel when you yell at me," she said.

I couldn't believe that with all the hostility, intimidations, ruptures to the soul that she would face as she grew up, that I, her mother, had taught her what fear felt like, as my mother had taught me. "I am so sorry," I said kissing her head. "I never, ever want to make you feel that. Do you forgive me, baby?" She did, but a tear rolled down my face.

When the children were asleep, I saw an email from Evan requesting "another interim meeting to the 90." He was at a nearby bar, and would wait there until 8:30 p.m. I had half an hour. The taboo had been taken out of sleeping with him. It was the taboo nature of relationships that had historically created my most fulfilling sexual encounters: massages, authority figures, sex with platonic friends, men and women, ugly people, people I'd judged as below me, above me, intellectually or physically. It was the inability to resist crossing the line, where intimacy was reduced, no elevated, to that place where unfettered need lives. Where it lived when I was nine, when I discovered one of my parents' porn films. Was that why I was predisposed to finding taboo situations so hot? Or was it that nothing could be blander than fucking my moral, intellectual, physical or emotional equivalent?

But I could think of nothing more I'd have wanted to do than to be with Evan.

"There are going to be ice pellets, an accumulation of eight inches by morning. Tell Mom she should keep your hot water running..." Jonathan was telling his father. This was the sort of weather that would deter Jonathan from going out except to buy jugs of water because "you never know, there could be riots for water." The exact weather that'd make it all the more fitting for me and Evan to have seen each other. I'd have had no way to explain it to Jonathan. But then I might not need to, since we weren't speaking.

"She's doing fine..." By his dismissive tone, I knew he was talking about me.

I sent an email to Evan: "I won't bore you with my guilt. But I'm drowning in it. We're only a few weeks away from ninety (assuming I accept that the Mandarin didn't reset the clock). Hold tight."

Evan emailed back: "I understand your reluctance. But I keep coming back to that place where I think about what would be if nature were allowed to run its course, if we didn't operate amidst all these safety cones. Where would we be if we weren't both married—it's not necessarily a permanent condition. How can something so natural be so equally destructive? It's a divine paradox. Or maybe I just want to get you back in a hotel room. Either way, you need to ask yourself what it is that you'll value more in fifty years, that you were true to yourself at the expense of your husband, or that you were true to your husband at the expense of yourself? Reread that line as many times as you have to."

I grew oddly infuriated. I wrote back immediately: "But we do operate between safety cones. This is nothing more than a tryst."

"A tryst? There's no denying the force of what we've been. Why can't you admit it? My mistake. I shouldn't have pushed the ninety days... if it helps, my intentions were partly inspired by my desire to follow up about your source."

"You know, our kids are growing up in a maybe lopsided culture where personal fulfillment at any price is okay. And yeah, I can't escape feeling like I somehow deserve what we've been doing. But it doesn't change that it's a superficial shellac on top of my real life, and it doesn't make it right."

I headed to my roof to smoke and call Sabrina. Enough procrastinating. I needed closure on Evan's closure. I needed my head clear of that issue, at least, and now, for the first time, it seemed silly that I'd waited this long. She was an adult. She could handle knowing what her husband did some twenty-five years ago, and even if she couldn't, she needed to know, in case Evan did. She picked up after one ring.

"I have to tell you something, and it's not good."

"Is it health-related?" she asked.

"No."

"Let me guess. You blew Paul?" she joked.

"Twice," I said, seriously.

"You're disgusting," she laughed.

"But it is about Paul. Remember I told you I was looking into the hit and run for Evan Roth?"

Silence.

"Hello?"

"Yeah," she said after a pause. "What about it?"

"This is really messed up," I said. She was oddly quiet. "I think it was Paul who accidentally hit Joy."

"Why would you think that?" she asked slowly. She sounded scared.

"I know. It's horrible." I downloaded everything I'd learned, how I'd lied to Evan that it was Tom Moretti driving to protect Paul, and to protect her, and that I thought he might have found out the truth on his own.

All I heard was the wind on my roof and the honking of cars for a few moments.

"Oh my god," she finally said and her voice got a tone deeper, the way it always did when she was about to cry.

"He isn't seeking revenge. I think just an apology. At this point, there aren't any legal consequences. Even if he doesn't already know the truth, I think he deserves it."

"Paul didn't kill anyone," she said.

"No, I know, it wasn't on purpose. It was an accident, a really terrible accident."

"No, he didn't do it," she said, sobbing uncontrollably now.

"Sabrina, please calm down. The baby. Listen, I'm not going to tell him. I'm just giving you a heads up that..."

"I'm sorry, I have to go. I really... I have to go..."

"Sabrina... it was an accident," I said becoming concerned. "Nothing is going to happen to Paul. You're okay."

"No, you don't understand!"

"What? What?" I asked, panicking from her panic.

"Not..." she was crying so hard that she sounded like she was hyperventilating. My chest tightened. "Paul... driving the car." She took a deep breath. "He let me... I... I... It was me. I was driving."

No. No. No.

My eyes were bulging as she confessed the details of how she'd been driving his car, that she wanted to turn herself in but Paul convinced her not to. That's why she was scared to drive at night, why she has had nightmares ever since, why she now had panic attacks and generalized anxiety—post-traumatic stress disorder a therapist had told her. Only Paul knew her worst secret, and that's partly why she'd never wanted to leave him.

"Do you think I'm terrible? I'm going to Hell," she said, but seemed to have stopped crying.

"You were only fifteen. I can't believe you've suffered with this secret all these years. I'm sure that's been punishment enough. At least you've had Paul, I guess."

"I don't know. He used to be sympathetic about how this tortures me. Now, he's fed up hearing about it. When we were kids, he acted like he understood how I felt. But now I think maybe he was just scared I'd tell the police, and that he'd get in trouble for letting me drive the car, or for not reporting the accident. When I heard she died, I thought the guilt would kill me."

"So that's why you stopped getting in as much trouble," I said.

"But you suddenly went totally nuts after Evan left. So, on top of everything, I felt like I ruined your life too. It wasn't until you got your shit together that I could finally breathe a little."

"How could you not have told me?" I asked.

"You would have had to tell on me," she said, as if we were still kids, "or suffer with covering it up the way I have. You were better off not knowing."

"Well, now I'm faced with that choice anyway," I said.

"How is there a choice involved here?" she asked, all traces of that guilt she'd supposedly been suffering, vanished.

"I think we should all get together and discuss what happened. It would bring you closure, too."

"Do you want me to go to jail?" she demanded. "Don't you care about your unborn niece? How could you even consider telling him?"

I explained, again, that there was no legal exposure anymore.

"I simply can't," she said.

I felt tenderness and pity equally. I had judged her so harshly, blaming her weaknesses on envy, mistakenly and egotistically. I knew I'd think both more and less of her now, and that our relationship would change.

I stayed on the roof wondering where she would be today were it not for the self-hatred and guilt that had dominated her. Then I thought, those same things were dominating me now.

By the time I got back down to my apartment, my head was spinning, and I actually wished I were talking to Jonathan, so I sort of hovered around him. He must have sensed it. We hadn't spoken an optional word to each other in the last few weeks, but now he did, as if it were no big deal.

"You know we have the holiday party at the new building next Friday. We should go even though it'll be months before the place is ready for us to move into. I found out that the uncle of one of our most important investors lives in our new building. And in case you forgot, we're supposed to leave for Grand Cayman the weekend after that."

I was thankful for these ordinary concerns that now demanded my focus.

"I'm not going anywhere, pretending to be your happy little wife, until you apologize," I said, playing hardball, but thrilled to be talking again.

"*Me* apologize? I'm supposed to apologize for what?" he asked. "For the way you speak to me? For the way you completely disregard me? For the way you barged in on me and freaked that morning because I asked you to take care of your children?" he asked.

How could he not *want* to apologize? How could he be so callous?

"You're an ingrate." *An ingrate?* I almost laughed, but he was on a roll, and I didn't want to interrupt this outpour of contempt. "You see the nuances in everything, analyze things down to quarks and leptons, but you really know nothing. Have you once thought about what I need from you rather than what you need from me? You're so self-centered!"

"Is it self-centered to expect affection when my face is paralyzed? It's not just sex I need," I said. "Our parents have fifty years of grievances behind them, but they're still married. Would you forgive them if they abandoned each other in the hospital when they were in need? No."

He looked hurt.

"You think intimacy wouldn't have helped me process this?" I asked. Now I got teary-eyed. I'd gone into observation mode, when the Palsy first hit. I didn't ask for affection. I went inside. Was it so I could document his failings and build a case for my future ones? Or was it to disguise the neediness and vulnerability that I no longer felt safe showing?

"In the beginning you had no legs to stand on when you argued with me," he said. "Now you do. I know you haven't been getting what you should be, what you deserved, physically and emotionally the last few years." *Holy moly, who is this man? Has he been cheating on me with a therapist?*

"I'm still here," he said, but it was a tiny voice, and neither of us felt sure of it.

Chapter 24

We went to the holiday party at our new building. It was all wine and cheese and shrimp cocktail, and unnecessary fur for a party in an interior lobby. Our neighbors coveted the shrimp, like it was last call at an all-you-can-eat buffet, as if they couldn't afford to start a shrimp farm. The president of the board told us that the reason we hadn't been approved right away was obviously not because of our finances, but because I was an attorney, and they were worried I'd start trouble. I saw Jonathan relax that his twenty-five million was respectable enough, and his surprise that I'd impacted anything.

It took me the next week to pack for the whole family. By the time I finished, I knew this trip to Grand Cayman was going to be an exhausting mistake. I considered backing out right until first class and handicapped were called to board and I realized that I was now both.

As I collected our things, Sabrina called.

"I'm about to get on a plane. Can I call you back?" I asked.

"Really quick," she said, insisting that I stay on the phone. "I've thought about it. You can tell Evan the truth."

I gasped. "I'm so proud of you." I felt my decades-old perception of her as self-centered and weak dissolving. "I'm going to hug you the next time I see you," I said.

"That would be awkward. Please don't."

I laughed.

Once we were seated, I looked out the window, thinking about the doctor. "You'll just have to figure yourself out," he'd told me, "you're beautiful." I looked at my precious daughter, and suddenly felt like crying, imagining how it'd kill me to see her struggle with her self-image.

A teenaged boy with limp legs, and a neck brace holding his head up, had boarded the plane and was being lifted from his wheelchair and carried to his seat. "What's wrong with him?" Ella asked.

"Don't stare," Jonathan and I said at the same time. We looked at each other tenderly with unspoken compassion for the boy and shared gratitude for our healthy children. This is where we had fallen in love, where the emotional tissue connected and radiated.

"I swear to God, I'd sleep with him just to make him feel wanted," I told Jonathan.

"I know," he said.

Why was our compassion unlimited for others and rationed for one another?

Nothing between us—money, the kids, the days I'd measured, wasted, by their proximity to the last one where Jonathan had plugged my physical hole—would be fraught with contempt if we'd felt a dose of the compassion for each other that we did so easily for this boy. It's your pills, it's your coldness, it's your tone, it's your negativity, it's your frank fill in the blank, because what it was, was, only the opposite of compassion, the incessant denial of our own destructive roles. We had, I had, been a bystander to the decay of my own marriage.

Once everyone had boarded, the captain announced that due to high traffic on the runway, we'd be delayed taking off. Our focus shifted away from compassion to the annoyance.

My phone started ringing. Sabrina again. I walked to the back of the plane.

"What's up?"

"Paul and I talked again. He thinks blaming Tom Moretti was genius. I've changed my mind. I'm begging you not to say anything. Nellie."

I gritted my teeth. "How am I supposed to look him in the eye?" I asked.

"Why would you be looking him in the eye?"

***

Ella invented a game in the pool on our third day of vacation, and I pretended to be interested while I tried to keep Charlie from swallowing chlorine.

"Let's all get dried off. We've had enough pool time," Jonathan said from the edge of the pool. I saw him noticing a young woman in a white bikini and I mouthed the word "stuff" to him, our code word for hot women. He turned his head away dismissively, and I felt like the aging mother that I was.

"Nooo," Ella said. "We just got here."

"Take a picture of us while your hands are dry," I told Jonathan. I'd been in no pictures since the Palsy began. I remembered when we used to do photo shoots on the beach, in my skimpy bikinis in the sand, when he'd tell me how to pose, and couldn't get through the shoot without fucking me. For the last few years, he'd acted as if taking a photo of me were as burdensome as taking out the garbage, but he'd maxed out the memory in his phone with pictures of the kids. I saw the aggravation in his eyes, but he acquiesced, because of the Palsy, because it meant I was feeling a little better. I took Charlie's hand to my face and used it to push the left side of my smile up.

"Alright, out of the pool, guys, let's shower," Jonathan said.

"You're the worst daddy ever!" Ella said, "I'm not going to shower!" She was screaming her head off. "It's my body, and you can't tell me what to do with it!"

"Ella, don't speak to your father that way. You have three minutes to get out of this pool and get washed off, and if you don't, I'm taking your Kindle away for good," I said.

"Noooo," she protested.

"That's it. I'm leaving you with a babysitter for the rest of this trip," I said, getting out of the pool with Charlie.

"No, Mommy, please, no!" she said. Of course, the tears had started.

"Alix!" Jonathan snapped at me, "Don't be so impatient with her!" Typical. I came to his defense and in turn he insulted me.

By the next day, my mood was light, because my face looked looser, maybe from the humidity, or maybe because I was having frequent sex with Jonathan. "Can you say 'whale?'" I asked Charlie, pointing to a picture on his sand pail. Although I couldn't fully form the "w", for the first time in a while, I entertained the possibility that I'd make a full recovery someday.

I felt lucky to have my children; they were growing and learning so fast.

I buried all but Ella's feet in the sand. Suddenly she noticed a wart on her toe. "DO SOMETHING!" she screamed. She was in hysterics. I wished I'd buried her feet, too. "DO SOMETHING!" She wouldn't let it go. We spent four hours in town trying to find wart remover. When I applied it back at the hotel, she said she'd miss her wart when it got better. Now, it was me that felt like screaming.

It'd been five days of "vacation" and we were leaving tomorrow. Jonathan and I were exhausted. Never again without a nanny, I told him. I had a headache behind my right ear. I told Jonathan that it reminded me of the one I'd had on the left side just before the Palsy began. He told me I was probably just dehydrated, and though he understood that I'd always be afraid of recurrences, maybe I should talk to someone about my anxiety when we got home. I placed an emergency call into the ENT and waited for a call back. Jonathan looked pissed, because he knew this would excuse me from having to bathe the kids, and leave it to him.

The doctor called back quickly. I described my headache, my suspicions, asked him if it'd be helpful to take a preventative steroid in case this was the precursor to a recurrence. Should I go to the emergency room? Find a flight home tonight? He told me there were a million reasons for headaches, that the chance of a recurrence, let alone this soon, and on the opposite side of my face, wasn't impossible, but beyond slim. Was he sure? He was.

When the kids were asleep, I suggested that we get a sitter and go to the hotel club to enjoy our last night of vacation. Jonathan declined because we had to get up early to go to the airport. I told him I was going anyway, because for all I knew this was my last night before my face fell off again. He rolled his eyes.

I put on a short dress with heels and headed out. I was standing just outside the hotel club, wondering if I should go back up to the room because I didn't really want to be in a club without Jonathan. Though we'd been having 'vacation sex,' we were still disconnected. All I really wanted was for Jonathan to hold me, make love to me, and give me back that feeling that, no matter what lay ahead, I'd loved and been loved. That at the end of grueling days with the outside world, we'd succeeded in creating a cocoon we could travel in and out of freely to recharge.

The girl we'd admired earlier at the pool walked past me. Jonathan would enjoy seeing her dressed up, I thought with displeasure.

And then it hit me that our misery was actually quite romantic. It reflected an unremitting fear of losing each other, our marriage, and all it represented—and the willingness to completely surrender to preserve it.

But what if we removed the threat of losing one another, by losing ourselves, together, not outside of our marriage, but within it, with another woman? I wondered. The 'safety cones' could be expanded. I suddenly heard Dr. Stearns' voice, "Do you think a ménage à trois indicates *mature* growth in your relationship?" We'd bank little more than an elusive rush. What we needed, I knew, was to grow together and accept each other's individual longings and yearnings—even if they had nothing to do with the relationship we'd once envisioned we'd have, without demanding unrealistic changes.

I texted him: "I'm coming back up. I miss you."

"You've only been gone five minutes."

"Closer to five years."

When I got back to the room, I mentally tightened my pigtails, and said, "My face is stiff. Will you massage it?"

"Lay down," he said. I spooned up against him on the bed. He propped his head up with one elbow on the bed, his hand under his ear, looking down at me.

"You have to stick your thumb into my mouth to get to where it's really bad."

Quietly, calmly, and for a good ten minutes, Jonathan massaged my face, maneuvering it into the most unattractive, contorted positions. I'd been scared that he'd say no when I asked him to massage me. Now, I thought I could feel love radiating through his fingertips, tenderness. I turned around so that my body faced his and looked up at him.

"It's good to just lay in bed together," he said.

I stroked his cheek gently with the knuckles of my hand and traced his eyebrows with my finger. I felt tears welling up in me, from where, I didn't know. I propped myself up on my own elbow so that our lips were nearly touching. I pressed the palm of my hand onto his chest, inhaled his scent—characterizing it as neither good nor bad, only familiar—and inched my whole body towards him as if I were trying to climb inside of it, hoping to be absorbed. He caressed my shoulder, tilted his head, and stared into me. I lifted my chin. We kissed, deeply, passionately, slowly, for a long while, leaving our bodies out of it.

"Is it too late?" I asked, "for us?"

"We do need to wake up early," he said. *I wasn't pressuring you for sex!*

"I know," I said. I wouldn't force the question. I wanted to stay embraced, cuddling in the crisp sheets. "Let me wash up and get ready for bed. I'm coming right back to this spot," I said.

But when I returned from the bathroom, Jonathan was already laying on the sofa in the living room of our two-bedroom suite, with a blanket and pillow, his back facing out.

I took a pill, feeling empty. There's been too much emotional erosion, I thought. Or perhaps I was being unfair. He'd given me what I'd asked, and simply needed sleep. He hadn't shunned me. *Don't be angry just because it's easier than feeling vulnerable*, I told myself. Yet I couldn't help wondering why it was Evan to whom I'd been so sure I needed to say goodbye. I fell asleep imagining us driving on a highway, the top down, surrounded by desert, my hair blowing in the wind.

Chapter 25

The hall light was still out, the apartment cluttered with toys, kitchen towels hung interchangeably as bath towels, the wood chipping on the antique book case, twelve cups of frozen yogurt glistened with freezer burn, articles Jonathan had clipped, though he'd never read, were stacked on the dining room table, our plush mattress, sloped to my side from wear and tear. It was good to be back.

The next morning, I woke to an email from Evan: "Hope your flight back was easy. Today is non-negotiable. It's officially Day 90. You don't have to tell me again—I get it, strictly platonic. See you at 5. -E"

I'd decided not to tell Jonathan about the situation with Sabrina because I expected things would fizzle. There was no point in risking Jonathan piecing together what I'd done.

I texted Jonathan: "I'm going to meet one of the moms at school for an early dinner. See you later tonight."

Jonathan replied: "I'll be home early... have fun. Hope your headache is better."

I dressed in a too sexy for midtown, elegant, trendy jumpsuit. This was, after all, going to be one of Evan's last memories of me. Mine of him were so vivid, and flash as fixed images, as I approached the bar. In the school yard in his sweaty t-shirt, reaching for his sister's hand, his nervous hand on my leg under that old tree, his paintings, his writing, the first night we met, the bench in Central Park, his words of encouragement, the massage, the night by the river, the night at the hotel, the sound of his belt buckle, the bizarre way our worlds had collided, how his entire life had changed direction because of my sister, how mine had, too, since we reconnected. He'd cooked up a tangible energy in me, and I wanted to keep it, without relying on him to stir the pot.

I smiled softly at him when I saw him standing at the bar. I took off my jacket and quickly removed the fuzzy white hat I was wearing before he could notice it was browning on the edges from my make-up.

"Good to see you," he said, and as usual, I crumbled, beneath his beautiful eyes. "Have you been playing good girl to make being bad girl sweeter?" he asked.

"No," I said quickly. "I accept my safety cones. This is where I am now."

"So, why'd you agree to meet me?"

"I did my homework. I went back to my source to convince them to let me reveal more to you," I said.

He smiled, and blinked hard, a look of relief on his face. "Thank you," he said, and cupped my cheek and ear in his hand, making me want to kiss it.

"I didn't succeed. But I'm convinced it was Tom Moretti." It sucked to lie. Here I was, holding the spray can again so Sabrina could escape unscathed.

"Is that so?" he asked, sharply withdrawing his hand. I nodded, and when our eyes met, he searched mine. I wasn't worried, because I knew my face gave little away now.

"Well, I did my homework, too," he said sternly. My heart free-fell. "Tom Moretti is dead." He looked at me waiting for the reaction I didn't give him. "But it's irrelevant. I don't need to talk to him." *Phew! He's letting it go.*

"See, a thing like that... you *don't* forget the details. They just replay, over and over again in your mind. I still hear it now—the thump of the car against her little body—like it was yesterday." He swallowed hard and looked lost in memory.

"I'm so, so sorry, Evan," I said, my voice cracking.

"It was like slow motion, when I turned around. That fucking redhead in the passenger seat. I saw him mouthing 'Go, go, go.' She looked like an ice statue." He paused to make sure I'd heard him.

"She?" I asked, in a whisper. Again, he searched my eyes.

"Stop the charade," he said. "Sabrina. She was in shock, frozen, not a strand of that blonde hair moving. To this day, her blue eyes haunt me. The redhead leaned over, grabbed the wheel. They drove off. Just drove off, as if they hadn't hit a human being." He raised his chin and breathed deeply. I saw his teeth clenching under his jaw. "All along, I figured you genuinely didn't know." He closed his eyes, but I saw his eyeballs moving beneath the lids. "It wasn't until you sent me searching for a conveniently dead guy, that I suspected you knew."

"So you knew the truth the whole time and you were just observing my behavior," I said bitterly, repeating my words from after the massage. "You were using me all along. Why not just tell me?" I asked.

"I intended to, the first night we met. I never expected..." He looked at me tenderly, "to fall in love with you. Had I told you, it would've changed everything between us. You'd have felt like I was pushing you against a brick wall..."

"I liked when you did that," I said, unable to resist.

"I thought you'd figure it all out on your own, and share it with me—that the whole thing might actually bring us closer. But then, you fed me that nonsense about Tom Moretti." He looked angry now. "I was confused. I asked if Sabrina was your source to test you. And your reaction was to invite me up to your hotel room. I didn't know whether your sister lied to you, and you really didn't know—or you knew I knew, and wanted me to punish you for lying to me, and leave it unspoken."

"I'm flattered by how perverse you believe me to be. I *didn't* know it was Sabrina until after that night," I said truthfully.

"Then why the wild goose chase?" he asked, wanting to believe me.

"After investigating, I thought it was her husband—she married the redhead, Paul." I couldn't tell if he already knew that.

"Why didn't you tell me?" he asked, his anger visibly dissolving now that I was being straight.

"To protect him," I said, unashamed, as if it were obvious. "Her, really."

"From what?" he asked, exasperated. "Tracking down murderers for revenge is for Hollywood movies. Did you think

I'd kill them? I'm not a thug. You know they can't be prosecuted now. Don't get me wrong. I'll never excuse them for driving away, or myself for not telling the police. It was as foolish for me to keep my mouth shut, as it was for Sabrina to get behind that wheel. But I don't want to hurt anyone. What I've always wanted is an acknowledgment, and an apology. At the very least, Joy deserves that."

"Why didn't you tell the police?" I asked.

"By the time they arrived, I was sure Joy would be okay. It was an adolescent decision, made on a whim."

"What whim?" I asked.

"I didn't want your sister to get in trouble." He laughed at himself. "It was crazy. My first thought, after I saw that Joy was alive, was that I wanted you to keep being my girlfriend. I thought that if Sabrina was arrested, we wouldn't be able to 'go out' anymore."

"All that for puppy love?" I asked.

"You were my world that summer. I figured Joy would be okay." He shook his head. "But if it weren't for Sabrina, she'd still be here today."

"Or if you'd been playing on the sidewalk rather than the street, or watched television instead of playing ball..." I covered my mouth with my hand, like I was surprised—but I wasn't—that the words escaped.

"Why didn't you tell the truth later, when she died?" I asked.

"I wanted to. But I'd told my parents and the police repeatedly that I'd seen nothing but a blue car. I didn't know how to admit that I lied, or why I lied. Then they sent me off to school. It was almost out of sight, out of mind. I wrote letters to them, telling the truth, and then shredded them. The more time that passed, the worse it seemed to admit what a stupid thing I'd done by lying. It wasn't until college that I was mature enough to own up to it. By then, my parents finally seemed normal again. I decided, after much debate, that it wasn't the right thing to put them through it all over again. What was the point? But with my daughter's every movement reminding me of her, now that she's the same age Joy was, and my mother's gone, I just couldn't ignore it anymore. I needed to finally confront this, for myself. I needed you to know what I did for you, and I wanted you to get Sabrina to face up to it."

"So you manipulated me," I said.

I explained that Sabrina had suffered from post-traumatic stress and panic disorder since the accident, and that though I told her—and agreed—that he deserved an apology, she was pregnant, emotional, and felt she couldn't handle it.

He squeezed my hands tightly in his. "I have no ill will towards Sabrina anymore. You've become my world again. Do you understand that I love you?" he asked.

I stared at him. I thought about all the mental energy I'd spent on him, how this was all I wanted to hear two nights ago in Grand Cayman when I was dreaming of running off with him. How desperately I'd wanted to believe that I was lovable, that I could evoke in someone what I no longer evoked in Jonathan—desire, curiosity, excitement, even with the Bell's Palsy. But now, with his lies and manipulation—despite my own—it didn't penetrate.

"My sister is gone. I know that an apology from Sabrina won't bring Joy back, or change what happened to me. Over the last couple of months, I've realized I don't need that anymore. I just want *you* to acknowledge that I loved you then, and that I love you now—even if you are running back to your husband."

I studied his handsome face, all that unrestrained emotion colored his cheeks, made his eyes glisten, made him seem thirteen and ninety all at once. What difference did it make that Evan thought he loved me? I wondered. Did it make me love myself? No.

"I love you, too," I said. The rock in my throat made it tough to swallow. "I'll miss you."

He smiled.

"What now? You're going to glorify an ordinary existence because I disappointed you?"

"I should just go," I said.

"Let me drop you off in a cab," he said.

We said nothing to each other in the short ride towards my apartment and I suddenly looked forward to getting home to Jonathan and the kids. *Imagine that!*

"I have to get out here," I told him and the cab driver, a block away from my apartment, "just in case."

He moved in to kiss my lips, and I turned my head and hugged him instead before getting out of the cab. The sun was glistening off the cement and buildings around me as I crossed the street. A man on the opposite corner was watching me and grinning. "You have a beautiful smile," he said as I passed him.

I was forty feet from the entrance to my building. I saw Lara leaving with her daughter, in a hurry. She waved, and as we were about to cross paths, I said, "Real quick, I need your email to send an invitation for Ella's birthday."

She'd already passed me, pulling her daughter by the hand, and over her shoulder, she said, in her flat monotonous way, "Thanks for thinking of us. It's lbj1779@gmail.com." That was familiar. I stopped walking, and squinted. Yes, I knew that email. Jonathan's sent messages, from the day of the Palsy! I remembered the email verbatim:

Regret canceling our first official meeting tonight. I'm unavailable due to issues at home. I cannot reschedule right now.

I pressed my lips together, but they felt numb and wouldn't purse. My jaw dropped open, and as if my racing thoughts were drinking all the excess fluid in my body, my tongue was suddenly dry and tingly. I saw Jonathan, twenty feet away, crossing the street against the light. My eyes were wide, fixed on him on, with disbelief, like I couldn't make him out, like I expected him to suddenly look like someone else. I felt like I couldn't blink as venom filled my veins.

A honking taxi sped toward Jonathan, the horn so loud I had to cover my right ear. I saw Evan holding my furry white hat out the window. Jonathan leapt toward the curb to avoid getting hit, and we both turned toward the taxi driving away.

Jonathan stared at me with the same horror with which I was staring at him, his horror visibly intensifying, and as he suddenly reached out towards my face, I thought he'd seen my hat, pieced it all together, and might just smack me. But he touched, just barely, the right corner of my mouth.

"Alix, when did this happen?" he asked.

"What?" I asked.

"When did the Palsy on the right side start?"

No! It was happening again. *No, please no!*

"I have to get to the doctor," I said, touching my face.

I left emergency messages for the neurologist, ENT, and acupuncturist, and headed to the clinic to get the steroids in me. I paced around the office waiting for the doctor, blurting, "Shit! Fuck! Shit!"

I studied my reflection on my phone. The paralysis was less dense than last time, so far, just the right side of my mouth drooping. More Edvard Munch than Dali. When the doctor came, I gave her the summary. After examining me, she told me, unsympathetically, that it was Bell's Palsy, again, and how rare an occurrence it was for it to present bilaterally, in such a short period of time, particularly for such a young woman. But it was mild, she told me, hardly different from the left side. *But the left side never recovered!*

"Okay, just give me a shot of steroids, please," I told her. How can I make you, anyone, see what I am, what I was, who I want myself to be?

"You should feel lucky," she said, tapping the shot, "it may not be full paralysis this time, maybe just paresis, a muscle weakness."

The originally afflicted side of my face, the bane of my existence, had now become my baseline. All traces of my old self were officially gone. There was no longer even half of my true smile intact. At least the normal side had provided a familiar focal point for my children, gave strangers an option in how to perceive me, captured my essence. My "bad side" had become my "good side."

I didn't want to go home afterwards. There was nothing Jonathan could say to make me feel better, and he might make me feel worse.

Dr. Lee, the acupuncturist, told me to come right away though the office was already closing. I thought about all the work he'd put into me, resuscitating me, patching up holes on a roof only to have the whole thing cave in. I cried when I saw him, when the needles were sticking out of both sides of my face, and when he touched my face like he was sifting through remainders of a wrecked harvest.

It was 9:00 p.m. when I left and I already felt the high dose of steroids coursing through me. There was nothing to say, nobody to talk to, an isolated speck. I was losing sensation, my cheek was numbing, smells were changing, only one eye was crying, despair was mounting. I was aware of every neuron attempting and failing to coordinate my facial muscles, defying logic and predictability.

The ENT called back. I agreed to see him tomorrow.

"I dare you to give me your spiel about mind over matter now," I yelled through the phone.

"You're going to be fine," he said, very calmly.

"There is no mind over matter! It's all so fucking meaningless! Whatever neurotic conflicts exist in my mind, exist on my face. All humanity evolved to endure their nothingness. But me? No. Apparently I'm ill equipped."

"What? It's just the steroids," he said. "Go right home. Take half a milligram of Xanax tonight. We'll talk tomorrow."

I was in bad shape in the morning. It was progressing. The right side of my mouth was numb, drooping, and thinned, and though my eye was still closing, it required effort. But my grinning face looked almost normal. The children might not notice if I didn't change expressions.

I bounced from doctor to doctor, amid their speculation. The kids were awake when I got home, but hadn't seen me come in. Jonathan seemed strung out in the kitchen. I needed reassurance. I needed to relay what the doctors said. I needed him to memorize the lines, or missing lines, of my new face so he could help me check for improvement. I couldn't do this alone. Alone, actually, yes. Alone, within a marriage, no.

Out of earshot from the children, I said, "I can't believe this. Again."

"What?" he said venomously, waving the sandwich he'd made in the air. "*What* can't you believe?"

I backed away like he'd threatened me with a knife.

"I hate you," I said, shaking my head. Was he so frustrated from handling the children himself for an hour? I headed to my bedroom, and lay staring at the ceiling until I was sure the kids were asleep. I knew Jonathan wouldn't check on me. So I went to find him.

"This is why I didn't come straight home last night, why I debated talking about my feelings last time, this time. It's not been forty-eight hours since my life has fallen apart for the second time. I'm not asking you to touch me like some shaman with healing power. But how can you possibly be so nasty at a time like this?" I asked.

"What did I do? You said you couldn't believe me... All disappointed, like *you* are ready for a fight. Over what? That I didn't cut the crust off a sandwich? What do I have to suck up, once again, because you're angry at life?" he asked, his lower lip thinning.

"No! What I said was that I can't believe 'THIS', not 'you'!" I said.

"That's not what I heard," he said. But I wondered if he hadn't heard exactly what I'd said, and because he had things on his mind other than my face, he was now just back-peddling.

"What do you think happens over time, to experience this lack of compassion from the person you most loved and respected and harnessed yourself to? Even if I had been nasty, why wouldn't you allow me to be whatever I need to be to get through this?" I asked, with my hands turned up. But then I wondered why I felt entitled to his unconditional love.

"I know exactly what happens over time when the person you married shows you no compassion!" he said.

He sighed heavily, entrenched in frustration. Nonetheless, I allowed the thought clawing at me to surface: I might never be capable of feeling compassion for him again after his has been so long absent.

We stayed silent awhile. I looked at him expectantly.

"You will get through this," he finally said. "You're a mother, and a wife. You have no choice." I knew he had to dig deep to say those words—words I'd said to myself—that were supposed to be supportive and encouraging.

"But I do have a choice," I said, more spitefully than I intended. "Every single day."

"No, you don't," he spat back without attempting to disguise his hostility. "A mature woman doesn't get to debate on a daily basis whether she really wants to be a wife or mother."

"Mature women adapt to an unfulfilling status quo?" I said sarcastically. "I'm not capable of just existing next to you, with an emotional cadaver between us for another decade."

I walked to the bathroom sink, feeling the incongruity in my face, like that between what I'd expected of myself—and what had become of me, like that between what I'd expected of me and Jonathan—and what we were.

I thought back to my analysis last time—that the cumulative stress of Jonathan's repeated rejections and having denied my passion had caused the Palsy. Wasn't that a convenient excuse to seek my revival in Evan? I knew now, though, that there was nothing to gain in attempting to prove that, de-winged, I was still lovable. Or, that marriage was the scalpel. I couldn't remain stuck in the muddy footprint of a teenager battling the ethos of convention, nor a thirty-year-old that had once found redemption embracing it.

Jonathan walked up behind me. Our glances met in the mirror.

"You're not the only one struggling with who you once were," he said. "I've given up everything to be your husband and a decent father."

I looked at him blankly, through the mirror.

"Youth! Control of my life, women, the freedom to take financial risks, my time, possibility, a real bed!" Jonathan said.

"But you take pleasure in the sacrifice. It fills you up." I turned to face him.

"Not anymore," he said. He looked lost.

"Maybe not," I said, thinking about his email to Lara. "But I believe this second Palsy suits you."

"How's that?" he asked. Neither of us could tell if we were fighting.

"Because it reinforces my dependency on you," I said calmly.

"You're the one that wants *me* to be dependent on you. If you had it your way, I'd be retired. My only interests would be inside these walls, with you and our children," he said, just as calmly.

Then I sighed heavily. I had felt abandoned when he started his new company. He'd given up on what I thought were our shared passions—I had wanted us to be extraordinary together. My flaw.

"We've both been suffering," I said.

We really had done a number on each other, I thought. We'd been on the same path as my face. Instead of the afflicted side working to gain back its full potential to match the healthy side, the good side brought itself down to match the unhealthy side; they'd brought out the worst in each other, just like me and Jonathan.

We exchanged pained glances.

"But I'm done suffering," I said, with optimism not spite.

"I am too," he said.

I'd done enough research to know that our brains were not static, permanent, and irreparable. The connections could be retrained, rerouted, and reestablished. We're wired to learn from mistakes and disappointments. That's what pushes us to be better, to correct, not just the paresis and paralysis of our brains, but also of our relationships, our hearts, and our passions.

"This recurrence on my face won't be the last. It's rare to happen twice, but once it does, it's more likely to happen again."

Jonathan looked alarmed. But I felt calm.

I knew that it'd happen again, and come and go in waves, like the passion in our marriage, any marriage, and if the core was intact, it could be weathered. I could weather it. I would choose to bounce back rather than wallow in grief. I would not hide from my children, or the world, this time, or next time.

"Come here," he said, opening his arms.

I briefly put my head on his chest, and then pulled away.

"I'm okay," I told him, running the water to wash my face and motioning with my hand that he should leave.

I was okay. I knew that I would delve into my business. I'd strip myself of the cloak of dependence I'd been wearing. I'd look back on who I once was, and what Jonathan and I once were, not with an anxious yearning, but with fondness—and leave it at that. I would find my value, and vitality, instead, in what I could become. Perhaps we'd slowly become inspired once more to continue on our solitary journeys together. But ultimately, it was a solitary journey, and one I would triumph over—with or without a smile on my face.

It was late, our usual bedtime. But, I felt like going for a run.

"Are you ready to head in for frozen yogurt?" Jonathan called from the bedroom.

But I'd already slipped on my sneakers and opened the door.

About the Author

Born and raised in Queens, Aliza studied psychology at Queens College and graduated from Fordham Law. As a litigation attorney, Aliza has specialized in complex civil litigation and white-collar criminal defense. She lives in Manhattan with her husband and two children.

Note from the Author

Word-of-mouth is crucial for any author to succeed. If you enjoyed *Asymmetrical Woman*, please leave a review online—anywhere you are able. Even if it's just a sentence or two. It would make all the difference and would be very much appreciated.

Thanks!
Aliza Ross

Thank you so much for reading one of our **Fiction** novels.

If you enjoyed the experience, please check out our recommendation for your next great read!

City in a Forest by Ginger Pinholster

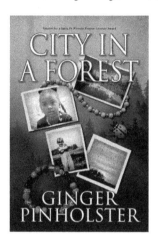

Finalist for a *Santa Fe Writers Project Literary Award*

"Ginger Pinholster, a master of significant detail, weaves her struggling characters' pasts, present, and futures into a breathtaking, beautiful novel in *City in a Forest*."

—IndieReader Approved

View other Black Rose Writing titles at www.blackrosewriting.com/books and use promo code **PRINT** to receive a **20% discount** when purchasing.

CPSIA information can be obtained
at www.ICGtesting.com
Printed in the USA
BVHW070331020321
601385BV00006B/156